TRUST

ME, I'M

TROUBLE

Also by Mary Elizabeth Summer

TRUST ME, I'M LYING

MARY ELIZABETH SUMMER

TRUST ME, I'M TROUBLE

DELACORTE PRESS

Text copyright © 2015 by Mary Elizabeth Summer
Jacket photograph copyright © 2015 by Carrie Schechter

All rights reserved. Published in the United States by Delacorte Press, an imprint of Random House Children's Books, a division of Penguin Random House LLC, New York.

Delacorte Press is a registered trademark and the colophon is a trademark of Penguin Random House LLC.

randomhouseteens.com

Educators and librarians, for a variety of teaching tools, visit us at RHTeachersLibrarians.com

Library of Congress Cataloging-in-Publication Data
Summer, Mary Elizabeth.
Trust me, I'm trouble / Mary Elizabeth Summer.—First edition.
pages cm.
Sequel to: Trust me, I'm lying.
Summary: Master con artist Julep Dupree has managed to stay at her private school, but now her life is in danger and, against her better judgment, she takes a shady case.
ISBN 978-0-385-74414-0 (hc) — ISBN 978-0-385-38289-2 (ebook)
[1. Private investigators—Fiction. 2. Swindlers and swindling.—Fiction. 3. Murder for hire—Fiction. 4. High schools—Fiction. 5. Schools—Fiction.] I. Title.
II. Title: Trust me, I am trouble.
PZ7.S953935Try 2015
[Fic]—dc23
2014031426

The text of this book is set in 11.75-point Goudy.
Jacket design by Ray Shappell
Interior design by Trish Parcell

Printed in the United States of America
10 9 8 7 6 5 4 3 2 1
First Edition

For my best brainstorming buddy,
my mother, Elizabeth

THE EMBEZZLER'S WIFE

If I could give fledgling con artists one piece of advice, it would be this: tacos.

Specifically, Cemitas Puebla tacos.

There might be a mark somewhere out there impervious to the fresh Oaxaca cheese and garden-grown papalo, but if there is, I have yet to meet him. The spit-roasted pork, the chorizo and carne asada, the chile guajillo . . . No one says no to tacos. At least, not these tacos. Which is why they are my secret weapon on my toughest cases.

Holding a bag of taco heaven, I knock on the back door of our very own windowless 1996 Chevy van and wait for Murphy to let me in. Murphy opens the door, the cord of his headphones stretched to its limit. He doesn't bother looking at me until he smells the tacos.

"You brought me dinner?" he says, eyes lighting up.

"Mitts off, Murph. These are for the mark."

Murphy grumbles something under his breath.

"Well, if you'd get out of the van and actually, you know, work, the tacos could have been for you."

"The van is an extension of me. I do not leave the van. The van does not leave me."

J.D. Investigations, which is the name Murphy and I finally settled on for our PI firm, purchased the van in March for all of the company's creeper spying needs. Murphy practically drooled on the bumper when he saw the extended wheelbase. I liked the monstrosity for its diesel engine, the price of gas being what it is. But what sealed it for us was the 1-800-TAXDRMY hand-painted on the side. I'd like to see the curious bystander brave enough to peek in that windshield.

"How does Bryn feel about that?" I can already tell you how Bryn, Murphy's girlfriend for the past seven months, feels about that. Her queen-bee social status tanks any time she gets within a five-foot radius of the van. A type A personality, she is constantly appalled at the grease spots the van leaves wherever Murphy parks it. And her nerd-limit is obliterated every time he brags about the latest gizmo he's added to it. Or maybe that's just me.

"Bryn loves Bessie almost as much as I do." Murphy pets the periscope controls on the surveillance dash he spent six weeks installing. It drove me crazy that it took him that long to get the van operational, but he insisted. His love of geek gadgetry is even deeper than Sam's is. Was. Is.

Anyway, tomorrow is the start of the last week of the school year and the van's been used on only one other job. Which means we're still working out the kinks.

I hop into the back of the van, setting the tacos down on the dash. "A, I seriously doubt that. B, for the last time, we're not calling it Bessie."

Murphy opens his mouth to argue, but I redirect the conversation before we can go down that road. Again.

"Any movement?" I whip off my frayed hoodie and slip a brick-colored polo shirt over my black tank.

"Not a blip." Murphy adjusts a knob. "Maybe this guy's legit."

"Maybe. But we'll find out soon enough."

"What are you going to do?"

"Tacos."

Murphy snorts. "An insurance scammer pretending to be paralyzed is not going to get out of bed for tacos."

"Well, it's either that or set his house on fire."

Murphy ponders this. "We could set his house on fire."

"We are not setting his house on fire, Murphy."

I miss Sam. He was more than just my hacker. More than just my partner, even. He was my best friend—the person I relied on to keep me from going off the rails. He should be the one arguing that we're not setting anyone's house on fire. It shouldn't be my job to reel myself in.

"Besides." I slide the temples of my fake glasses over my ears and don a Cemitas Puebla visor I conned the cashier out of. "Tacos always work."

"If you say so," Murphy says, tapping something on the tablet he'd had custom-built into the dash. "Camera's aimed at the front door in case you're right."

"I'm always right." Well, almost always.

I slip out into the dying light, goose bumps prickling my arms in the slight chill of a Windy City evening. Even in May the wind finds a way to make its presence felt. Live here long enough and you start taking the wind for granted. That's what Tyler used to say. And if anyone had known what the wind was capable of, Tyler had. I shiver thinking of him, of the night he died in front of me. Ghosts don't haunt people. Guilt does. And on Thursday, I'll turn all pruny marinating in my guilt when St. Agatha's hosts a memorial vigil for him.

I stuff thoughts of Tyler into the box in my brain marked Do Not Open and walk up to the one-story bungalow with drooping carport where the alleged insurance scammer lives. If I can prove he's faking, I get a nice, fat check from the insurance investigator who contracted me.

I ring the bell.

The intercom speaker above the doorbell crackles. "Hello?"

"Taco delivery!" I say brightly, smiling for the tiny camera that the mark had installed with the intercom.

I have to hand it to the guy. He's not taking any chances with his potential six-figure insurance payout. I'd feel bad about calling out another con, but this guy's just a dabbler. He's not really my people. He is thorough, though. Installing the intercom was a nice touch. Most insurance scammers fake their injuries for their doctor's visits and court appearances and then resume waterskiing the next weekend. This guy is maintaining character even when he thinks nobody's looking, which makes him a tough nut to crack.

Or he could be legitimately injured, I suppose. The tacos will tell us for sure.

"I didn't order anything," he says.

"Really?" I pause, pretending to check an address on my phone. "The order says 675 North Hamlin Avenue."

"Must have been a typo," he says, sounding grumpy.

"Man, my boss is going to kill me," I say, scrolling through my phone with my thumb. "This is the second time this week. And it's a prepay."

I pretend to fret, weighing my options. "I don't suppose you want these tacos? I can't take them back. Cemitas Puebla has a strict policy about taco delivery time."

"Cemitas Puebla?" the mark says.

I can almost hear the pros-and-cons debate going on in his head. Risk detection. But tacos . . . I've got him interested. Time for the shutout.

"I've got to get back. Thanks anyway, mister."

"Wait!" he says. "Is it the Orientales?"

"Yes, and the Gov. Precioso."

A few seconds of silence follow, and then the door opens. The mark—a skinny man in his midforties with a receding hairline and an honest face—stands in the doorway, fully erect and lacking any mechanical aid. Bessie's camera had better be getting this, or Murphy will be on paperwork duty for the next three months.

"Extra cheese?" he says.

"Salsa on the side," I say, and hand him the bag.

I could have kept the tacos, I guess, but the man is about to lose a five-hundred-thousand-dollar insurance settlement. He deserves a consolation prize.

"Thanks," he says, smiling, as he shuts the door.

"No sweat," I say, more to myself than to him.

Five minutes later, I'm climbing into the van's passenger seat. I toss the visor into the back for Bryn to pick up later and stow in the disguises compartment. She likes to feel useful.

"You couldn't have kept the tacos?" Murphy asks when I fasten my seat belt.

"Home, Jeeves," I say, taking off the glasses.

"That's not as funny as you think it is."

I smile around the pang in my chest. God, I miss Sam.

• • •

At 10:28 p.m., I stretch back in my office chair, yawning and rubbing my eyes. Murphy left Café Ballou with Bryn at eight, but I'd wanted to finish the report to the insurance company investigator before calling it a night.

The footage Murphy captured seems clear enough evidence to me, but I learned early on that if I don't write out my own observations in agonizing detail for the lawyers, I'll end up on the stand giving testimony. And I seriously never want to see the inside of a courtroom ever again.

Julep Dupree, you are under arrest. . . .

I'd never seen the inside of the juvenile detention center,

thanks to Mike Ramirez, the FBI agent who arrested me. Why he stuck his neck out for me I'll never know, but he did. And because he and his wife, Angela, took me in, I've mostly evaded the travesty that is the foster care system. I have a social worker, Mrs. Fairchild, who I see on a semiregular basis as part of my punishment for getting Tyler killed. That's not how the judge put it, of course, but that's how it feels, since Mrs. Fairchild asks me about him all the time. She's totally missing the point, though. I'm not supposed to forgive myself for what happened to him.

My phone buzzes and lights up. Mike.

Curfew. Crap.

I tap out my standard apology:

At work. Sorry.

There are few things worse than going from running the streets at will to a ten p.m. curfew. Ten p.m. On a weekend, even.

My phone buzzes again:

Grounded.

This is a game we play.

You rly want me stuck in your house with nothing to do?

I'd nearly typed *at home* because it's shorter, but, well, no. It's not my home.

Buzz.

Serious this time.

Tap.

Suuure.

Buzz.

1 week. No phone.

Good lord. That's like saying "No coffee."

Tap.

Ouch.

Buzz.

No Dani.

Ha. I'd like to see him try to stop her. For real, I'd probably pay admission. Dani is a nineteen-year-old mob enforcer. She does exactly what she wants, and no FBI agent, let alone Mike, is going to get in her way. I'm not even sure she would listen to me. In fact, I know she wouldn't.

Tap.

Good luck with that.

Now he's calling me. I sigh and tap the Answer button. "Who is this and why do you keep stalking me?"

"Funny," he says. "I could consider this a violation of your probation, you know."

"Blowing curfew by accident is not grounds for probation violation."

"Blowing curfew repeatedly is good enough grounds to try."

"If you wouldn't insist on instituting these silly rules, I wouldn't be forced to break them."

"The point of these 'silly rules' is to keep you safe. You know, from vengeance-seeking Ukrainian mobsters."

"Spending years up to your neck in a covert government agency has skyrocketed your paranoia. No one's conspiring to kill me."

"Yet," Mike growls. He's probably referring to himself rather than Petrov, the mob boss I took down last October.

"Seriously, Mike, if it were two in the morning, I'd understand. But ten o'clock? Middle schoolers are still out peddling Girl Scout cookies."

Mike echoes my earlier sigh. I can see him in my mind's eye rubbing his bald boulder of a head in agitation. "I don't want to babysit you. Believe me, I have better things to do with my time. But I can't follow you around to keep you out of the crosshairs either. I'm responsible for your safety. The ten o'clock curfew is the best compromise I can make."

None of this is new territory. Since I moved in with him and Angela, we've had multiple arguments about my safety. But if Petrov had wanted to make a move to hurt me, he'd have done it by now. I remind Mike of this, but he shrugs it off.

"Whether Petrov is out to get you or not, you'd better get your butt back home in the next half hour or I really am grounding you this time."

"All right, all right. I'm leaving now," I say.

"One more thing," he says. "I'm leaving town for a couple of weeks. I have a bank robbery assignment in New York."

"Bank robbery? Aren't you in the organized crime division? And anyway, doesn't New York have its own FBI agents?"

He pauses. Just a tiny fraction of a pause no one else would notice. But I notice. "It potentially relates to one of my cases here in Chicago, so I'm going to check it out."

My gut says he's holding back. "Anything having to do with me?"

He chuckles. "It was the pause, wasn't it? Look, kid, not everything is about you. I'm just worried about leaving you here without somebody to hassle you when you don't make curfew. I don't want you to feel alone. I am coming back."

Ugh. I hate it when I'm blindsided by sappy crap. Especially when it's tough-as-a-tire-iron Mike trying to be sensitive to my abandonment issues. Yes, my mom left me when I was eight. Yes, my dad's now in prison for the remainder of my high school years. That doesn't mean I'm going to break down when the closest thing I have to a parental unit is going on a business trip.

"Don't worry about me, G-man. I've got this."

"I know," he says. "Just make sure you keep Angela up to date on where you are."

I hang up and quickly email the insurance scammer report and video to the insurance investigator. I'm pulling on my jacket when the tarnished bell hanging over the door rings.

"We're closed," I say as a joke, because I assume it's Dani checking up on me.

When there's no acerbic comment in return, I look up. But it's not Dani's black-clad, steel-sharp form standing in the doorway. It's a woman in her early fifties with chestnut hair and a haggard expression.

"Can I help you?" I ask.

Instead of answering, she ducks past me to my desk and collapses into the beat-up chair I keep for clients. I sigh and shrug out of my jacket. I'm going to be late, which means I'm going to get another Mike safety lecture. And he might actually ground me this time. Awesome.

"Mrs. . . . ?" I say, having noticed the plain gold band on her left ring finger.

"Antolini," she says.

The name sounds vaguely familiar, but not enough to raise red flags. "How can I help you, Mrs. Antolini?"

She takes a tissue from her floral purse. I wait as patiently as possible while she dabs at her eyes and blows her nose. I never try to comfort weeping clients. For one thing, it drags out the crying. For another, it's just as likely to cause awkwardness as it is to cure it. Most people prefer I just wait it out.

"My husband was arrested a month ago for misappropriation of government funds. He worked for Lodestar. They do informational architecture for several government programs. If he's convicted, he'll remain in the maximum-security prison they're holding him in for the next eighteen years. I can't find the money he supposedly stole, so I can't even get him out on bail."

She stops to sniffle. So far, I'm not really hearing anything I can help with.

"I'm sorry that happened, Mrs. Antolini, but I'm not sure I—"

"It's not that I think he's innocent. I'm not that naive." She wrings the rapidly disintegrating tissue in her manicured hands. "But I know my husband, Ms. Dupree. I know he'd never have done something like this on his own. *They* put him up to it."

"'They' who?"

"The New World Initiative. It's a cult my husband joined just over a year ago."

Well, that's interesting. I remember now where I heard the name Antolini before. Mike has CNN on twenty-four seven, and I remember overhearing a story about Mr. Antolini's arrest. I don't recall the embezzlement angle, but I did hear the New World Initiative mentioned. I noted it at the time, because NWI is a leadership and personal development organization that St. Agatha's sponsors an internship with. Then I get why Mrs. Antolini is coming to me.

"You want me to take them down," I say, crossing my arms.

"I want justice," she says quietly.

And don't I know what that feels like. When Tyler died, I wanted to tear the world down. It didn't help at all that the man who pulled the trigger was behind bars. I wanted *justice*. But there is no such thing as justice when you've lost someone. Mrs. Antolini just hasn't figured that out yet.

"Fair warning: I only ruin people when I can prove they deserve it."

"They deserve it. They *used* my husband to get money for themselves. All you have to do is find it and you'll learn the truth."

"Find the money?"

"No," she says. "The blue fairy."

THE ROOKIE

"*The blue fairy.*"

I hear the words on repeat as I sit in the chapel of Holy Mother of God Church during my study hall period. I claim matters of spiritual pursuit, but I'm pretty sure Mr. Ulrich doesn't buy my piety. Luckily for me, the academy bylaws don't allow him to turn me down. It's one of the benefits of going to a private Catholic school with its very own campus church. There are disadvantages as well, but right now I'm not complaining. I slouch in the straight-backed wooden pew and prop my ankles on the top of the bench in front of me. Not the most humble of postures perhaps, but I'm not exactly a god-fearing person. God has far bigger fish to fry than me.

To explain the blue fairy, I have to take you back to the bad old days seven months ago when I took down a Ukrainian mob boss to save about a hundred girls from his human-trafficking ring. It's a long story that started with my dad, Chicago's second-best grifter, contracting his forgery skills to Petrov, the Ukrainian mob boss, for a significant sum of money. During the job, my dad found out that the forged documents he was making were being used to smuggle Ukrainian girls into the country. So he tipped off the FBI (enter Mike Ramirez), and subsequently got himself kidnapped.

But my dad is nothing if not a planner. He knew he was gambling with more than his life trying to save those girls, so he hid a series of clues to keep me safe should anything happen to him. It mostly worked. Well, it helped. Okay, it was a terrible idea, and he should have known it wouldn't stop me.

Anyway, the first clue came with a gun. My mother's gun. On the gun was an inscription: PER A.N.M., LA MIA FATA TURCHINA. *For Alessandra Nereza Moretti, my blue fairy.* At the time, I had no idea my mom owned a gun. I still don't know where it came from, why she had it, or why she hadn't taken it with her when she walked out on us eight years ago. But Alessandra Nereza Moretti was undoubtedly my mother, and the thing in my hand was inarguably a gun, and whoever called her "my blue fairy" was definitely not my dad. I gave the gun to Sam, and as far as I know, he still has it.

In any case, Mrs. Antolini's mentioning a blue fairy can't be a coincidence. Coincidences don't exist. Somehow the New World Initiative is connected to my mother. The question is, what is the blue fairy and what truth is it going to show me if I find it? That the New World Initiative is a cult? That Mr.

Antolini was manipulated into stealing the money? Or that my mother was somehow involved?

Mrs. Antolini was marvelously unhelpful in providing intel. She had no idea what the blue fairy was—only that the two men in suits who questioned her about it wouldn't tell her anything else. She couldn't even tell me what agency the men worked for. Which means that the people looking for the blue fairy are likely not legit lawmen. If they were, they'd have identified themselves.

"Julep Dupree?"

A young girl of ambiguous Asian descent is standing in the row in front of me. She looks about twelve, and she must be a recent transfer student, because I've never met her before. She does look familiar, though, so I must have seen her wandering around campus.

"Excellent day for devotion," I say, gesturing for her to take a seat. "How can I be of service?"

Skipping study hall is not my only motive for hanging out in the chapel. After Dean Porter—St. Aggie's dean of students and my personal nemesis—nearly busted me outside the music room last semester, I realized I needed a place on campus to meet potential clients where Porter couldn't go. Then I found out a couple of months back that, per the strict orders of the school's president, Sister Rasmussen, the dean doesn't police the chapel. I'm not sure if that's Sister Rasmussen's way of protecting the sanctity of the church or the secrets of one Julep Dupree, but I'll take it.

My visitor stares at me for five full seconds without saying anything. I raise an eyebrow and start to tell her she should take a picture, it would last longer, but she moves before I do, taking the seat I'd indicated and staring straight ahead. It'll make conversation awkward, but I have a feeling that the conversation is going to be awkward anyway.

"I'm Lily," she says. Simple enough introduction, but the way she says it is weird—assertive, angry. This girl has some kind of baggage.

"What can I do for you, Lily?"

She lowers her gaze to her lap, her glossy black hair swishing over her secrets before I can tease them out.

"Do you have a job for me?" I prompt.

"No," she says forcefully.

"Then what do you want?" I'm too amused to be annoyed. "You came to me, remember?"

"I—" She stops and glances over her shoulder at me. "I want to . . . work for you."

I laugh. "You want to what?"

"I need a job," she says.

I roll my eyes at this outrageous lie. She's clearly well cared for—designer haircut, perfect makeup, professionally pressed St. Aggie's uniform. She needs a job like she needs a makeover. Which is to say, she doesn't.

"I don't think so," I say. "I don't hire liars."

"Aren't you a professional liar?"

"Good point," I admit. "Still."

"Okay, I don't need a job." She turns in the pew to face me. "I want a job. Not just a job. I want to work for you."

"You can't join me like you would a country club. I'm not hiring."

"I was a research assistant for one of my teachers at my previous school. I type fast, I don't charge, and I make a mean caramel macchiato. Can Murphy Donovan make a caramel macchiato?"

"I don't have an espresso machine."

"I can throw in an espresso machine."

"I have no *need* for an espresso machine." I stare at her, trying to figure her out. Why is she doing this? "Are you trying to piss off your parents or something?"

She's silent for several moments before she answers.

"No," she says, finally. "I'm trying to learn."

"Learn what? How to pick locks? Spy on people?"

She's quiet again, thinking. If she doesn't give me an answer I like, this conversation is officially over.

"I'm trying to figure out who I am," she says softly, the suffering in her voice so apparent that I wince. I know too well what that feels like—not just the pain, but not being able to hide it.

I have no idea what the right thing here is. Giving her what she's asking for isn't necessarily a kindness. I grift partly to keep myself afloat and partly because I don't know who I am without it. But I'm under no illusions that it's a good thing to be doing. Sure, I use it to help people now. Since everything went down with the mob, I'm on the Captain America side of the law (well, mostly). But I'm still not really a great person. No one, least of all me, thinks I'm a good influence on young girls.

Lily must sense that she's losing me, because she says, "I'm looking for the Julep Dupree who saved a hundred girls from a life worse than death. Is that person still around?"

Fabulous. One act of brainless idealism, and I am never going to live it down.

I size her up again. The last time I trusted a classmate, he ratted me out to a mob boss. The last time I trusted a barista, he arrested my best friend and then me. You could say I'm a little gun-shy in the trust department these days. But I have a hard time believing she's duplicitous. I'm practically gagging on the waves of innocence rolling off her. She couldn't be an FBI agent, and I can't imagine her in league with someone like Petrov.

And then her lower lip wobbles, ever so slightly, and she immediately firms up her features. The show of resolve is what breaks me. What can I say? I'm a fixer.

"One-week trial," I say, shaking my head at myself. I can't believe I'm doing this. "If it turns out you're a spy, I *will* sic my enforcer on you. And yes, she bites. Give me your phone."

Lily hands me her phone, and I type my number into her contacts app.

"When should I start?"

"Right now," I say, switching from her contacts to the Web browser and pulling up the page for New World Initiative. I hand back her phone. "You'd better be right about that caramel macchiato."

She turns to go, glancing at me once before walking out. I settle back into my angst. I wish she hadn't brought up the Ukrainians. I wish I hadn't been thinking about all of it before she even showed up. I have too hard a time stuffing it all away after it comes popping out. The weight of it all presses down harder on me here. I lost so much more than I saved that day. Tyler. Sam. My dad. Not to mention Ralph, who I still haven't managed to track down despite all my and Murphy's searching.

I just want to go back to what it was like before all this started happening.

Amen to that. I light a candle on my way out.

• • •

After school, Dani takes me to the firing range in Des Plaines. Dani and I have been going regularly since January, so it's a familiar route. I spend this particular trip lost in thought.

I usually talk Dani's ear off during the drive, getting her criminal-underworld insight on cases, keeping her updated on the Ukrainian girls, and, in general, telling her about my day. She's a great listener. Not so much a sharer, unless she's giving me the smackdown for being stupid. Like last March when I was struggling with my anger over Tyler's death and daring the world to try to take me down. She said I didn't have to suffer to earn forgiveness. But maybe I just suffer either way. . . .

"You did your job. You saved me from Petrov. Your promise to my dad is done, but you're still here. And you still think it's your job to protect me. Just so we're clear, I never asked you to."

"You are right. You did not ask. But I was not doing it for you."

"*Dani—*"

"*Enough. It is your life to risk as you want. Just as it is my life to risk in your place.*"

"What are you thinking?" she asks, breaking into my memories.

"Work," I say, more lie than truth. No need to rehash the many ways in which I've been an idiot. So I fill her in on the particulars of the NWI job instead. Well, most of the particulars.

"And your new associate has found information on the New World Initiative?"

"As much as can be found without joining up," I say, thinking back to the two-page report, typed and double-spaced, that Lily had emailed me that afternoon.

"You are considering joining a cult?" Dani doesn't sound thrilled.

"It's not really a cult. Or at least, not openly. It's a leadership organization. Businesspeople pay to attend a series of leadership workshops that supposedly help them turn their mediocre lives into satisfied, happy ones. They advance to higher levels, bringing in new members to earn rewards and greater status."

"It sounds like a cult."

"It's more like a pyramid scheme. It promises a big reward it never intends to deliver."

"Which is?" Dani backs into a parking spot next to the firing range just as the horizon turns a dusky rose. I open my door and step out, stroking the hood of Dani's Chevelle as I walk to the sidewalk. This car and I go way back.

"That's what worries me," I say. "What kind of 'reward' would convince someone with no priors to commit something as severe as grand larceny? Antolini had to know he'd get caught."

Dani holds the door to the range open for me. Steve the gun-desk guy smiles at us. He's seen us enough times now to recognize our faces.

I fork over my fake ID and Firearm Owner's ID without his asking. Dani, he never ID's. Possibly her black coat and perpetual glare are ID enough for Steve. They'd be enough for me to make her as a mob enforcer. And no one who wants continual use of his fingers cards a mob enforcer.

We pay our rental fees, grab safety gear, and head to the firing range. It's busy, but not so busy that we have to wait for a booth. I lay the Beretta I always rent on the table so I can adjust my safety glasses before loading the gun. The glasses are too big and constantly slide down my nose. Dani never seems to have that problem. Somehow she looks just as lethal wearing plastic glasses and headphones as she does without.

She waits as I inspect the gun and load it. She's a stickler for proper procedure. Always point the gun downrange. Always assume the gun is loaded. No coffee on the shooting line. Blah. Too many rules. But both she and Mike insisted I learn how to shoot in case another Petrov tries to use me as a body shield—which is hardly likely given that I turn down the dangerous cases these days, but as it's probably the only thing they agree on, I took a note.

"There is something you are not telling me," Dani says over the dull roar of the other shooters. She's leaning against the wall of the booth, her arms crossed, looking relaxed. She always seems most at ease when there's a gun in the room.

I fire a few rounds into the distant target. It's hard to tell from the booth, but I may have managed a reliable group. It's down by the lower left quadrant of the target, but it's a group.

"Move your right foot back," Dani says, her expression shrewd and assessing. "Lean more over your left."

Dani didn't exactly volunteer to teach me. She prefers to keep me completely separate from her day job as hired muscle for whatever criminal syndicate happens to be shorthanded. Training me in the fine art of killing people is too close to that part of her life for comfort, I guess. But I insisted. Mike gave me exactly one (totally unnecessary) driving lesson during which I nearly booted him from the car for stomping on an imaginary brake pedal on the passenger-side floor every time I rounded a corner. I figured that subjecting myself to his teaching style while I was in possession of a loaded weapon was not the best way to stay out of prison.

Besides, I like being around Dani. She doesn't push me to be something I'm not. She doesn't judge me, as long as I'm not acting stupid. And she doesn't need protecting. I can just *be* with her. No expectations, no apologies, no guilt. She is to me what a gun is to her—I'm most at ease when she's in the room.

She arches an eyebrow, still waiting for me to spill my secrets. I adjust my stance and my aim. "I'll tell you later," I say, because hell if I'm shouting about my mom issues at the top of my lungs.

I take a few more shots, but they end up hitting the same

place on the target. Dani leans forward and fixes my grip on the gun, her movements patient but firm, her fingers warm against mine.

"Holding it like this feels clunky," I say.

"It applies rearward pressure to counteract the forward pressure of your shooting hand. Try again."

I do as told, and this time my shots end up in the lower right quadrant of the target.

Dani sighs, which I see more than hear, and comes over to stand behind me. She wraps her arms around me, placing her hands over mine on the gun. She still has to shout despite her mouth being right next to my ear, but that's not as weird as the chill that zips down my spine at the thought of her mouth being that close to my ear. Earth to Julep—you're supposed to be paying attention.

"You are working too hard to align the sights. You won't have time to do that in a fight anyway. Focus on the front sight. Now take a breath and let it out halfway. Squeeze the trigger slowly so the movement does not change your aim. . . ."

Bull's-eye.

She hesitates, and then steps back. The sudden absence of her body heat makes the ambient air that swirls in feel colder than before.

As much as I prefer Dani's company, I don't actually *get* her. I'm a grifter. I can usually read people like a shopping list left abandoned in a grocery cart. But Dani's more like *The Brothers Karamazov*, the nineteenth-century Russian novel Mrs. Springfield bludgeoned us with last semester—all intricate imagery that's a bitch to decipher. I'm sure it's because my knowledge of her life is patchy at best. She won't tell me about her present, and I get only rare glimpses of her past. She keeps too much hidden, like why she goes out of her way to help me.

I freeze my position and fire off another three rounds. All of them end up just to the right of center.

"Better," she says.

I change the clip and hand her the gun. She pulls the slide back to check the chamber. In one smooth movement, she aims and shoots the target dead center. She waits a breath and shoots another. Then another. The hole in the center of the target widens to an oval.

"Control is everything," she says. Her ice-blue eyes are set at serious, but then they always are. I've seen her laugh maybe three or four times in the eight months I've known her. Whatever demons she's carrying must weigh as much as the cathedrals she has etched into her skin. And I know a thing or two about carrying demons.

I see the moment her thoughts shift from guns to something else. I don't know what they shift to, but her expression turns bleak. She's about to say something when Steve bursts through the door, minus headphones and safety glasses. His gaze falls on us like he's a smoke alarm and we're on fire.

"You'd better get out here," he says.

THE INITIATIVE

"Ooo, yikes—that's going to take a while to buff out," Murphy says as he joins me on the sidewalk. Not-Bessie is cooling her tires next to the curb rather than the parking lot to give the battered Chevelle its space.

"Thanks for that, Murph. Perhaps you could rein in your exorbitant sensitivity when you talk to Dani." Sarcasm is my superpower.

"At least it's fixable," he says, surveying the shattered windows, dented fenders, and spray-painted hood. "Who did you piss off this time?"

"It's probably just a fluke." I wave with a dismissiveness I don't feel.

"Just a fluke?" he says, eyebrows raised behind his just-this-side-of-hipster glasses. His latest haircut is even more rakish than the one Sam had him get when he orchestrated his

geek-chic makeover. Bryn might be the true grifter here—
her transformation of Murphy is more absolute than mine. "I
thought you didn't believe in coincidences."

I did tell him that, didn't I? Con artist rule number 489:
Keep your philosophies on life to yourself. Sadly, I suck at following this rule.

"Besides," he continues, "flukes don't usually come with
strange messages."

I look over at Dani's poor Chevelle, its smashed windshield
a radiating web of milky glass. Toothy shards litter the asphalt
around the tires. And worse, the words NO GAME are spray-
painted in red on the hood.

NO GAME. I haven't the faintest idea what it means, but my
list of suspects is pretty short.

"It's not too late for Witness Protection," Murphy says,
though he's only saying it to irk me. He knows I hate it when
anyone brings it up.

"This isn't Petrov. If he had this kind of reach, he'd have
gone for me directly."

"As someone who stands next to you a lot, that's really comforting," he says. My sarcasm appears to be rubbing off on him.

"It's not meant to be comforting. It's pragmatic. This isn't
his style. Property damage? Petrov is a razor, not a baseball bat."

"Nice. You should say exactly that to Agent Ramirez when
he asks you about it," Murphy says, smirking.

I play through that conversation with Mike in my head.
"Yeah, not going to happen. It's Dani's car, so it's not like the
police are going to call him. And if the police don't tell him,

how's he going to find out? He flew to New York this morning, and it'll be fixed before he gets back, so . . ." I let Murphy fill in the you-better-not-say-anything blanks himself.

"That's one way of handling it, I guess," he says, shaking his head at me.

Dani and Steve, the gun-desk guy, are talking with a couple of police officers near the building's entrance. The officers are taking notes, Steve is gesticulating with his long, scrawny arms, and Dani is quietly brooding. I see the lines of tension in her body. She's a coiled spring about to pop through the leather upholstery.

"I'd better get her out of here," I say.

As I approach the group, Dani's eyes snap to mine. She looks like a caged animal. I imagine I looked much the same when I waltzed into the MCC to try to post bail for Sam after Mike arrested him at the dance last year.

It's not that we criminals are afraid of cops, exactly. I certainly didn't hold back when I railed at Mike for betraying me and arresting my partner, despite being in the heart of FBI territory. But there's something inherently wrong about being within spitting distance of someone who's your polar opposite. It's like it messes with the space-time continuum. If Sam were here, he'd use some bizarre hacker analogy about mutual exclusion programming. But Sam isn't here, so I have to settle for imagining him saying it.

I take Dani's arm and begin to slowly extract her from the group. "You got this, right, Steve?" I give him my most winsome smile.

"Sure," he says.

"Wait, we're not done with our questions," says the female officer. She's shorter than her partner, but not by much.

I hand her my card. "I'm sorry, we need to be somewhere. But you can call me anytime, and I'll be happy to answer any further questions." I'm backing away, pushing Dani behind me. "I can't tell you how much we appreciate everything you and the Des Plaines police force are doing for us. And rest assured we will continue to help in whatever way we can."

And before Officer Lady can get a word in edgewise, I'm shoving Dani into the front seat of the van. I climb over her, shutting the door behind me and strapping myself into the jump seat Murphy installed behind the driver's seat.

"Next stop, coffee," Murphy says as he starts the engine.

"Thanks, Murphy," I say, inching over enough to put my hand on Dani's arm. "Dani?"

She's staring out the window as we pass the Chevelle. I can't help but feel like we're leaving an injured friend behind in enemy territory. I'm sure Dani feels ten times worse.

"I can fix it," I say.

She doesn't answer.

● ● ●

St. Agatha's in late May is an explosion of roses. I don't know who the rose nut was who planted them all, but now the poor groundskeepers are forever pruning, deadheading, spraying, and staking. The ivy up the side of the administration building is bad enough, but the roses add a whole new level of angst. I mostly try to ignore them and how they smell like my mom.

I open the door leading to the Brockman Room and pass the portraits of dead white men frowning knowingly at me as I climb the stairs. They don't bother me anymore, though. We have an understanding. I keep playing Robin Hood, and they keep their judgment to a minimum.

I trot up the carpeted stairs to the administration offices. I always feel a bolt of dread when my feet hit the second floor. Dean Porter's office is up here, so it's a conditioned response. But I'm not here to see the aggro dean of students today. Besides, at four in the afternoon, she's usually out doing campus rounds.

"Can I help you?" asks a freckled student assistant. A junior. Karla . . . something.

"I want to apply for the New World Initiative summer internship program. It says online that I need to fill out the application through the Professional Development Office."

Karla taps something into her computer. "The application deadline for that was in February. Besides, both spots are taken. One of the students would have to bow out. Even then, you wouldn't get in. There are two alternates selected, and both of them would have to pass. Plus, there's no guarantee the program director would accept your application. The internship starts next week."

"May I ask who the accepted students and alternates are?"

Karla gives me a suspicious look—I am Julep Dupree, after

all—and then scrolls to the bottom of the screen. She reads me the names. I thank her for the information and walk out.

Once in the hallway, I pull out my phone and scroll to a number in my contacts app. I press Send and wait for Kurt Peddleton to pick up.

"Kurt, hi. It's Julep. Remember that favor you owe me?" He answers in the affirmative, though reluctantly. I don't know why everyone is so apprehensive about the favors I make them promise me when I do a job for them. I've never asked for anything crazy. Well, except that one time. But it's not like his eyebrows will never grow back. "Well, I need you to back out of the NWI summer internship program." We go around about it a few times before he finally caves. They always cave eventually. They have to. I have too much dirt on them, and they know it. "You're a gem, Kurt. Thanks."

Then I call Rajid Ahmed, one of the two alternates, and have an almost identical conversation with him. He finally agrees (after much whining), and we hang up.

Sonja Warrick is another story, though. I don't have anything on her, and I don't know what leverage there is to use against her. So I call Bryn.

"What is it this time?" she says when she picks up. Bryn likes me, I'm fairly sure, in spite of how I manipulated her into going with Murphy to the formal last year. In the end, she's happy dating Murphy, so she mostly forgives me for duping her into saying yes. But on some level it still irritates her.

"What do we have on Sonja Warrick? Anything I can use?"

Bryn sighs heavily. "I don't know, Julep. She's a nerd. She

does all her own work. She keeps to herself. I can't remember the last time I even talked to her."

"There has to be something. Does she like someone? Does she hate someone? Everyone has a secret."

"Ugh, that is so . . . you. Why don't you just ask her for whatever it is you want? Maybe she'll give it to you."

I frown at the phone. "I don't understand the words that you are speaking."

"Oh, for— I don't have time for this." She hangs up on me.

I pace back and forth, thinking. And then I get an idea. I call Murphy.

"Hey, Murph, I need you to change Sonja Warrick's bio grade to an F."

"Hello to you too," he says, but I hear him tapping his keyboard in the background, so I don't berate him for insubordination. "Why are we changing Sonja Warrick's bio grade to an F?"

"I need her disqualified from the NWI internship. The powers that be will figure out the grade 'mistake' in a week or two, but it'll take them long enough to verify everything that she'll be disqualified from accepting the internship until after it's already started."

"You know, there's a note here that she's accepted an international internship in Mumbai for the summer."

"Oh," I say, sheepishly. "You can change her bio grade back, then." Bryn was right. I could have just asked.

I hang up with Murphy and walk back into the Professional Development Office. Karla is on the phone.

"All right. I'll make a note of it. Thank you for calling," she says, and hangs up. Then turning to me, she says dryly, "Apparently, one of the students backed out of that internship you were asking about. And then mysteriously, one of the alternates backed out as well. If the other alternate backs out—" She taps a few more times on the keyboard. "Actually, it looks like that alternate is out of the running as well. Interesting."

I smile innocently at her. She hands me an application and a pen.

"Thank you," I say, and fill out the form.

When I hand her the completed form, she takes it with an arch expression. "You'll still have to convince the program director you deserve special consideration."

"Who's the program director?"

"Dean Porter."

• • •

Murphy enjoys a hearty guffaw at my expense later that night as we're sitting in the Ballou office, regrouping. I lean against my desk and tap my fingers on the scratched wood, waiting for him to get his hilarity under control.

"Why is that funny?" Lily asks, referring to my news that I have to get special permission from Dean Porter to get into the NWI program.

"Julep and the dean are like orcs and elves."

Lily looks at Murphy blankly.

"Meaning they loathe each other," he explains. "There's no way the dean is going to let Julep in."

"There's a way. I just haven't figured it out yet," I say. Really, he should have more faith in me. I did get Bryn to say yes to his invitation to the formal, after all. If that's not a miracle, I don't know what is.

"Well, while you're chewing on that, I have something else for you. Which do you want first, the bad news or the slightly less bad news?" Murphy swivels his chair around to grab a couple of papers from his desk.

I pinch the bridge of my nose. "Why is it never good news?"

"Slightly less bad is slightly good," Lily points out.

"Thanks for the input, Lily," I say. "Let's go with the bad news first."

"I just wasted the greater part of two days—which I can never get back—following the paper trail for the New World Initiative. Every publicly available document confirms they're legit. There's not so much as a building code violation on these guys."

"There has to be something," I say. "Even companies entirely on the up-and-up have a little dirt under their nails."

Murphy shakes his head. "I've checked property records, incorporation documents, court records, police reports. I even checked UCC lien records. No red flags. Not even yellow ones. And get this . . ."

Murphy rolls his chair across the floor. He sets some papers on my desk, turning them to face me. A printout of the pristine Better Business Bureau reviews of the New World Initiative Corporation glares mockingly at me.

"There are no complaints," Murphy continues. "Not one."

"That's . . . weird," I say.

"Because it means there's nothing shady going on? Or because it means there is?" Lily asks.

I think of Petrov's pet senator, Tyler's dad, who ended up in prison, but not before he paved the way for Petrov to wreak all sorts of havoc on a lot of innocent girls' lives. If NWI has that kind of connection, that's more power than I really want to pit myself against. Even if the blue fairy lies on the other side, even if Mrs. Antolini is another kind of innocent in need of my help, I don't know that I can go through another Petrov.

"What have you got, rookie?"

"Not much," Lily says. "Duke Salinger is the founder and CEO. Several articles mention his checkered past, but nothing I found spelled out what that past was. Almost every article was a glowing endorsement of NWI. The only detractors were crazy, tinfoil-hat-wearing types who live off the grid and write manifestos. And even they were luke-brimstone at best. The NWI is just—"

"Too clean to be real," I finish for her.

A quiet moment passes as we all consider the implications of this.

"Maybe we should just let this one go," Murphy says at last.

I skim through the Better Business review. None of them convinces me continuing this job is a good idea. "Maybe we should," I say.

"Why?" Lily asks. "You brought down an entire mob. What's one little pyramid scheme compared to that?"

I look up in surprise at the note of bitterness in her voice and catch a glimpse of pain before she manages to cover it up.

"Sometimes a pyramid scheme is more than a pyramid scheme," I answer before turning to Murphy. "What's the slightly less bad news?"

"I think I have a lead on your mom," Murphy says.

I nearly fall over. "What?"

"It's not a good lead."

"Murphy," I say sharply. "What lead?"

"Up till now, we've only been scratching the surface in our Internet search. There's so much the search engines don't index. So I started combing online databases—university libraries, media archives, that kind of thing—to see if I could find anything. And, well . . ."

He grabs his laptop, clicks something, and turns the computer to show me a grainy scanned image of a newspaper article from February 2012. A picture of my mom dominates the left side of the column. Her name, Alessandra Nereza Moretti, is the caption. My heart climbs into my throat as I start at the top of the article.

> Thirty-three-year-old Alessandra Moretti reported missing. Last seen at Deer Run Café on Mercator Dr. Reward for information leading to her recovery. Call 555- . . .

I pull back in confusion, then scroll to the top of the page and down to the article again.

"This can't be right," I say. "It's a missing person report. It says she disappeared three years ago."

"I told you it wasn't a good lead."

"I don't understand." It's definitely her. Dark brown hair, blue eyes, the same smile I used to see in the mirror before everything went haywire last year. I may not have seen my mom in eight years, but I'd still recognize her in a picture. "Why wouldn't I have heard about it? Who would have reported her missing if not me and my dad?"

"I don't know," Murphy says. "It's a local article from some nothing town in Alabama. A missing person is hardly national news. Still, it seems like they would have notified next of kin if they knew her name."

I pull out my phone and dial the number listed in the article, but all I get is a "This number is no longer in service" message.

Then my stomach drops. "Wait. Did it say February of 2012?" I scan the newspaper header for confirmation.

"I think so. Why?"

My knees shudder, and I sink into my chair. "I would have been thirteen. And that's about the time of year my dad took off and was gone for two weeks with no explanation."

Murphy goes quiet, digesting this. "Do you think he knows about it?"

"I—I never asked him where he went or why. I just assumed it had to do with a job that had gone wrong. I thought he left to protect me. But now . . . It can't be a coincidence."

Murphy shoots me a sympathetic look as he resumes control of the laptop. "Speaking of coincidences . . . ," he says, pulling up a web page he bookmarked.

WELCOME TO THE ALL-NEW BAR63.

"What is this?" I ask, the sixty-three pinging around in my head like an eight ball.

"Maybe nothing," he says. "But it might be worth checking out."

> Located in the vibrant Rogers Park area, just steps away from the campus of Loyola University, the new Bar63 offers something for everyone . . . opened its doors in March. Talented bartender Victoria Febbi . . . live music every Thursday night . . . designed for sports enthusiasts, with more than twenty giant flatscreens . . .

"What is it?" Lily asks, no doubt tired of our cryptic discussion.

"It's a bar that just opened a couple of months ago called Bar63."

"Why is that significant?"

"My father has this saying: 'You, me, and sixty-three.' He used it as a clue last year when everything went down with the mob. I always thought the sixty-three was meaningless, something he just made up because it rhymed and it was catchy. But now there's this bar." I look up at Murphy. "I don't know, Murph. This one really could be just a coincidence."

"I thought so, too, when I first read the article. But something about it kept nagging me. So I dug around a bit, and I found something else pretty coincidental."

He uses the keyboard shortcut to bring up the next browser window. The Wikipedia page for Victoria Febbi appears. Except it's not Victoria, it's Vittoria. And it's not a page about a bartender. It's a page about the actress who voiced the Blue Fairy in an Italian production of *Pinocchio*.

"We already know from the inscription on the gun that the blue fairy somehow relates to your mom," Murphy says, his bespectacled gaze intense. "What if the sixty-three relates to her, too?"

I stare at the screen without really seeing it. Is that what my dad meant? Every time he said *You, me, and sixty-three*, did he mean my mom? All these years, I thought it was just me and him against the world; I thought my mom had left us without a backward glance. But maybe that's not what happened at all. Maybe my dad was trying to tell me something.

"Well . . ." I shut Murphy's laptop. "There's only one way to find out."

THE CONTRACT

Forty minutes and a fake Loyola student ID later, Murphy slows the van to a stop on the street just outside Bar63.

"Are you sure you want to see what's behind that door?"

It looks like a harmless enough door. Dark wood siding, lanterns above it. People bustle by, some of them bona fide Loyola students, and their reflections in the bar's front window follow them from pane to pane.

"I think I can handle it," I say, giving Murphy a halfhearted smile and slipping out of the van.

I thread my way through the passersby and pull open the heavy oak door, the darkness inside greeting me like a shill roping a mark. It's packed for a Tuesday night. All the seats at the bar are filled, and I can make out only the bartender's back in the dim light as she hustles to make drinks for the sports-cheering patrons.

Taking advantage of the crowd, I loop around the perimeter, scanning the walls for clues. But if there are any among the vintage team shots and event posters, they're too well hidden for me to find. The room is long and narrow, with a row of two-seater tables along the right wall. It connects in the back to a series of adjoining rooms, some filled with high tables, others with sofas. One of the rooms contains a closed door marked OFFICE.

The crowd explodes into a simultaneous cheer that makes me jump. I look over at the screens they're riveted to and see a brown diamond surrounded by a green field. I lean against the rough granite wall across from the bar, which is still too crowded for comfort. I want to actually talk to the bartender, not just order a drink and have her flit off again. I can afford to wait, though. It's the bottom of the ninth, and the Cubs aren't doing very well.

Since I'm waiting anyway, I pull out my phone and open Contacts. As I scroll up to Mrs. Antolini's number, I happen to pass Sam's number. And as I often do when I see it, I hesitate with my thumb over the Call button. I've talked to him only once since he left for military school—only one time since that night. I tried to call him on his birthday. I tried to call him on my birthday. But he won't answer my calls. So I gave up trying. And soon maybe I'll stop hesitating every time I see his name in my contacts.

Of its own volition, my thumb moves to the Delete Contact button. I might as well save myself. I could do it with a simple press of my finger. But then I hear Sam's voice in my head, telling me why he'd decided to accept his dad's military-school ultimatum. That he didn't know who he was without me. That he needed to find that out before he had anything to offer me. I don't pretend to know what the hell that means, much less how the hell I feel about it. But regardless, he's still the best hacker I've ever met, still my partner . . . always my best friend. Whether or not either of us still believes it, it's the truth.

My thumb moves again, past Sam's number and up the alphabet to Mrs. Antolini. I tap the number, and then clear my throat as I press my phone hard to one ear to block out the sound. I move to a quieter corner of the room and put my palm over my other ear. I should probably wait until I'm outside to do this, but I don't want to lead her on. If I'm changing my mind about the job, she deserves to know as soon as possible.

After three rings, her voice mail picks up.

"Hi, Mrs. Antolini. This is Julep Dupree. I'm sorry, but I've reconsidered taking your case. Based on my preliminary research, I don't think it's a good fit for my team. I have a list of private investigators who might be able to help you. I can email it to you in the morning. Thanks for your understanding."

As I press the End button, I get a text message from Mike.

Twenty-minute warning.

Halfway across the country, and he's still tracking my curfew.

Angela's making me cookies as we speak.

That's proof? She always makes cookies on Tues. How about I call her?

Chuckling, I reply,

You got me. I'm on my way back now.

Better be.

Just then, the crowd heaves a collective sigh of disappointment and breaks into smaller groups of twos and threes. Most groups head for the door, while some stay to finish their drinks. A stool opens up at the south end of the bar. I pocket my phone and make my way over to it.

After sliding onto the stool, I signal to the bartender that I'm ready to place my order. She's probably in her late thirties or so, and looks like a cross between a biker and a hippie— dark jeans, a form-fitting tie-dyed tank revealing a barbed-wire tattoo, and bleached dreads piled messily on her head. Her brown eyes linger on me a beat too long before she goes back to smearing the guts of a lime wedge on the rim of the glass she's holding. If she's the famed Victoria Febbi, then we can pretty much chalk this one up to coincidence. She's about as far from my überfeminine, fashion-forward mom as it is possible to get.

"What'll you have?" she says, wiping her hands on a towel as she comes over to me.

"Club soda," I say. "With a twist."

She snorts. "Can I see some ID?"

"For a club soda?"

"For being in the bar at all. No minors."

"I didn't see a bouncer," I say, producing my fake Loyola ID.

She glances at it and hands it back. "I need a license."

Wow, not even a smile. Such customer service. I take out my fake driver's license and hand it to her.

She pulls a black-light flashlight from under the counter and checks the hologram. Good thing I know what I'm doing in the fake-ID department—just ask the hundred or so St. Aggie's students I made IDs for last year to cover rent while my dad moonlighted as the mob's pet bullet-cushion. On second thought, don't ask them. They'd probably give me a lousy reference, since I threw them all under the honor-code-violation bus to save the Ukrainian girls from both Petrov and deportation. And speaking of getting kicked out of places . . .

"Is it the Catholic schoolgirl getup?" I say to the bartender, heaping on the charm as she pores over every molecule of the license. "I'm in a play. Dress rehearsals all this week. I just came in to catch the end of the Cubs game."

She studies my face, and then hands back the license. "Club soda?"

"With a twist."

She stows the flashlight, grabs a glass, and fills it using a soda gun. She's watching me with an expression that's half suspicious, half befuddled, and there's a certain tension in her shoulders that, in my experience, usually indicates fear. Which makes no sense. Even if I were busted as a minor in her bar, I'd be the one with a black mark on my rap sheet. She carded me. She did her job. So why the fear?

The bartender plunks the glass down on the bar in front of me, sans twist, and starts her retreat. I have to act now if I'm going to figure anything out.

"I read about this bar online. Are you Victoria Feb—Fab—Fib— Help me out here."

"Yes," she says, eyeing the other patrons, but she doesn't

elaborate. My heart sinks an inch or two as her admission confirms my guess that my errand here has been for nothing. As much as I don't believe in coincidences, this bar really must be one. There's nothing here but a bevy of masochistic sports fans, a surly staff, and an unusual couple of names. Nevertheless, I'll give it one more shot.

"You know, you remind me of someone," I lie, sipping my soda. "Her name's Moretti. Any relation?"

The bartender doesn't so much as bat an eyelash at the name. "Nope. I have a niece Sylvia in Spokane, though."

I slump over my drink, depressed. Looks like I may have to take that NWI job after all. I need to find my mom. Especially now that I know she's officially missing. I pull out a five and leave it on the bar. I didn't really want the soda anyway.

I slide off the stool and head for the door. Just as I reach for the handle, my phone buzzes with a text notification. I glance back at the bartender, but someone else has taken my stool already, so all I see are her bleached dreads. My phone buzzes again. I pull it out of my pocket, and when I read the two messages from Dani, all thoughts of biker-hippie bartenders fly out of my head.

Where are you?

You are in danger.

I don't bother texting back as I swing the door open and step out onto the sidewalk. Dani picks up on the first ring.

"Where are you?" she says.

"I'm on North Broadway, near Loyola," I say, scanning the

street for Dani's rental car. It's not in sight, though, which doesn't do much to improve my anxiety. "What do you mean I'm in danger?"

"I just heard from one of my contacts. He is not reliable, but if he is telling the truth about this—"

"Back up. Telling the truth about what?"

"There's a contract out on you."

A contract. Perfect. "That means the Chevelle was about me, wasn't it? Dang it. I hate it when Murphy's right."

"This is not a time for jokes," she says, her accent getting thicker.

"It's not a joke. Murphy is unbearable when he's right. Thank god Mike's out of town, or I'd be on a one-way flight to Albuquerque before I could say—"

"Stop talking," she says sharply. "I am coming to get you. Go somewhere bright and full of people and text me the address."

I agree and hang up, checking over my shoulder, because it is physically impossible not to when someone's just told you there's a hit man targeting you.

The Popeyes across the street definitely fits the bill for brightness, and its proximity to a college means it's relatively populated, even at nine-forty-five at night. I glance at the number on the door as I start to cross the street. Unfortunately, I'm too busy tapping the address into my phone to notice the headlights barreling toward me until it's almost too late.

The squeal of accelerating tires betrays my would-be killer. I throw myself behind a Corolla parked illegally in front of the bar. Glass shatters as bullets rip through the car's rear wind-shield. I cover my head instinctively and curse when the glass nicks my skin.

Gunshots are almost unheard of in Edgewater, so of course people pour out onto the street like idiots when they should be barring their doors. Popeyes is out of the question now. I make a run for it, my heart slamming against my rib cage. The rational part of my brain says the hit man won't come back, not with so many witnesses on alert. But the rational part of my brain is no match for survival instinct.

The "L" station is packed and full of light. I jump the turn-stile and sprint across the platform, but I don't feel safe here. I won't feel safe until I see Dani. I curl up behind a nice metal map display, wrapping my arms around myself to keep my body from shaking to pieces.

Granvlle L staiton.

I tap to Dani, typos rampant from clumsy fingers.

Two things on my to-do list: First, force myself to breathe, and second, figure out who the hell would want me dead.

THE CONCESSION

"Are you all right?" Dani asks. The soothing glow of street-lights washes over the car as we pass from one pool of light to the next. I want to think about the light, or the oral report I have to give in history, or anything other than bullets flying at my head. And as soon as I think that, the pools of light turn to pools of blood under Tyler's body.

"Yeah," I say, blinking back the image for the fiftieth time. "I got away. Total amateur hour."

"You or him?"

I'm still too rattled to snort, though I appreciate her efforts at distraction. "Both."

She reaches across the console to lay her hand on top of mine. I must be pretty out of it. She never touches me voluntarily, not without a specific purpose. I'm not sure her touch helps, though. It makes me nervous for a different reason, one that involves me leaning on her too much when I'm clearly a danger to anyone stupid enough to be friends with me. Her job is already dangerous enough. She doesn't need my crazy life adding to that.

Despite my reservations, my tremors eventually subside under the warmth radiating from her hand.

"I should be stronger than this," I say. "I used to be invincible."

She squeezes my hand. "The first time I was ordered to kill someone, I shook so badly, I missed at point-blank range."

Seriously. This is what she comes up with.

"That's supposed to make me feel better?" I say.

She smiles at me, unapologetic. Sometimes I forget that most of my friends can take care of themselves.

"The *first* time you were ordered to kill someone?" I continue.

She releases my hand, moving hers back to the wheel. "Do you really want to know?"

Do I? Or would I rather exist in this fantasy I've built up that Dani is as much a victim as the other girls I rescued from Petrov? I know she's a mob enforcer, but knowing is a far cry from witnessing. I've never seen her do any actual enforcing. Do I want to go down that road, or do I want to leave Dani in this nice gray area where she's just like me—a crook with an unfortunate weakness for the innocent?

I'm not much for truth, generally. But in this case, I think I do want her to tell me. I want to know her better, and that includes all the pieces that she usually keeps hidden. She shows up every time I need her. She tells me what I need to hear every time I need to hear it, whether I want to hear it or not. Since the day we met, she's never hurt me, left me, or asked anything of me I couldn't give. I can't say that about anyone else I've ever met. But I still don't *know* her. And I need to know her to have even half a chance of repaying her someday.

"Yes, I do," I say. "But not tonight. Tell me a happy story instead."

She falls silent for a moment, thinking. "In Kharkiv, a group of us orphans lived in an underground maintenance area for the city heating system. Lots of pipes that steamed, kept us warm in winter."

Holy crap. This is a happy story? I keep my mouth shut, though. This is the first time Dani's ever actually talked about her past.

"One day, Tatyana—she was six or seven then—came through the manhole carrying a bedraggled cat. It had only one eye and a chunk out of its ear. The fur was patchy and covered in so much grime we could not tell what color it was. The cat took one look at us skinny gutter rats and thought it was about to get eaten. It clawed free of Tatyana's arms but couldn't figure out how to get back through the manhole, so it flew around our shelter, bouncing off kids and pipes and yowling at the top of its lungs. We were all scrambling, trying to catch it and throw it out before it drew *militsiya* attention. Mykola finally forced it out. He was covered in scratches, but he was the hero for the day, so he got the largest portion of food. Poor Tatyana. We teased her about it for months afterward."

I laugh. I can't help it. It's a horrible thought, Dani as a child living underground in a post-Soviet concrete jungle, dodging cops and scrounging for food, but the mental image of a bunch of kids hopping around trying to catch a cat that's gone nuclear is like something out of a sitcom.

"Did it ever come back?" I ask.

"The cat?" Dani says, smiling enough to actually show teeth. "No. But Tatyana couldn't help herself when it came to animals. She was always dragging in some poor unfortunate creature with a limp or when it was zero degrees outside. Sort of like you."

"Ha. Ha-ha. You're so hilarious." I'm itching to ask her for all the details—how long did she live in Kharkiv, how did she hook up with Petrov's crew, what happened to her parents, how is she even still alive—but I don't. I may not know her history, but I know her personality enough by now that digging for information directly is the fastest way to get her to clam up. "Do you ever think about going back?" I ask instead.

"I do," she says. There's more she's not saying. The silence that falls is heavy with it. She wants me to figure it out, but I think I already have.

Dani pulls the car up to the curb in front of the Ramirezes' house.

"Thanks for coming to get me, Dani."

"I will always come and get you," she says.

I'm not sure what to say to that, so I don't say anything.

With a deep breath, she leans back and taps the steering

wheel. "Before you go in, we should figure out how to keep you from getting shot."

I'm proud of myself for not wincing at that. "There's not much we can do beyond figuring out who's behind the contract, is there?"

"No more riding the 'L'—it is too exposed."

"I can't call you for rides every time I need to go somewhere."

"Yes, you can. For now. If I am working, you can call Donovan. No more public transportation. Promise me."

I sigh. "Okay. No more public transit."

She scrutinizes me. "Are you crossing your fingers?"

"Jeez, I'm not five years old." I uncross my fingers.

"Your school is safe enough. I could never get closer than across the street."

Now who's the liar? "You put the rat in my locker, remember?"

She gives me a confused look. "What rat?"

"What do you mean, 'What rat'? The dead rat you put in my locker. Tyler said he saw you put it in there."

"I don't know what to tell you. I did not put a rat in your locker."

"Are you kidding me?"

Then it clicks. *Tyler*. That brilliant bastard. He was the only one who gained from the rat incident. He needed an excuse to earn my confidence. He planted the rat himself and said he'd seen who had done it so I'd open up to him. He must have seen Dani in passing while getting his orders from Petrov and decided to use her description. This is what I get for not confirming details.

"Rats are not the problem now," Dani says, interrupting my self-recrimination. "School is safe. Your coffee shop is not. Too many entrances, not enough exits. And not enough population."

"Aw, man."

She searches my face, but I can't tell what for. Understanding or agreement, or something. "This is important, *milaya*. This isn't a game."

I close my eyes and see NO GAME spray-painted across the poor Chevelle. It'll take at least the rest of the week to get it back from the body shop.

"I get that it's not a game, I do. But it's a pain in the butt working without an office."

"Then stop working until we know what we are dealing with."

I give her a sour look, but her face is set, and even if it weren't, I know she's right. About the Ballou, anyway. There's no way I'm not working.

Dani's gaze softens into uncertainty. She opens her mouth to say something more when my phone buzzes.

"It's Mike," I say before I even pull out the phone. "I'm late for curfew."

"You should tell him."

I don't really want to argue about it with her, so I answer the phone. "Hi, Mike. So, funny story . . ." I climb out of Dani's rental Nissan, mouth *Call you later,* and shut the door before returning to the phone conversation with Mike.

"I imagine it's a gut-buster," he says sardonically. Ha. If he only knew.

"See, I thought I had a lead on my mom, so I went to this bar."

"You went to a bar."

"Yes, and I knew you'd be upset, but see? I'm telling you everything like I promised." I feel a small twinge of guilt at the lie. Because I have no intention of telling him about the contract. He'd fly back on the next plane out here, and I'd be immediately reassigned to some new cop in some new city, and I'm just not risking that. Death? Sure, I'll risk death. Exile? No.

"Were you drinking?" Mike asks, voice hard.

"Yes. Club soda. Notably lacking the twist I ordered."

He sighs heavily. "Just get home, will you? It's bad enough I'm not there to chew you out in person, but you're making Angela worry."

I walk in through the front door and note that Angela is curled up on the couch with a book and a cup of tea. Yeah, she looks really worried.

"Hi, Angela," I say.

"Hi, Julep," she says, and smiles at me.

"I'm only"—I check the clock in the kitchen—"twenty minutes late."

"You'd be amazed what can happen in twenty minutes," Mike says.

"Yes, well, nothing happened," I say. Angela looks up again, a small frown on her face. "The lead at the bar turned out to be a random coincidence. But I do have a favor to ask." Misdirection—a grifter's greatest asset. It's even better when you can get something extra out of the misdirection. "Murphy found an article in an Alabama paper about my mother being reported missing. Can you pull a few strings and see if there's an official police report on it?"

"Pull a few strings? Julep, that's a state police issue. It's outside my jurisdiction."

"But kidnapping's in your jurisdiction, right?"

"Sometimes. But usually only when it involves ransom or a child. Do you actually think your mom was kidnapped?"

Not really, no. "It's not out of the realm of possibility," I say instead.

He sighs again. "Fine. I'll look into it, if you *promise* you'll be home by curfew *every night* until I get home. *No bars.*"

I think about Dani making me swear off the "L," the Ballou, and pretty much everywhere that isn't Mike's house or school.

"Done," I say.

He mumbles to himself about grifters and headaches and something else I don't catch. Then we sign off for the night.

"Interesting day?" Angela says.

"I turned in my history paper," I say, smiling a little too brightly. It took all my reserves maintaining a front for Mike. I'm worn out and starting to lose my focus.

"That's good," she says, assessing me.

I should probably explain about Angela. First of all, she's a saint. I mean, what kind of woman lets her FBI-agent husband take in a known criminal for an indeterminate length of time? Angela, that's who. She's a NICU nurse. She literally saves babies for a living. But she's no fool. She knew what she was getting into letting me stay. And she hasn't held it against me even once.

"Well, I'm turning in," I say. "I have two finals left to study for."

"All right," she says, but she doesn't say good night, which is kind of awkward.

I make it to the guest room and shut the door behind me with a soft click. Then I lean against it and slide down till my butt hits the floor. I wonder if Angela noticed that I didn't have my backpack with me. I left it at the Ballou, because I couldn't take it into the bar. I'll have to risk the Ballou in the morning. If I make Dani go with me, she'll be less likely to object.

I rest my head on my knees. For the first time since the attack, I start running through my mental list of usual suspects. A scant handful of angry perps I caught in the act of either breaking the law or breaking their spouses' hearts. But none of them had this kind of reach. Or vindictiveness. I can't see any of them going to the trouble of hiring a contract killer. Which leaves Petrov. I guess it's possible he did it. He's in a max-security facility serving nine consecutive life sentences or something, but stranger things have happened.

This is all so far beyond my ability to handle. For a split second, I even consider telling Mike. But then I dismiss it as the

Really Bad Idea it is and come to the conclusion that I'll just have to rely on Dani's underworld contacts for more information.

A light tap pulls me from my circling thoughts. I stand and open the door, admitting Angela to her own guest room. She sits in the desk chair, and I sit on the bed.

"Checking up on me?" I ask.

"I just saw the news. Gunshots near Loyola."

I could lie and tell her it has nothing to do with me, but I can already tell she won't believe me. "Are you going to tell Mike?"

She pauses, thinking. "I should tell him. But . . ."

"But?"

"Mike is kind of an idiot," she says.

I smile. "You're not getting an argument from me on that."

She smiles back. "He has a big heart, but he often acts when he should listen. Especially when it comes to you. It doesn't sit well with him, feeling like he can't protect someone he cares about."

My throat tightens. "You should try to get him to stop. Caring about me, I mean."

She laughs. "Right. Like that's possible. He's more stubborn than anyone else on the planet, present company included." She looks pointedly at me. "Besides, even if I could, I wouldn't."

I shift, uncomfortable. She settles more deeply into the chair.

"You probably wonder why we don't have kids," she says finally. "It's not because we don't want them. We came close several times. But I had too many miscarriages to keep trying. We almost adopted once, but it fell through at the last minute. Eventually, we got old enough that we decided to throw ourselves into our work instead. It was a painful decision, but it was the best for us at the time. And then you came along—a Molotov in a china shop."

"Oh, Angela," I say, intensely regretting having agreed to live here. I've done more damage than I realized. "I'm not that kid. I can't be normal. And I'm an awful person anyway. You don't want me."

"That isn't why I told you," she says, her eyes a bit shinier than usual. "I'm not trying to keep you. It would be pointless and selfish to try, I know that."

"Then why did you tell me?"

She's thinking hard about what to confess. I know that particular expression well. I invented it.

"It's Mike's job to keep you out of trouble, but he won't always be able to. I'm hoping that when trouble finds you again, and he puts himself between you and whatever's out there, that your understanding him will help you protect each other."

She gets up and touches my shoulder, holding my gaze for a moment before leaving.

After she shuts the door, I crawl under the covers into a miserable heap. Dani, Mike, Angela. Their care weighs heavily on me, because I care about them, too. But every time I think I might be able to have normal relationships, I remember the people I've failed—Tyler, my dad, Ralph—and I realize I can't let any of them depend on me.

I rub my face into the pillow and pretend I don't still notice the foreignness of the fabric-softener smell. It's a nice smell, but it'll never give me the same feeling of peace and safety it would have if I'd been born Mike and Angela's daughter. Which is appropriate, I guess. I shouldn't be allowed to feel peace and safety while sheltering with people I constantly put in harm's way.

I comfort myself with the idea that I'm not completely useless—that even if I can't wield my skills to save the people I love, I can at least use them to save total strangers. After a criminally long time, I finally drift off to sleep, clutching this meager consolation to my dysfunctional heart.

THE PROGRAM

Dani pulls the Nissan up next to the Ballou's front door. She wasn't thrilled when I explained that I needed to make a quick stop for my backpack, but she agreed on the condition that she go with me.

I wave a quick hello to Yaji, the barista, as I head up the back stairs to my office. Dani squeezes past me, the hand under her leather jacket no doubt resting on her gun. She gestures at me to keep quiet as we ascend the stairs. This time yesterday, I'd have rolled my eyes at her excessive caution, but this time yesterday I didn't know there was a contract out on my life.

As she rounds the stairwell corner, she stops suddenly, causing me to run into her, and says sharply, "Who are you? Why are you here?"

I lean to the right so I can look over Dani's shoulder. Mrs. Antolini is standing next to the closed office door, clutching her purse like it's about to get snatched. Dani's shoulder stiffens as if she's about to draw her gun.

"Mrs. Antolini," I say loudly in Dani's ear as I step around her. "How nice to see you."

"Oh, I'm so glad you're here," Mrs. Antolini says, her voice quavering. "I didn't know where else to go."

"What happened?" I ask as I unlock the door to my office and usher her inside. I hear Dani's grunt of disapproval, but really, it's just Mrs. Antolini. And anyway, who ever heard of a hit attempt at seven-thirty in the morning? Dani follows us in and shuts and locks the door behind her. Then she stations herself by the front window to monitor traffic in and out of the coffee shop.

"I got your message," Mrs. Antolini began. "I know you said you couldn't take the case, but I'm hoping you'll reconsider."

"Mrs. Antolini, I'd love to help you, but . . ." *But someone is trying to kill me, and I really can't add a possibly evil corporation to the list of Julep haters right now.* "But something's come up and I don't have the time to devote to your case."

"I know it's probably far-fetched. You probably think I'm crazy—"

"Not at all," I say, reaching across my desk for her hand. "In fact, I know you're on to something. That's why I can't take the case. I can't give it the time and attention it deserves."

"It's just, I don't trust anyone else. There's something I haven't told you yet. It only occurred to me last night after I got your message."

"I'm sorry, I—" I start. Then I make the mistake of looking

at her devastated expression and cave like the softy I am. But really, how much damage could looking at one piece of information do? Maybe it would help me steer her toward a better PI for the job. "All right, what is it?"

She opens her purse and pulls out an envelope. "I didn't think anything of it until I saw on the news about that shooting outside the bar."

The bottom drops out of my stomach and I reach for the envelope. I pull out a stack of receipts with Bar63 printed at the top. A folded sheet of paper shows an accounting of every expense corresponding to the receipts. The NWI logo is printed in the top-right corner of the expense report. The receipts are dated from before the bar officially opened.

"Where did you get this?" I ask.

"My husband's files. Apparently, he wasn't just a member of New World Initiative. He did some work for them on the side that I didn't know about. Something having to do with that bar."

I lean back in my chair, staring at the receipts and expense report. What could Bar63 possibly have to do with the New World Initiative? The only thing that connects them is . . . the blue fairy.

"Please, Ms. Dupree."

I lift my gaze to her face, and then farther up to Dani, who is shaking her head at me.

"All right, Mrs. Antolini," I say, standing. "I can't promise anything, but I'll see what I can do."

"Thank you so much," she gushes, grabbing my hand. It

takes me several minutes to see her to and out the door. I tell her I'll be in touch, and she thanks me about fifteen more times before I can finally shut the office door.

"Are you out of your mind?" Dani hardly waits for the latch to click before starting in. "You need to focus on staying out of the line of fire. Not infiltrating a cult."

"I told you, it's not a cult," I say. Semantics, but still. "Besides, I can't ignore the connections happening right under my nose." I shove the report and receipts at her, but she barely glances at them.

"I don't care about connections. I care about keeping you alive," she says, her glare frying me to cinders.

"What's the point of being alive if I have to stay in hiding? I cannot stay holed up at Mike's house all summer. I'll go insane."

She grabs my wrist. "You are not taking this seriously enough, *milaya*. Someone is trying to kill you. Someone we don't know anything about. I cannot protect you from that if I don't know where you are."

"I *am* taking it seriously," I say, staring her down. "One of your contacts is going to know something. We'll figure out who it is and we'll stop them, like we always do." She's still not convinced. I'm not even sure I'm convinced. But I have to do this. "I can't lose this chance to find my mother."

And just like that, all the intensity gutters out of Dani like the death of a cheap tungsten filament. She pulls back, releasing my wrist. "All right. It is your decision. But nothing else has changed. No public transportation, no office. Just school and the Ramirezes'."

School. Crap. "What time is it?"

I grab my phone. Eight-fifteen.

"Crap! I have a lit final that started five minutes ago."

I snag my backpack and start to make a dash for the door when Dani grabs my upper arm to stop me. Giving me a grouchy look, she precedes me into the hallway and down the stairs.

• • •

Three hours and several rounds of mental gymnastics later, I finally stagger into the dining hall for lunch. I set my tray across from Lily's and slump into a plastic chair.

"I have an explication hangover," I say, downing a glass of grape juice. "Ugh, Flannery. And people think *I'm* twisted."

"Only half of that made any sense to me," Lily says.

"See what I mean?" I prop an elbow on the table next to my tray and rub my temple.

Murphy and Bryn join us. Bryn actually brings her lunch from home, such as it is. I don't understand her obsession with acai-berry-flavored everything.

"How'd it go at the bar?" Murphy asks. I shoot him a dirty look and motion at him to keep his voice down. I'm not trying to get busted before I even have a chance to investigate.

"It was a dead end." I almost laugh at the unintentional play on words. "Or at least, I thought it was until this morning."

"What happened this morning?" Bryn asks, snagging one of Murphy's fries.

"I had another visit from Mrs. Antolini." At Bryn's blank look, I add, "The client."

"What does that have to do with Bar63?" Murphy asks.

"She shouldn't have anything to do with it. But she had these receipts of her husband's. There was a whole stack of them, and they were all for Bar63 from before it opened."

"Before it opened?" Murphy says, perplexed.

"Exactly."

"I don't get it," Lily says, her face drawn into a frown. "What does a bar supposedly connected to your missing mother have to do with the New World Initiative cult?"

"That's what we're going to find out."

"There's still the dean problem," Murphy reminds me. Unnecessarily.

"What dean problem?" Bryn asks, stealing another fry. Murphy, the doormat, doesn't appear to mind.

"Julep has to get special permission from Dean Porter to get into the NWI student intern program," Lily says.

Bryn's eyes widen, and she bursts into peals of laughter as loud as Murphy's last night.

"Glad I can be such an overflowing font of amusement for all of you," I say.

"What are you going to do?" Lily asks.

"I'm going to wing it," I say.

Had this been last semester, I could have used Heather's connection somehow to get Dean Porter's "approval" without the dean ever knowing about it. But the dean didn't ask Heather to renew her student-aid job this semester, no doubt due to all the crap she pulled for me during the mob-boss take-down. Not that Dean Porter was ever able to prove Heather was involved. But proof isn't something the dean ever really concerns herself with. Especially when it comes to me.

The rest of lunch falls into typical last-week-of-school conversation about finals and summer plans. Yearbooks are making the rounds of the cafeteria, though none of them find their way to me. I'm not exactly a social pariah, but my reputation has definitely taken a serious hit since last October. Bryn and Murphy hang out with me in spite of the grief it causes them with their respective social circles. Sure, the students still come to me to fix their problems, but it's not all just a game anymore. They're at least as much afraid of me as they are respectful of my skills.

It certainly doesn't help that I'm responsible for the death of the most beloved student at St. Agatha's. People might have forgiven me, but they haven't forgotten. Nor are they likely to after the memorial tomorrow afternoon.

St. Agatha's is renaming the gym after Tyler. Honestly, I'm glad of it. I'd rather have that knife of guilt in my gut every day than have even one person forget him. He deserves better than that.

My chest grows heavy at the thought. I try not to think too much about Tyler when I'm with other people, because once I start, I have trouble stopping. And when I get too caught up in it, I start snapping at people. Poor Murphy caught the brunt of my rage during Skyla's case, but Dani and Mike got their share as well.

I wish like crazy that I could bring him back. He may have been spying on me for Petrov from the beginning. He may have ruined my con, selling me out to Petrov in some misguided attempt to save me. I have no illusions about who should have died that day, and it wasn't Tyler. But since I can't bring him back, I wish instead that I could let him go. Neither seems to be happening, so I'm stuck in this weird limbo place of being chained to a ghost.

And just as I think that, a yearbook appears on the table just beyond my elbow. I look up at the silent intruder, a girl with long, chestnut-colored hair and shy brown eyes. She doesn't look like Tyler, not really, but her hair and eyes are close to the same color as his. It's almost as if his shadow is sending me a message. Hell if I know what it is, though.

"Thank you," the girl I've never before talked to says in a heavy Ukrainian accent. I study her for a moment, and then notice out of the corner of my eye that the entire tableful of Ukrainian girls is watching me, waiting to see what I'll do. I mean, it's just a yearbook for crying out loud.

I fish around in my backpack for a pen, but the girl waves it away before clasping her hands together. Confused, I open the front cover of the yearbook and see this inscription on the title page:

Для Julep Dupree, Покровителя загублених дівчат

On the inside of the cover, there's a wall of tiny words scrawled in different colored pens. Some of the words are in

English, some in Ukrainian. But all of the blocks of text are addressed to me, as if this were my yearbook and the girls had all signed it.

"It is our wish to say *dyakuyu* . . . thank you." Then she hastens back to her table, falling into the group of girls as a droplet is absorbed back into the sea.

Bryn and Murphy lean over my shoulder to look while Lily kneels in her chair to get a better view from the other side of the table.

"Wow," Bryn says. "It looks like nearly all of them signed it. Good luck deciphering it, though."

"Dani can help you," Murphy says.

Lily doesn't comment, but she's staring at the book as if trying to make sense of a Rubik's Cube.

"Look at this one," Bryn says, pointing at an inscription in loopy, purple cursive. "It says she lost all hope after her sister died until the night you saved her. It's like they think you're Mother Teresa or something."

Fantastic. If I'd felt guilty earlier, I feel ten times guiltier now. Yeah, I put those girls on the way to being saved, but I didn't really *do* the saving, and I certainly didn't pay the price. Tyler did. Sam did. My dad did. Pretty much everybody did *but* me.

"Why do you look like someone died?" Murphy asks.

I give him a withering glare.

"Oh, right. Sorry," he mumbles.

I look back down at the book, brushing a hand along the cover's edge. All these girls had lives before Petrov wrenched them away from everything they knew. My actions forced them into a system that, hopefully, will treat them well, but they're stuck in it now. Whether they get deported or worse is not up to them. It's up to a bunch of bureaucrats who have no idea what it's like to have to choose between slavery and death. The girls' lives are better, yes, but their choices are still not theirs. And here they are thanking me for it.

Lily walks out, leaving her tray on the table as if this were a four-star restaurant instead of a fourth-rate cafeteria. I barely notice.

"Well, on that note, I have a chem final to study for," Bryn says, giving Murphy a peck on the cheek and fleeing almost as quickly as Lily did. At least she takes her tray with her. Murphy gets up as well, pulling Lily's tray over so he can take it up with his.

"Wait, Murphy," I say, coming back to the present enough to remember I have more to say to him. "Something else happened last night that I need to tell you about."

He sits again, trays forgotten, as I lay out everything that happened with the contract killer. He leans forward and rests his forehead in his hands as I finish the story.

"You're serious," he says. "This is really happening."

"I'm telling you because I want you to be careful, but I don't want the whole world to know."

"What can I do?"

"Nothing. Let me handle it. Just steer clear of the Ballou for a few days."

"How many days?"

"As many as it takes," I say, getting to my feet. "I have to go see the dean."

"Now? After everything?"

"I have to do something, Murph. It's what I can do."

• • •

Dean Porter's office is every bit as god-awful as it always was. Walking into the loud mishmash of floral and plaid patterns is an assault on the senses. I think longingly of my sunglasses tucked away in my locker. They probably wouldn't help much, but some eye protection is better than none.

"The dean will see you now," says her secretary. He's new. Younger than the last one. Hopefully, he doesn't wash out in one semester like all the others.

"Ms. Dupree, how nice to see your shining face." The dean gestures me to a plump, too-bright chair. "I trust your mental health is improving."

I smile to derail this below-the-belt comment. I'm not that easy to taunt. "One day at a time," I say.

"To what do I owe the pleasure?"

She's dressed, as always, sharp enough to cut. Her titian hair is just as severe as it was the day I started at St. Aggie's. I wouldn't be surprised if she'd been born with its ends razored into the fine points currently brushing her shoulders.

Sadly for me, the dean has only one weakness, and that weakness is currently behind bars, serving who knows how many decades for conspiracy, trafficking, and really poor taste in associates. Nope, not Petrov. She had the hots for Senator

Richland, Tyler's dad—a fact Tyler exploited for my benefit on more than one occasion. But it's not a weakness I can exploit at the moment. I have to find another way into the New World Initiative.

Maybe Bryn's suggestion is worth trying. The direct approach.

"I'd really like your permission to—"

"No."

"But I didn't even finish—"

"It's not necessary for you to finish. Whatever you are asking for, I am positive you have an underlying motive I would not approve of. Therefore, no. You cannot have my permission."

"But, Dean Porter, if you just—"

"As a rule, I am bound to grant every student who requests one an audience. I have given you yours, and I have answered your question. Have a good day, Ms. Dupree."

"But—"

She gives me a look like she's daring me to continue, so I click my jaw shut and stand to go.

"Thank you for your time," I say as I pull my books to my chest. I can admit defeat. Temporarily, at least.

I walk out of the dean's office into her waiting room, my head spinning and discarding con after unlikely con. I can't figure out how to get around her. This may be the one time I can't find a way to get something I need. She'll be suspecting something now, but maybe I can use that to my advantage somehow.

As I step into the hallway, I nearly trip over Lily, who is sitting just outside the door to Dean Porter's office. She looks up at me, frowning.

I open my mouth to ask her what she's doing here, but she cuts me off. "No luck, huh?"

"No—"

She pushes herself to standing, and then brushes past me into the office. She's gone for two full minutes before coming out again.

"What's going on?"

She looks at me, her expression hard. "It's done," she says. "You're in."

Then she walks away.

THE FALLEN

After school, Dani drives me back to the Ramirezes' house. Since Angela's not there, Dani comes in with me. She rarely sets foot in the house, too close to a cop for comfort, probably. Even when Mike and Angela aren't around, Dani usually just drops me off at the door. I guess having a contract out on me changes things.

"What did she say to convince Dean Porter to agree?" Dani asks.

"She didn't tell me. She just walked off. I don't know what leverage Lily could possibly have over the dean that would get her to give up any leverage she has over me. She'd never cave willingly, and certainly not that quickly. It must be huge, whatever it is."

"So you're really going through with this, even though someone is trying to kill you."

I sigh. "Do you have any leads on who put the contract out on me?"

"No, which is all the more reason for you to stay where you know it's safe."

"No, which means there's absolutely nothing I can do about that situation right now, so I might as well work on something that I *can* move on."

Dani's expression turns stonier than I've seen it in a while. I forget how much her demeanor has softened over the past few months until she gets irritated at me. Then I remember what it was like in the beginning, when she was running me off the road and dragging me out of warehouses and trying to force me across state lines.

Time for some misdirection to soothe the savage enforcer.

"I do have a favor to ask, actually." I try to sound as insecure as I feel to help nudge her out of her bad mood.

Her eyebrow lifts, changing her frown from forbidding to receptive. Looks like my cunning vulnerability worked.

"I was hoping you could translate something for me," I say, pulling the yearbook the Ukrainian girls gave me out of my backpack. I open the cover and point at the inscription on the first page. Для Julep Dupree, Покровителя загублених дівчат.

"*Pokrovytelya zahublenykh divchatok,*" she whispers, her voice sending a shiver up my spine. "'For Julep Dupree, patron saint of lost girls.'"

I lean against the bar in the kitchen, absorbing the words like a blow. It's worse than I thought. The idea of me, of what I did, has become completely twisted in their heads.

"Can you talk to them?" I ask Dani, grasping at straws. "Make them see I'm not who they think I am?"

She looks at me, her eyes unreadable. "Why would I do that? They have hope. Is it wrong for them to hold on to that for a while at least?"

"I didn't really save them, Dani. They're better off, yes, but they're still shackled to the system. They're still not free."

Dani stares at me for a long, silent moment. See? This is why I felt insecure when I asked her to translate the inscription for me. I knew it was going to get awkward.

She edges a step closer like she can't help herself, though she's careful not to touch me. "You grifters value your freedom above all other things," she says. "But freedom is not the only gift there is. These girls appreciate you for the gift you gave them, not the gifts you could not."

I wish I had the luxury of looking at it that way. I'm not a good person, much less a saint. Letting them believe that I am feels like a lie I can't live with. Which is saying something, since I live with a lot of lies.

My gaze flicks up to Dani's and is caught like a fly in honey. I have the strangest feeling just north of my solar plexus, like a cross between a magnetic pull and a spike of adrenaline. I can't tell what she's feeling, as usual, but there's something about her, something different. Her short blond hair and white skin are practically glowing in the sunlight that's streaming through the bay window, which makes her look the part of saint much more convincingly than me. But that's not what's causing my breath to stutter, to stop. That's not what's drawing us toward a cliff, not touching but barely an inch apart. I wish—

"Hello, girls." Angela's voice comes from behind a couple of paper grocery bags. "Help me with the rest?"

And just like that, the connection snaps. My heart starts pumping again, faster to make up for lost time. I move past Angela at a pace just shy of running.

Later that night, I'm circling the drain of studying for my environmental science exam when I finally give up and chuck the book at the unfortunate desk chair. I can't get that scene with Dani out of my head. What the hell is wrong with me? Didn't I learn my lesson with Tyler and Sam? Caring too much is a one-way ticket to graveyards and good-byes.

Tomorrow is the vigil for Tyler, and still, after seven long months, I'm not sure how I feel. Did I love him? Honestly, I don't know. I loved the idea of him. I could easily have fallen in love with him if I'd had the chance to get to know him without bullets and bad guys dogging us at every turn. Mostly, I feel the lack of him where he should have been. I should have been able to yell at him for betraying me. I should have gotten to key his car and frame him for some petty theft so he'd have to spend a night in jail. I should have had months to get over my anger and forgive him, to hear him explain. Instead I had minutes. And then anguish. And then nightmares.

I'll never get to sleep at this rate.

"I miss you," I say to no one.

• • •

After an exhausting night of not being able to sleep, I have an exhausting day of forcing myself to stay awake. This is not helped by the fact that I'm not allowed at the Ballou. I begged Dani to take me there on the way to school, but she is a soulless herbal-tea drinker and doesn't understand the imperative of caffeine in the morning. By three o'clock in the afternoon, I'm about to take Lily up on her offer of an espresso machine for such emergencies.

"Looks like you went about five rounds with a Glaakmaar monster and lost," Murphy says as he comes upon me lying lengthwise across the overstuffed couch in the lobby.

I yawn, my jaw cracking with the intensity of it, and then tug my hair from a knotted ponytail into a half-assed French braid.

"Better?" I say.

"Ish," he says.

"Where's Bryn?"

"She's meeting us in the bleachers."

"I'm not sure I'm up for this," I say, bugs crawling the walls of my stomach.

"No one would blame you for skipping it. You don't have to go," Murphy says, his tone supportive rather than sarcastic. Which feels weird, because that's just not how we are with each other. In our line of work, we often witness people being awful. How we combat that is by never taking ourselves or each other too seriously. So it throws me when he tries to be earnest. I don't want him to be, and yet I appreciate it at the same time.

"Thanks, Murphy, but I need to be there."

When we arrive, the shiny, newly renovated gym is already packed, as expected. Tyler was beloved even when he was alive. And then he died young and a hero.

The ambiance reflects the somberness of the event—dimmed lights, the guidance counselor's office staff handing out electric candles to everyone. A podium stands resolute in the center of the portable dais the janitorial staff erects for special events. A poster-sized picture of Tyler mounted on a freestanding easel stares me down. The guilt deluge is about as overwhelming as I wanted it to be.

Bryn waves at us from six rows up. We thread our way through the unusually subdued crowd. You'd never know it was nearly summer break with how dejected everyone looks. Bryn moves her bag to free up the spot she saved for Murphy. I squeeze in on her other side, counting on my damaged reputation to clear me a spot. Sure enough, two freshmen get up and move out of my way.

"You okay?" Bryn asks grudgingly.

"Yeah," I lie.

She sighs and loops an arm around me, pulling me in for a close side-hug. "It's okay if you're not."

Dani said something similar to me once, after finding me wandering around in the rain. *You con yourself into believing you're fine, but it's okay if you're not.* I wish I could agree with them.

"I'm a grifter," I say. "I don't have real feelings."

"I think you're confusing grifters with sociopaths."

"Who says they're different?"

She rolls her eyes at me. "Whatever."

The lights dim further as the program starts. Sister Rasmussen takes the stage. She doesn't wear a traditional nun's habit, though she does wear the customary black polyester-blend vest and matching pants. Her gray hair reflects the lights directed at the makeshift stage. She's the youngest president St. Agatha's has ever had, but she's still in her sixties. I sometimes forget her age when I talk to her, because she seems so in tune with everything happening around her. But today, when she seems to be shouldering the weight of the entire student body, I can see every day of her sixty-some years etched on her face.

She clears her throat, and the low hum of dispirited conversation trickles to silence. My heart founders, lumbering lower in my rib cage than it should.

"Seven months ago, we lost one of our brightest students. Tyler Richland was a brilliant pupil, an esteemed classmate, and a Christian example to all of us. He made the ultimate sacrifice to save the lives of friends, both old and new. And his memory will be forever synonymous with integrity, compassion, and valor."

Each word is a chiseled letter on a flat stone in a snowy graveyard. I haven't been to Graceland Cemetery since I said good-bye to Tyler in December, but I will never forget the deep grooves of his name under my fingertips, the negative space of the lettering echoing the hole his absence left in my life.

Leaves. And not just my life, if the sniffling and nose-blowing around me are any indication.

"Before we ask Tyler's family to perform the dedication ceremony, designating this gymnasium as the Tyler Richland Athletic Center, I would like to turn the podium over to you. You knew Tyler best. I can think of no more fitting way to honor him than to have those of you whose lives he touched share your most treasured memories of Tyler with our community."

The next hour is torture as student after student walks up to the podium and tells a tearful story of how Tyler affected them. I listen to every single one, trying desperately to suppress my memories with theirs.

"I was convinced I'd never be able to remember all my lines. I panicked and told Tyler I was going to quit the play. But he wouldn't let me. I still remember him dressed in that ridiculous costume, putting his hand on my shoulder and saying, 'You can't leave me here alone with these yahoos.' He barely even knew me. We'd talked maybe once since I started at St. Agatha's. But he ran lines with me for a month. . . ."

The voice from the stage fades into ambient noise as a too-strong memory bubbles to the surface. . . .

"Well, I have the perfect remedy," Tyler says. "Close your eyes."

Out of curiosity, I humor him.

"Okay, open them."

When I do, he's making a ridiculous face—eyes crossed, head tilted forward, one finger stretching his mouth into a clownish grimace. I laugh reflexively. His face snaps back to its normal gorgeousness, his delighted smile echoing mine.

"Works on my little sister every time," he says. *"Ready for another one?"*

I nod and close my eyes. . . .

I come back to the present, holding my head. Another student has replaced the last. I focus on his words.

". . . thought for a second he was going to flatten me. I mean, it was a crappy thing to do, I know. I hadn't meant for things to get that out of hand. And he'd have had every right to beat me to a pulp. But Tyler stepped in, totally diffusing the situation before I ended up in the hospital. I owe him all my remaining teeth, if not more. . . ."

And then I swirl under again. . . .

Only when he pulls me to his chest and I am bound by his arms do I notice that I'm shaking.

After a few minutes, he says, "Where can I take you?"

"I don't have any place. I don't have anyone."

"You have me," he says, *and my heart feels a little less like a prisoner of war. . . .*

Stop, I beg my sadistic brain, fixing my attention on Tyler's best friend, Nick, who's taking his turn onstage.

". . . a thousand little things that all added up to my best friend. We did everything together from the time we were twelve. Every sport, every class, every party. It's hard to feel like my life didn't end when his did. Every day is a struggle. And the worst part is that I never . . . I never told him . . ."

And don't I know how that feels? I finally give in and let Tyler drag me under.

"You mean everything to me. And that means I do whatever it takes to save you. Even if saving you means losing you."

I stop arguing, but I'm breathing hard and glaring at him.

Tyler's gaze softens. "Sam is not the only one who loves you . . ."

Bryn hands me a tissue. I stare at it, my eyes dry as a desert. But as soon as I touch the lotion-infused paper, the waterworks start. Thanks, Bryn. Thanks a lot.

After the last masochist leaves the stage, Sister Rasmussen steps up to the mike. "Thank you, everyone, for sharing those stories. As long as you carry Tyler's memory with you, he will never truly be gone. Now, for the dedication, I will turn the podium over to Mrs. Richland."

Tyler's mom looks like a different person. She's still the ice queen I remember, but there are deep cracks in her facade that weren't there before. I flinch, dropping my gaze. This is the part I was dreading the most, seeing her. I avoided the newspapers, the online "news" articles, the media circus surrounding Tyler's death and his father's incarceration as much as I could. I didn't want to see what I'd done to his mother or the rest of his family. I couldn't stand the thought of watching stoic Mrs. Richland fall to her knees, knowing that I was responsible. I accidentally came across one grainy photo taken of Tyler's family at his funeral and it almost choked me. Seeing her now is even worse.

"I officially dedicate this gymnasium to the memory of my beloved son, Tyler Atticus Richland. Lily, if you would light the candle. . . ."

My eyes sweep to Mrs. Richland's left, where Lily is openly weeping and lighting a lone candle on a table. The electric candles around me switch on as the community conveys its solidarity to Tyler's memory.

"Why is Lily up there?" I whisper to Bryn and Murphy, as I recall that grainy photograph. It was small, black-and-white, and taken from a distance. The people were all dressed in heavy black clothing with black hats and sunglasses. But there was a girl. Half hidden behind Mrs. Richland. Her head down, long, dark hair shielding all but a sliver of her face from the camera . . .

"She's Tyler's sister," Bryn says. "Didn't you know that?"

THE SISTER

I'd be mad, except what right do I have? She played me. And anyone who can do that has my grudging respect. Besides, she didn't exactly try to hide her relationship to Tyler. She just never told me her last name, and I never asked. Tyler mentioned his sister, telling me that she was enrolled in an all-girls' school across town. But he never said she was adopted, or that her name was Lily. Which just shows again how little I actually knew him.

"How long have you two known?" I say, glaring at them.

"Since she transferred here in March," Murphy says. "You really didn't know?"

Bryn gives him a look, and he shuts up. "We didn't mention it, because you were having a rough time getting over Tyler's death, and then everything happened with Skyla, and it just sort of . . ." She gestures vaguely. "You never brought it up, and we thought you didn't want to talk about it, so we never brought it up. After a while it had been too long, and it just felt awkward. . . ."

I count down from ten in my head. I really have just the worst minions ever.

"Well, this explains how she got Dean Porter to let me in the program. The dean is probably still wrecked over Lily's dad."

"Shhh," says Carter, Murphy's tech-club buddy, who elbows Murphy in the ribs and nods toward the bottom of the bleachers where Dean Porter is giving us the evil eye. "Moment of silence."

Lily. Lily is Tyler's sister. And everyone knew but me. . . . Awesome. I pull out my phone and text Dani to come pick me up. I'm not interested in spending more time in Murphy's company right now.

After the ceremony, Lily leaves the stage with her mother, not so much as glancing in our direction. Sister Rasmussen comes over to our group, though. Part of me wonders if we'll get chastised for interrupting the moment of silence. But recrimination is not really Sister Rasmussen's style.

"Ms. Dupree," she says. "I wonder if I might have a word with you in my office tomorrow, after you finish your finals."

"Sure," I say, though I'm on guard. Sister Rasmussen has been lenient with me, and I suspect has gone out of her way to shelter me from the dean the past few months. But we're not exactly besties. "Is something wrong?"

"Not at all," she says. "I'd like to discuss your summer internship with you."

"All right."

Several PTA parents pull the president into a conversation, giving us the opportunity to join the river of students leaving the gym.

"What was that about?" Murphy asks.

"I guess I'll find out tomorrow."

My phone beeps with a text. I check it, expecting to see Dani's name pop up. Instead, the message is from Mike.

You okay?

Angela must have told him about the vigil. Or maybe he just remembered it was today. Or maybe he found out about the hit on me. Most likely scenario: Angela told him about the vigil.

Dealing. When are you coming back?

Next Saturday. Why?

The Chevelle should be done by tomorrow, so at least I won't have to explain its absence. I'll have a harder time explaining the contract killer if I haven't gotten that taken care of by then.

No reason. How's the investigation going?

"Who is it?" Murphy asks, peeking over my shoulder.

"Mike. He's still in New York."

"Good thing."

It's classified.

"Typical," I say.

"What?"

"Nothing." I pocket my phone. I have better things to do than wonder what Mike is up to anyway. "I'm going for coffee. Anybody want some?"

"I thought Dani said no Ballou," Murphy says. I level a glare at him, and he throws up his hands. "All right, all right. It's your funeral." Bryn smacks him in the chest. "Ow. You know what I mean."

When I walk through the door to the Ballou, Yaji, my barista buddy, takes one look at me, cuts off his chat with the customer at the register, and heads directly to the espresso bar. Good man.

Two and a half minutes later, I'm sitting in the far corner of the café, huddled over my cup like I'm all the passengers on the *Titanic* and it's the only life vest. I lay my cheek on the plastic lid and close my eyes. For the briefest of moments, I manage to push away all the stress and fear and unanswered questions, and there is only the cup and me. It lasts for a mere handful of heartbeats, but it's enough to slow my breathing and clear the mental clutter. It's enough to make space for my inner grifter to take stock.

One: Lily. What is she up to? Why would she want to work for me while keeping who she is a secret? Did she transfer to St. Agatha's just to take me down? If so, why help me by getting the dean to let me into the NWI internship?

Two: The contract killer. Who would put a contract out on my life? The only person who hates me that much is Petrov. And while I'm not naive enough to think that Petrov wouldn't have influence outside of his jail cell, I just can't see him hiring someone to kill me. It's personal between him and me. If he ever gets even with me, he'll pull the trigger himself. So then who? Someone who doesn't want me getting too close to NWI? It's possible, I suppose. The Chevelle wasn't vandalized until after I first met Mrs. Antolini. And the first hit attempt happened after I wandered out of Bar63, which is somehow connected to NWI. But it's not like I've gotten very far. I haven't even made it to the NWI office yet. Besides, the timing might not mean anything.

I take a long swig from my coffee cup, and then rub my forehead. Too many connections, too many coincidences, too much going on at once. Like . . .

Three: The blue fairy. I'm no closer now to figuring out what that means than I was when Mrs. Antolini first mentioned it. Does it have to do with Victoria Febbi?

And if so, does it have anything to do with my mom or that tuition check I got in December?

Or maybe it has something to do with . . .

Four: The Morettis. The dean is keeping a giant file on me with dossiers of people I've never heard of and can't track down. On top of which, I have no idea how I fit into that picture. I can't ask my mom. My dad either doesn't know or isn't telling me. And the dean sure as hell isn't going to clue me in until she's already tightening the noose.

The itch of someone watching me causes me to look up. Standing just in front of the coffee bar is Victoria Febbi, the dreadhead bartender from Bar63, holding a Ballou cup. She walks over and pulls a chair next to the couch I'm sitting on. She's wearing jeans, a leather vest over a puffy cream-colored peasant shirt, and an uncertain expression.

"Look," she starts, rolling the coffee cup between her hands. "I'm sorry about what happened at the bar the other day. I heard about it on the news."

I lean back, confused. Why are we having this conversation? But then I realize it doesn't matter *why* we're having this conversation. *We're having a conversation.* Perfect opportunity to pump her for info.

"No apology necessary. Unless you're the one who put a hit out on me."

She snorts dryly. "Nope, not me." When she catches me studying her, she says, "Wait. You're serious. Someone put a hit out on you?"

I shrug, careful not to reveal too much.

"You don't know who?"

"I'm still working on the who."

"Strange for a Loyola drama student to have made that serious an enemy."

"It's possible I wasn't as honest about myself as I could have been."

"It's possible I guessed as much." She smirks at me.

"I suppose that's what makes you a 'world class' bartender."

She huffs in irritation. "That stupid article. It wasn't my idea. But the boss thought it would be good publicity."

"The boss?" I ask. "I thought you owned the place." I didn't really think that, but I need to transition the conversation over to her side.

"Nah, I don't own it. I'm just a peon."

"Why Bar63? It's kind of a weird name."

"Why so curious all of a sudden?" she asks, raising a dark eyebrow.

"Just making conversation." I bump up the wattage on my smile. "That's what drew me, actually. The name." Pro tip: A little truth goes a long way.

"Well, hopefully this doesn't disappoint you, but it's named after the address: 6341 North Broadway."

"Oh," I say, somewhat deflated. I regroup quickly, though,

thinking of Mr. Antolini's receipts. "And you've been open since March?"

She nods.

I peel the sleeve off my cup, feigning nonchalance. "I heard about the bar from a friend who went before it opened. In February sometime. He said the booze was fifty percent off because you hadn't gotten your liquor license yet."

She snorts. "Your friend lied to you. Our first patron was served—legally—on March fourteenth. You should get better friends."

The denial is not surprising. No one would admit to a stranger that they'd done anything illegal. And it's entirely possible that the bar served Mr. Antolini and his NWI associates without Victoria's knowledge. But there's something twitchy in her answer—a microexpression that seems off. I surprised her just now, and she's doing her best to hide it.

"Well, I should go. Try not to die, kid," she says as she stands to leave.

"I always do," I say. "Nice talking to you, Victoria. I'll see you around."

"Tori's fine," she says. "And no, you probably won't." She walks out the door without a backward glance.

I check my phone for the time. No fewer than three texts from Dani at varying levels of panic asking me where I am. I totally forgot I'd texted her to come pick me up. At school. She knows me, so she's probably on her way here, which is not going to end well for me.

I jump up, sloshing foam onto my hand. I swing my backpack onto my shoulder and head to the door. But before I get there, someone else walks in. I drop the cup and coffee splatters everywhere.

It isn't Dani.

"Sam," I say.

THE STRANGER

Dani comes in on Sam's heels. Her angry expression turns surprised when she sees Sam. I barely notice her entrance, that's how shocked I am myself. I didn't realize until just now that some part of me thought I'd never see him again.

"Sam." I clear my throat, which is clogged with so many conflicting emotions—fury, hurt, fear, hope—it doesn't know which feeling to swallow first. "What are you doing here?"

"Getting coffee," he says, his eyes as riveted to me as mine are to his. "And looking for you," he admits.

My heart both shrivels and soars. I've missed him more than I thought. "I mean, why aren't you in Georgia? At school?"

"I—" He blinks, his expression shuttering to guarded. "School ended last week. I met my parents in New York over the weekend. I just got back."

"Why didn't you text me that you were coming home? Or, you know, at *all*?"

"I'm here now."

I'm distracted from needling him further by the catalog my brain can't help but make of the differences this Sam has from my Sam. This Sam is roughly the same height but broader in the shoulders, with shorter hair and a haunted look. He's torn. He's harboring secrets and he's not happy about it. He breaks eye contact first, bending to pick up my forgotten coffee cup. He even moves differently, with more purpose. More like Dani. I don't like it. I want my Sam back. I want my Sam to never have left.

Dani skirts the spilled coffee to reach my side. "Why are *you* here? You were supposed to wait for me in the lobby."

"Bad day," I say, recalling the vigil. "I needed coffee. And then the bartender showed up and I lost track of time."

"What bartender?" Dani asks, her expression turning stormy again.

"From Bar63. But she's not—"

"Julep, can we talk?" Sam asks as he returns from dumping the coffee cup in the trash.

I open my mouth to answer, but Dani speaks before I do. "Not here," she says, grabbing my hand and shouldering past Sam.

"Why not?" Sam hurries to catch up.

"Keep him out of it," I say to Dani. "It's enough that Murphy's involved."

"Keep me out of what? Involved in what?"

"*You* involved him by being somewhere you should not have been," she says to me. "It is out of my hands."

"What's going on?" Sam's voice booms. I wince. Sam is not supposed to sound like that.

Dani finally lets go of me when we reach the Nissan. "Get in," she says, sliding in on the driver's side without looking at me. She's definitely pissed this time. I'm not that sorry, though. The conversation with the bartender might prove useful.

"You're not the boss of me," I remind her. She's only three years older than me, and in no position to judge. I climb into the passenger's seat anyway, but only because I want to.

"No, I'm your bodyguard. Stop making my job so"—insert Ukrainian curses here—"difficult."

Sam gets into the backseat without asking. "Somebody better start talking to me, or so help me, I'll put you both on the FBI's most wanted list."

I heave a loud sigh. "Some idiot put a hit out on me, and Dani's overreacting."

"Overreacting? You think I am overreacting? Someone shot bullets at you not two days ago. Bullets. You should know better than anyone the damage that bullets do."

I glower at her. That was a low blow, especially after having to endure Tyler's vigil.

"Shit," Sam says under his breath.

Dani pulls out into traffic. "I'm calling Ramirez," she says.

"Don't even think about it! He'd bury me so deep in Witness Protection I'd never see any of you ever again."

"Maybe it would be better that way," she mutters.

I take a deep, shuddering breath. How does she get under my skin like this? Anyone else, I would have shifted into grifter mode at the first sign of dissension. But Dani derails me the way Tyler used to. She's always been protective, since the day my father asked her to look out for me, protect me from Petrov. But she's taken it way past Petrov. And somehow in the process, she managed to get unrestricted access to my inner workings. Most of the time, she greases the cogs, makes me run better, smoother. But she's equally capable of mucking up the machine when she wants to.

"Fine. I'll call him myself," I say. "I'll text him right now."

I pull out my phone and open up a string of texts I sent to Mike a while back. I type,

There's a contract out on me. Please come back and fix it.

Then I tap Send.

I show the sent message to Dani. She reads it, glancing up to the road and then over at my face. She's suspicious, but she drops it. I don't tell her Mike recently changed his phone number, and I sent the text to his old one.

"Welcome home to me," says Sam from the backseat.

• • •

"Pass the *jajangmyeon*."

I hand the box of Korean black-bean noodles to Angela

without comment. On my right, Sam silently dishes some *bulgogi* onto his plate. On my left, Angela eyes both of us as we quietly seethe. Okay, maybe it's just me doing the seething. Now that my first flush of mixed feelings on seeing Sam is past, my anger has ratcheted up.

Dani dropped us off twenty minutes ago. Angela, who had never actually met Sam and didn't know about all our drama, invited him to stay for dinner, which took my day from fabulous to just freaking outstanding.

"So, Sam. You're home for the summer?"

"Yes, ma'am," he says after swallowing a forkful of beef. "The colonel wanted me to go with him on a business trip to Abu Dhabi, but I think I successfully talked him out of it." He cuts a look over at me before taking another bite.

"The colonel" is what Sam lovingly calls his father. Sam's dad hates that Sam is friends with me. Admittedly, I'm a horrible influence on Sam. And after I got him arrested last year, the colonel insisted Sam go to military school. Sam didn't exactly fight him on the issue, though, giving me that line about needing to find himself or some crap. Whatever.

In any case, Sam mentioned him on purpose. He's telling me that he's back to stay. He's saying that he's choosing me. Or at least that's what the old Sam would have meant. I can't be sure of anything with this new Sam.

"Why don't I give you two some time alone to catch up? I'll be in the family room if you need me."

I watch Angela go, both grateful and annoyed that she's

handling me. Sam opens his mouth to talk, but I beat him to the punch.

"What do you think is going to happen here, Sam? You left, remember?"

"I know," he says, holding up a placating hand. "I know leaving was a shitty thing to do. I still think it was necessary, but that doesn't mean it wasn't wrong."

"It wasn't just you leaving. You wouldn't take my *calls*, Sam. How can I trust you'll have my back when you wouldn't even pick up the phone?"

He sighs, rubbing his ear like he always does when he's thinking. "I'll just have to prove it to you."

"I can't take that kind of risk right now. I have a killer on my tail, not to mention all this stuff with my mom. Even I have limits."

"You trusted Tyler, and you barely knew him."

Why the hell is everyone poking my Tyler wound today? It's like I have this giant neon sign hanging over my head that says FREE EMOTIONAL PUNCHING BAG—TAKE YOUR BEST SHOT.

"And look where that got me." I toss my napkin on my plate. I'm losing my appetite a lot lately. "He was spying on me for Petrov the entire time."

"I'm saying I'm not him. You've known me for half your life—"

I shake my head roughly. "The Sam I knew vanished that night at the warehouse. I don't know you."

He flinches, like I sank a knife in his chest, which I guess I did metaphorically. "I deserved that," he says, slumping in his chair. "I know to you it seems like I left you, but everything I did, I did for you. Not a day went by that I didn't hear you in my head. I don't expect—" He cuts off before finishing the thought. "Can I please just help you? That's all I'm asking."

I scan his face, though I'm not sure what for. I know he means it. He means it with every fiber of his being. He still has that much of the Sam I knew about him. But the rest . . . the rest is what worries me. It's not just that he looks different. There's something about his bearing, his core, that's different. I can't put my finger on it, and the fact that I can't place it makes me crazy. I'm afraid of it, because if I can't define it, I can't plan for it like I do all the other variables.

"Go home, Sam."

He sighs and gets slowly to his feet, holding my gaze with an intensity that makes me shiver. That is also *not* my Sam. My Sam was a puppy. This Sam is a wall.

He leans over the table, trespassing ever so slightly on my personal space. "I am not giving up that easily. You need my help. And this time when you call, I will answer on the first ring."

Then he leaves, taking all the air in the house with him. I watch the door for several minutes after he shuts it. I could go after him. It'll take him at least ten minutes to make it to the "L" station. But I won't. The less he knows, the better for him. And for me. I won't be the death of anyone else I love. Even if the people I love morph into pod people I no longer recognize.

Angela appears in the doorway between the kitchen and hallway. "Want to talk about it?"

"Not much to talk about. He left. He tried to come back. I told him to take a hike."

"You know, he might have left to protect you the way you just chased him off to protect him."

"How do you know I'm not protecting myself?"

"Because you're still looking at the front door," she says, walking to the table and clearing a few plates. "He doesn't strike me as the kind of guy who needs protecting."

"I'd rather not test that theory if I can help it."

She gives me a pitying smile. "I don't think you're going to be able to help it."

The sound of the garbage disposal accompanies my thoughts as I sit watching the door.

• • •

"Is she in?"

Janet, Sister Rasmussen's timorous aide, flashes me a tiny smile and dials the president's office number. "Sister Rasmussen? Julep Dupree is here to see you." She pauses, listening. "Yes, Sister." Then she hangs up the receiver, gesturing for me to go in.

I open the door and poke my head around it. "Hi, Sister Rasmussen," I say. "You wanted to see me?"

"Yes, please. Come in, my dear."

I obey and take the seat she reserves for guests.

"I wanted to ask how you are doing. You've had an eventful year."

Well, that's not open-ended or anything. I don't even begin to know how to answer that question.

"I'm fine." Which is classic opposite-speak for "not fine." So, there's that.

"I hear you'll be participating in the New World Initiative summer program for independent study credit," she says.

"Yes," I say.

"It's a good program, to be sure, but I wonder if you'll find it as effective at paving the way for you with your Yale application as you hope. You might do better to have a company in a recognized field on your transcript."

This is . . . interesting. What does Sister Rasmussen have against NWI? The program is practically dripping with networking opportunities. Not to mention I'm pretty sure that at least some of the students who interned at NWI ended up at Yale.

"I'm only a sophomore," I say instead. "I have plenty of time to add more targeted experience."

"But precious few summers. Besides, I'm not sure the philosophy behind the program will align with your worldview."

Oh. She thinks my sarcasm will be too harsh for the delicate spiritual types who buy in to all that positivity crap.

"Don't worry, Sister. I'll behave myself," I say, winking at her.

She presses her lips together, which is the closest I've ever seen her to betraying frustration. Weird.

"I'd like you to consider an alternative." She slides a paper across her desk. It's a printout of a brochure for a company called Brillion. I skim the subheads but not the content. It doesn't matter if it's the best internship there ever was. I need *this* program—NWI. I'm not signing up for my own betterment. I'm on a job. And anyway, I'm not sure about the whole Yale thing anymore. I can't imagine they'd be thrilled to have a crooked, friend-sacrificing professional con with a criminal history on their roster. Normal is not a thing I'm ever going to be, no matter how hard I try to convince myself otherwise.

"It looks great, really. But I already committed to NWI."

Sister Rasmussen gestures at the brochure. "There's still plenty of time to reconsider and apply for something more appropriate. The recommendation of a school president goes a long way."

"I appreciate you looking out for me. I'm surprised you would, considering how much trouble I've put you through this year." Deflect. Distract.

"It hasn't been dull, that's for certain," she says.

"Well, I'll give your proposal serious thought. I'll let you know if I decide to change programs."

"I strongly urge you to do so," she says. I'm struck again by the strange route this conversation has taken. I've never seen her so committed to an opinion. Even when I brought her the heads of more than a hundred of her students on a silver platter, blackmailing her into helping a bunch of Ukrainian strays, she didn't show this much personal investment. She's always kind but distant, like an observer or witness, not a player. She knows something about NWI that I don't. Something she's decided not to tell me, despite her concern.

"Thank you for taking an interest in me, Sister."

"Always," she says with a smile that doesn't quite reach her eyes.

THE PRISON

When Dani picks me up at seven the next morning, she doesn't say much. I guess I should be grateful that she agreed to take me to see my dad at all. We didn't leave things well on Thursday, and she was working yesterday, so Angela took me to school and Murphy drove me back to the Ramirezes'. I haven't seen Dani since she was epically pissed at me and I lied to her about texting Mike.

Now that my initial irritation at her attitude has passed, I can see that going to the Ballou was perhaps not the most responsible thing for me to do. Plus, I'm going to have to fess up today that I didn't text Mike, if she hasn't guessed already. She's not an idiot, and I'm not looking forward to that conversation.

Par for the course, I owe her an apology. The last time I was in this boat, I'd made a similarly poor decision in the personal safety department. I'm sensing a theme. I'm sure she is, too. And after what happened with Sam, I'm doubting my ability to keep friends. An hour-long drive to Ransom Correctional Facility seems a good time to amend that.

"Look," I say as we exit onto I-57 and reach minute five of stony silence. "I'm sorry. I didn't mean to make you worry. I should have listened to you."

Dani blows out a breath she'd been holding. "I cannot believe you actually apologized."

"Shocking, I know," I say, smiling.

She drums her fingers on the steering wheel. "Well, I am sorry, too. I should not have lost my temper. But I—" She clenches her jaw and tightens her grip on the wheel. "When I imagine bad things happening to you, permanent things . . . It just cannot happen. Do you understand?"

"Yes, but it isn't easy for me. It doesn't come naturally, working with people, even after all these months. I'm going to screw up."

"I realize that, and I try to adjust, but some things are non-negotiable."

I nod. "I'll work harder at it. Though why you stick around is the real mystery." I mean it as a joke, but she doesn't laugh.

"If you are the patron saint of lost girls, then I am your crusader. My fate is linked to yours until one of us is martyred. But I prefer that does not happen soon."

I am floored by her response. It's one thing for the Ukrainian trafficking survivors to believe I'm an avenging angel. It's entirely another for Dani to believe it. I'm strangely reluctant to disabuse her of the notion, though. I'd trade a lot to keep her good opinion of me—just not her life.

"I'm not a saint, Dani. I'm a thief. You know that. And neither of us is dying over this."

Her smile holds a tinge of regret. "If you are a saint, *milaya*, you may even be able to pull off that miracle. Just remember when the time comes to stand behind me."

I'm trapped again in a breathless moment as her gaze captures mine. Her eyes flick back to the road almost immediately, but the contact, for all its brevity, liquefies my insides. What I thought I knew to be true has gone fuzzy around the edges. I can't think right. I can't even breathe right. And the rest of the drive I spend desperately reconstituting my poker face.

Unfortunately, pulling into the prison parking lot doesn't make me feel a whole lot better. Lots of ways to die in a prison. Or worse—get locked up. I hate prisons. And police stations. And doughnut shops. Being surrounded by cops makes me feel claustrophobic. But then I've said that already, haven't I? Let me just say it again. Cops make me edgy.

"Will you be all right?" Dani asks as I shift to get out of the car.

"Yeah, fine." I lift the door handle. "No hit man in his right mind would try anything this close to a prison."

"I meant about seeing your father. About asking him about your mother."

I dredge up enough courage to look at her. "I'm okay. He's the one you should be worried about."

She nods, and I take that as permission to leave. I sign in at the front desk and walk down the familiar hall to the visitors' area. Thanks to Mike, my dad ended up in a medium-security prison, which means no bulletproof glass walls with phones on either side. It's more like a conference room with tables and chairs. Only the tables and chairs are bolted to the floor.

I'm the first visitor of the day, which is not my favorite thing. I hate having guards overhear my talks with my dad. It's a pain having to censor everything. My dad enters from the inmate door and gives me a big smile. He looks older every time I come. Being imprisoned is taking its toll on him.

I give him a hug. He feels thinner. I swallow the rock in my throat and take a seat across from him.

"Any news on your mom or Ralph?" It's his first question, always. Usually, my answer is no, but today . . . There's so much to tell him that I don't have a clue where to start.

"You found her," he says quietly, sorrow shadowing his face.

"No," I say. "I found a missing-person article. From the same time you left thirteen-year-old me stranded without a word for two weeks."

He looks down at his hands.

"What aren't you telling me about her family? About my family?"

"All I know—all she would ever tell me—was that she had a falling-out with her family. That she didn't want to talk about it, wouldn't even consider reconnecting with them. Ever. After a while, I stopped pushing."

"You could have gotten it out of her if you wanted to. You're one of the best con artists there is."

He smiles halfheartedly. "Thanks for the vote of confidence, Julep. But your mom would not bend on it, and I figured it was her right. Whatever happened to her, it never interfered with us . . . until it did."

"You think she left us because of her family?"

"Honestly, I don't know. It's a guess at best."

But his guesses are always more than just guesses. His grifter instincts penetrate other people's motivations with laser precision.

"Was she running away from them, or back to them?"

"I don't know, honey. I really don't. Her going missing at the same time I was . . . out of town . . . It's just a coincidence."

Right. Coincidence.

"What does sixty-three mean?"

He eyes me sharply. "It's your mom's favorite number. I'm not sure why." He smiles at some memory I'll never share. "She had it tattooed on her right hip."

"Did you know there's a place called Bar63 in town?" I don't tell him it's new. I want to see if he'll let something slip.

"I didn't," he says. And he's so good that I can't tell what he's lying about. "I'd never been to Chicago before the three of us moved here."

"With all the grifting, you'd never once been to Chicago," I say suspiciously.

"I spent a lot of time in Thailand."

I used to trust my father. When did that change? When he didn't tell me he was working for the mob and then got abducted for his trouble? Or before that? When he abandoned me for those two weeks during which my mother also went missing?

It doesn't really matter. The fact is I don't trust him anymore. Not completely.

He takes my hand, interrupting my fidgeting. "Whoever her family was, your mom loved you."

"Not enough to stay."

"Maybe she loved you so much she had to leave."

I pull my hand away and stuff both into the pockets of my vest. It's time to change the topic.

"I need your advice on a job I'm working. Have you heard of the New World Initiative?"

He pauses. "It's some kind of pyramid scheme, I think."

"Yes, maybe. It sells leadership skills and self-confidence to pencil pushers." I explain about NWI, about the imprisoned embezzler and his wife, my new client.

When I finish, my dad leans back in his chair, arms crossed. "I guess it could be legit. But it's strange that your client is so insistent that her husband was coerced. Most people don't need additional motive to steal money."

"An otherwise honest man might. If he thought his place in heaven would be secured."

"I thought you said it was business-oriented. Not religious."

"It's not religious. I meant it figuratively. But if Duke Salinger is half as charismatic—"

"Did you say Duke Salinger?"

"Yes, why? Have you heard of him?"

"He was a financial investor arrested for fraud in the nineties. A grifter in the Wall Street sense."

I make a face. I don't have a lot of respect for that sort of criminal. It's a lot easier to lie convincingly to someone over a phone than to their face.

"He was something of a legend, actually. He stole a lot of money from a lot of gullible people. But then something happened, and he got caught. Last I heard, he was in the pen."

"And?"

"That's it."

That's it, my eye. He's holding out on me for some reason. But I know better than to try to come at him about it directly. "Well, he's been out of jail long enough to form a lucrative leadership skills–building organization."

My dad stays silent, his eyes glazed with the preoccupation of his own thoughts. I don't know whether to push him more or to let it go for now. The last thing I need is for him to shut down completely. So I try a subtler approach.

"There's more. Mrs. Antolini found a bunch of receipts linking the New World Initiative to Bar63. And she mentioned that the authorities questioning her were looking for a blue fairy."

He gives me a blank look. "Lots of organizations keep receipts from company outings. It might be nothing."

"But the blue fairy?"

He rubs his forehead. "If this company is somehow affiliated with your mom's family, stay away from it. I may not know anything about her past, but I know that she was terrified they'd find her. *Terrified.* Anything that scared your mother that much—your mother, who wasn't afraid of anything—should be avoided at all costs."

"But what about Mr. Antolini? If Mrs. Antolini is right that there's more to this than a trumped-up embezzlement charge . . ."

My dad gives me a pointed look. "Don't get too attached to the mark."

"Mr. Antolini is not my mark."

"He's somebody's mark. It's a slippery slope, Julep."

Says the man who got himself shot trying to save a warehouse full of marks.

"Time's up," says Bob the prison guard. I kind of hate Bob.

We get out of our chairs, and my dad hugs me tight. "I love you. Be careful."

"I love you, too, Dad."

And then he's through the door without a backward glance. I wish I didn't know that it's because it's the only way he can force himself to leave. Sometimes being a grifter sucks.

It isn't until I'm back in Dani's rental car buckling my seat belt that I realize I forgot to tell him about the contract killer.

"How did it go?" Dani asks.

"About as well as you'd expect. He either doesn't know anything or he's doing a damn good job of hiding that he does."

"Yes. That is irritating, isn't it?"

"What?"

She just smirks in response. I stick my tongue out at her, because yes, I am that mature.

We rehash my conversation with my dad and everything I know about NWI on our way back. It doesn't amount to much.

Salinger found the light, repented his ways—up to and including jail time—and started a company with the purpose of training people in the fine art of grifting without actually using it for evil. At least, that's my take on it. Technically, it's a leadership cult—we'll teach you how to "lead people," and then you lead them to our program. To some extent, it is a pyramid scheme, in that it builds its power base by turning its members into recruiters.

But in order to be a true pyramid scheme, by definition, it can't return on its patrons' investments. That's the real question Mrs. Antolini's accusations raise. Is NWI secretly an evil corporation bent on using and abusing its initiates for its own gain, or is it a benevolent, possibly misguided group of people passing on their version of the keys to success?

My money's on evil. Duke Salinger is a grifter, and a grifter never quits, not really. I'm a prime example of that. I wanted to quit, and now look at me. Is it possible to get out once you're in? I look over at Dani and wonder if she would ever go straight, if she even could.

"How'd you get into being an enforcer?" I ask her, though it's not really hard to guess. Street urchin to mob lackey is not a large leap.

She coasts to a stop at a crosswalk. "It was a particularly

brutal winter." A woman crosses in front of us, holding on to a little boy with one hand and waving at us with the other. "Temperatures hovered below freezing for weeks. We lost little Olena first. She was too small to forage, and we could not feed her and ourselves. We tried. We even took her to the orphanage, but they were almost as bad off as we were. No government money. No food or fuel. She did not last long after that. And then the others. We lost nine in all."

"Jesus, Dani." I put my hand on her arm, because how could I not? For once, she doesn't brush me off.

"When the frost broke, I swore I would never go through that again. For *syrota* like us, there are two options—crime and prostitution. I chose crime. I joined Petrov the next week. He fed me, trained me. He taught me to read himself. He was a good boss. Paid us fairly, even by American standards. I did what I could for those who were left. And when Petrov came to Chicago, I came with him."

I realize then how hard it must have been for her to pull that trigger to stop Petrov from killing me. He had literally saved her life. For someone like Dani, that means a hell of a lot.

"I'm—I didn't know. You shouldn't have had to save me from him."

She blinks, confused. "What do you mean?"

"Petrov. You shouldn't have had to choose someone you barely knew over someone you cared about."

She casts me a quick look. "I betrayed him when I started helping your father gather evidence to free the girls, which was before I met you."

"But you shot him because of me."

"I did. And I would have shot him again, if you had not stopped me. I have regretted listening to you every day since."

That shuts me up. Maybe I don't know as much about Dani as I think I do.

"Do not be so presumptuous as to take all my transgressions as your own, little saint. You have quite enough of other people's sins on your shoulders as it is."

When we get to the Ramirezes' house, she puts the car in neutral and pulls up the parking brake. She looks like she's about to get out and walk me in. But there's one order of business I've been putting off. I need to get it over with before I lose the guts to do it.

"What?" she says, reading the hesitation on my face.

"I . . . may have, um, liedabouttextingMike. Okay, bye."

"Hold it!"

Damn. I'd almost made it to the curb.

"You didn't text Ramirez?"

I bite my lip and drop my gaze, trying to look penitent.

She sighs and then laughs. "You are . . ." She shakes her head. "Just go."

"See you tomorrow?"

She looks at me sideways as she releases the brake. My stomach does this flippy thing that I wholeheartedly disapprove of. Then she drives away without answering, because she knows I already know.

THE ROPES

Let me tell you a little something about grifters. We are a breed of criminal that is a cross between thief and illusionist, and most of us suffer from a complete lack of conscience. I know this, despite the deep, black scar of sympathy marring my grifter soul. So going up against a grifter, practicing or not, is not my idea of a good time.

I can tell when most people are lying like they're admitting it themselves. They are, in fact, admitting it, with their unconscious facial expressions, their body language, and their vocal inflections. It's almost too easy, most of the time.

But a grifter is a whole other prospect. Con men have spent years observing and controlling their expressions. Learning Salinger's tells is going to take time, and honestly, I'm not at my best right now. Sam coming back, all this stuff with my mom, the hit man stalking me. I'm rattled, I'll admit it. And if I'm too distracted with looking over my shoulder, I might tumble into the trap right in front of my feet.

It doesn't help that Sister Rasmussen was against me taking the internship. Does she know something I don't? If so, why not just tell me? Is she hiding something, or am I just growing increasingly paranoid? And if it's the latter, can you blame me?

I take a deep breath and let it out slowly, my hand resting on the ostentatious sunburst that serves as the handle to the New World Initiative's heavy glass door.

"Are you going in?" says a pleasant, rumbling voice behind me.

I turn to see a thoroughly built guy in his late twenties with boyishly messy brown curly hair under a beanie. His white T-shirt stretches tight over his muscles, and his jeans are the perfect balance between relaxed and fitted. He looks a little too put-together to be real—like a model who's wandered off a photo shoot.

"Eventually," I say. "Are you in a rush?"

He smiles, the tips of his perfect white teeth showing. "I have an appointment."

So do I, actually. It's the first day of my internship. I'm due to meet the intern coordinator and the other interns for orientation at seven-thirty. It's seven-twenty-five, and I still have to check in at the front desk. I really shouldn't be dawdling, especially over something stupid like anxiety.

I fold my arms and step back from the door so he can go past me. But instead, he opens the door, gesturing for me to precede him inside, as if saying *It's now or never.* He's not wrong. It has to be now. I have to know if this place is connected to my mom, to my family. And if so, what that says about me.

I blink, my eyes adjusting to the dim lighting of the lobby. The tile floor is a soothing mottled blue and tan. The walls are a shade of green that shifts into blue tones in peripheral vision. Potted plants soften the edges at regular intervals. And the bank of windows looking out onto the street seems to beckon outsiders in.

"Welcome to the New World Initiative," Beanie Guy says as he walks past me and then past the receptionist into the offices beyond.

The reception desk is substantial, rib-high and curved slightly outward. Though there are stations for two, a single receptionist sits behind the desk, a middle-aged, black-haired woman with too-bright lipstick and a nose ring. Her nameplate says Brigitte. Judging by Beanie Guy and Brigitte, I'm a little overdressed in my slacks, blouse, and heels.

I ask for directions, and she points me toward a conference room on the second floor. Only it turns out to not be a conference room at all. It's a large, brightly lit obstacle course with blue foam-mat flooring under thirteen structures of rope, wood, and metal.

Several small groups of people are loitering around the room. Most of the groups seem to have a facilitator leading them in some ridiculous-looking icebreaker activities. One group of five is leaderless, though, and, coincidentally, its constituents appear to skew younger than the other groups. They're sitting on the floor in a loose circle, chatting with each other. The conversation trails off when I walk up.

"You a new intern?" says a pale hipster guy in skinny jeans, glasses, and a sweater-vest.

"Yep," I say. "You guys, too?"

"Oliver Ackley," the hipster says, reaching out his hand. I bend down and shake it. He introduces the others, showing off his memory and inherent leadership potential. This guy is clearly the gunner of the group. He cares way too much about being the best.

I've already forgotten the others' names. Strad-something, Hayes, and Gallagher? I think. The last guy's name I can't recall at all. Three girls, three guys. One of the guys is black, and one of the girls is wearing a hijab, but the rest are over-privileged white kids. In other words, they're all dismissible—not relevant to the job.

I set down my mostly empty satchel and move to sit in the last open spot in the circle when someone new comes over. Or not new, exactly.

"Settling in?" the guy with the beanie asks as he strolls up to us, rubbing his hands together. "Excellent. Everyone stand up."

We comply, each of us getting to our feet with varying amounts of enthusiasm. I'm the slowest.

"My name's Joseph, and I'm the intern coordinator," he says, flashing his perfect teeth again. "You all think you know who you are. Let's find out if you're right."

• • •

"You have to be kidding me," I say, staring up at the twelve-foot wall I'm supposed to climb. "Where was this in the internship application? I'm pretty sure I'd have noticed 'physically impossible feats of strength.'"

Joseph laughs. "It's in the fine print under 'team building.'"

I glance around at the groups of older people, NWI's stable of "initiates," busy with various obstacles. It's my first exposure to the marks who my mark is allegedly targeting. So far, they seem like ordinary people. Not as many traditional-looking business execs or government officials as I'd expected. I heard one woman say she was a special-needs teacher. Her trust-fall partner replied that he was a marketing copywriter for a distributor of HVAC units. How either of them might be valuable to a grifter is beyond me. Maybe they're just the chaff that comes in with the wheat. Still. All of this is disappointingly healthy-seeming.

"I have to climb a wall to be part of the team?" I say, turning back to the monolith in front of me.

"You have to climb a wall to prove to yourself that you can. The team building is just gravy."

I heave a sigh. "I so did not wear the right shoes for this."

Joseph laughs again. He laughs a lot, actually. It's easy for him, and the fact that I'm not used to it shows how damaged the people I hang out with generally are.

Anyway, it turns out the whole second floor of the NWI building is dedicated to the ropes-course challenge, complete with commitment bridge, swinging log, tightrope cables, spider's web, trust-fall platform, and, my current nemesis, the twelve-foot wall.

I kick off my heels and stretch, judging the height with an unpracticed eye. I back up several steps. Then I take a running leap at the wall, smacking into the wood embarrassingly short of the top and smearing to the floor like a cartoon character. I grumble curses under my breath and pick myself up again for another go. My lame efforts injured more than my pride—I'll probably be sporting a few bruises by morning.

I look around for something I can use to boost my five-foot-four height. Some of the initiates are using a small, square trampoline for one of the other challenges. I sidle over and ask to borrow it. They agree, nice as pie, and a couple of them even help me drag it in front of the wall.

I position it where I think it will give me the biggest advantage. Then I resume my previous position and take another running leap, this time onto the trampoline. Unfortunately, I didn't take into account how much the addition of the trampoline would add to my acceleration. I gain height, but also velocity. I smack so hard into the wood that it stuns me for a split second. By the time I start scrambling for a handhold, I've already slid down enough to grasp the top by a bare couple of fingertips—not enough to get a solid grip. So once again, I slide ignominiously to the floor mat.

Joseph comes over and offers me a hand. Despite my irritation and additional bruises, I'm not too proud to take it. I push myself up and smooth the wrinkles out of my pants.

"Try just once more," Joseph says, smiling encouragingly. I must admit—for a laugher, he hasn't laughed at my failure. That alone persuades me to give it another go. But before I head back to the trampoline, he stops me. "Jump from here," he says, pointing to the floor directly in front of the wall.

"Are you on crack?" I say, craning my neck to see the top. "I'll never make it."

"Just try," he says.

I shrug and turn to face the wall. At least I won't get smacked as hard before falling down.

I bend my knees, coiling my muscles for the jump, and then push against the floor as hard as I can while reaching up as far as possible with my right hand. I'm still three or four feet shy of the top, as I knew I would be. But as I start my descent, I feel hands under my feet, pushing me up again.

I flinch in surprise and fall forward into the wall. But when I look down and see Joseph and two of the other interns— Blondie (Hayes?) and Gallagher—pushing me up, I force my knees to straighten and arms to reach up again. Three feet, two, one, and then I grab the top of the wall and pull with all my strength. I take a chance and swing my left foot over the top. I barely clear the wall with my foot, but once I do, I manage to pull myself up and over the edge to a platform a couple of feet lower than the top with a ladder going down to the floor.

I sit for a second to catch my breath, as well as the point Joseph was trying to make. The wall is *supposed* to be impossible to manage alone. Jerk. He's trying to draw me in as much as I'm trying to draw him out.

I pop my head over the top to glare down at my audience. "Hey, why didn't you tell me this side has a ladder?"

After that, our intern team hooks up to a team of initiates. Let me just say this, the trust fall freaking sucks. Or maybe I suck at it. But the rest of the obstacles are actually fun. The initiates are all surprisingly well adjusted for adults pretending that the green mat under the spider's web is full of alligators. We end up laughing a lot and bonding over tasks set seemingly at random by Joseph and the other facilitator, who appear content to torture us in new and inventive ways.

Unfortunately, concentrating so much on the rules of the game has knocked my own internal walls down almost completely. It isn't till we're almost through the last obstacle that I remember I'm on a job. If this were a war, I'd have lost today's battle for sure. But I can't help feeling a measure of relief. Today was fun. Even Ackley dialed down his obnoxious tendency to micromanage as we made it through each challenge. And just for a moment, I felt a little less alone.

"All right, interns," Joseph says after our debrief of the last activity. "Time to meet the head honcho."

Or maybe today's battle isn't over yet. Crap. Better put my game face back on.

We all troop up to the elevator, me tucking in my blouse and straightening my hair. I really should have read that packet they posted for the interns on the site more carefully. I missed that whole "come dressed for activity" memo.

The elevator takes us up to the executive floor. Stepping onto the plush carpet is a strange sensation after spending the day bouncing around on spongy foam flooring. But at least I'm dressed the part for meeting a CEO.

Joseph opens one of a set of frosted-glass double doors and enters the room behind it. Ackley and the others follow. I take a breath and head in last.

The office is huge, with bookshelves lining one wall and windows along another. There's even a fireplace and a seating area with two overstuffed leather couches facing each other across a frosted-glass coffee table that matches the doors.

The high-backed chair behind the sprawling mahogany desk on the other side of the room swivels away from the floor-to-ceiling bank of windows to face us, revealing the man behind the curtain, so to speak.

He's tall. I can tell even though he's sitting, which means he's at least as tall as Senator Richland, if not taller. His hair is sandy and styled in a classic executive cut. He's not muscled like Joseph, but he must work out to maintain his trim frame. He's in his late forties, but he looks younger. His eyes are an arresting blue, which probably helps him hold people's attention. The grifter part of me wonders if he's wearing colored contacts.

"Welcome to NWI," he says, rising to his feet. He reaches his hand out for each of us to shake. "I'm delighted that each of you, leaders in your own right, have chosen the New World Initiative as your summer internship experience. I have no doubt we will learn a lot from each other. I encourage you all to explore every facet of our leadership program over the next few weeks. However, there is one rule that must be followed.

The confidential information of our participants must remain confidential. Beyond that, help yourself to all the information we can offer. We want you to be invested in the program, and you can only become so if you thoroughly understand it."

"Yes, sir," says Ackley.

Aadila, the girl in the hijab, surreptitiously rolls her eyes. I make a mental note of it. She might prove useful.

"Joseph started as an intern himself a few years ago. He knows this place inside and out," Duke Salinger continues. "If you have any questions, any concerns, any suggestions, he's your first stop. He can point you in the right direction. If for some reason you manage to stump him, come to me. My door is always open."

That seems to be the agreed-upon signal for the end of his speech, as Joseph gathers us up like ducklings and ushers us to the door. I'm not sure whether to be relieved or bummed. The meeting went well enough, but I didn't glean any actual intel from the exchange. I may have to devise some other way to get a one-on-one with NWI's founder.

"Ms. Dupree, if you wouldn't mind staying behind a moment."

Or maybe I'll get a one-on-one now.

"Sure," I say, turning on my heel and reapproaching Salinger's desk. He nods at Joseph and Joseph nods back, shutting the door behind him.

"Julep Dupree," he says, coming around the side of his desk and gesturing me to the leather sofas. "Interesting name."

I sit on one sofa, and he sits opposite me.

"Do you know what the purpose of our organization is?"

I pause, searching for the right response. I have to be careful. He's a grifter, so he'll see right through the wrong answer. "To give people the skills to make their professional lives better."

"Professional and personal, actually. The two often go hand in hand. But that's just the window dressing. What is our real purpose?"

I blink, confused. Is he admitting to me that there's a hidden agenda for NWI? Should I be recording this conversation? Damn it. Where is Murphy when I need him?

"To help people grow?" I offer lamely.

He shakes his head. "It's to help people *connect*. Too much of our lives is spent in mental and emotional silos. It's what makes us most vulnerable. If we connect with each other, really connect, nothing external can break those bonds. We're far stronger together than we are apart."

"I'm not sure I follow. Why are you telling me this?" Sadly, that admission is simply the truth. I'm not playing him. I honestly have no idea where he's going with this or why he singled me out.

"Building those connections takes time and trust. I need to preserve that trust by maintaining a safe space for the initiates and the other employees. I hope that you'll respect that safe space during the course of your investigation."

Wait. What did he just say?

"I'm sorry, sir. I don't understand what you mean by 'investigation.'"

"I assume that's why you're here," he says, his expression

mild. "You look shocked. Did you think I wouldn't recognize a fellow grifter?" He winks at me. "You're not as anonymous as you like to think, in certain circles, at least. But don't worry, I'll keep this just between us. I want you to continue your search. I have nothing to hide, not anymore. I am exactly who I say I am."

I gape at him.

"Would you like to shake again?" he says, smiling and taking my hand. "It's good to meet the daughter of Alessandra Moretti."

THE SHILL

"How could he possibly know who you are?" Murphy asks as he drives me to NWI the next morning.

"I have no freaking idea. I mean, my dad told me he was a grifter. Maybe he heard about my dad somehow."

"But he didn't say, 'Good to meet the daughter of Joe Dupree.'"

"I know. That's what's so weird. My mom wasn't the grifter. She had no ties to the criminal world." I say it, but I don't believe it. A gun inscribed with her initials is a pretty good indication that I don't know everything there is to know about my mom. Not to mention all the stuff my dad said about her family. Who *are* they? And what does any of it have to do with NWI?

"What are you going to do?"

"Now that my clueless-intern cover is blown, my options are limited. I need help. Inside help."

"Who? The intern coordinator guy?"

I shake my head. "Too obvious. Salinger would have planned for that."

"The other interns?"

I lean my head against the headrest. "Maybe. But they're all so intern-y."

"Meaning . . . ?"

"They're invested in the outcome, but not my side of it. It's in their best interest that NWI stay up and running. They're not going to be in a rush to expose and bring down their ticket to the Ivy League."

"Could be one of them was forced by their parents."

"That's why I said 'maybe.' But it'll take time to determine that."

My grifter senses are tingling. I'm itching from the inside out, and it's driving me nuts.

As we pull up to the curb, I consider my first line of attack.

"So. Crime?" Murphy says, reading my mind.

"Crime." I shoot him a quick and dirty smile before hopping out of the van and into the gutter. He doesn't wait for me to get inside and I don't watch him drive away. For a sidekick, he shows an admirable lack of codependence sometimes.

"Hi, Brigitte," I say, approaching the reception desk.

Without looking up from her computer she points down a row of cubicles. I veer in that direction, scanning the rows for wandering interns. It takes me all of three minutes to find them.

"You're late, Dupree," Ackley says when I slide into the only seat left within the fabric-paneled walls of the intern pen. "Joseph already gave us our assignments."

I don't bother to respond. Instead I pick up the assignment lying on my keyboard. Photocopying. Awesome.

The other interns are either chatting with each other or starting their assignments. I take a lap around our tiny pen, glancing over shoulders to see if there's a better project I can trade for. There has to be something that will give me a legitimate reason to spend some unaccompanied quality time in the file room. Let's see. Shredding, no. Spreadsheets, no. Ah. Filing. Perfect.

"Hey, Aadila," I say, smoothly, eying her sizable pile of manila folders. "Quite the stack you've got there."

She narrows her eyes suspiciously. "Yes. It's why they don't pay me the big bucks."

"Any chance you'd be willing to trade?"

"For what?"

"Photocopying and a Lunchable."

She snorts. "You're going to have to do better than that."

"Photocopying and my undying devotion?"

"Please. Do I look like I just fell off the rainbows-and-cat-GIFs truck?"

"Photocopying, the Lunchable, my undying devotion, and fifty bucks?"

She hands me the first of several stacks of folders. "Better not be that pizza-with-pepperoni crap. I'm a turkey and cheddar girl."

I'm starting to like this intern. She kind of reminds me of me. Well, before I got soft, anyway. I hand her the presentation packets I was supposed to photocopy, the Lunchable, and the fifty bucks I'd gotten from the ATM this morning in case I needed to bribe somebody. She counts it in front of me, which just makes me like her more.

"Nice doing business with you," she says, then swivels back to her computer to check her email.

I heft the stack of folders and make my way deeper into the bowels of the building. After a few wrong turns, I end up at a heavy, solid door with several industrial-strength padlocks. Out of professional curiosity, I set down the folders and palm the nearest lock. A Brinks shrouded shackle padlock. Tough to pick. Very tight cylinder. You have to rotate it backward to get past the security pins. I've managed it only once, and that was at home under ideal conditions. The other locks are of similar caliber. Which makes me wonder what the hell is behind this door. Must be something worth seeing. I make a mental note of its location for future perusal.

After asking for directions, I finally track down the file room, tucked away on the third floor. There's a file room attendant, a Filipina version of Brigitte with dark blue hair instead of bright red lipstick. This pretty much wrecks my snooping plans. I spend the next two hours filing Aadila's folders and asking every stupid question imaginable to frighten off blue-haired Brigitte, whose name turns out to be, ironically, Scarlet.

I'm filing attendance records and accounting data. But without the personal records of the initiates, the info I have access to is meaningless. I need names to go with dates and numbers. Salinger says that the initiates' profiles are confidential, which means if there's anything to find, it's probably in those files. Unfortunately, those files are locked in a file cabinet in direct line of sight from the attendant's desk.

There's no point in wasting my time checking into what Salinger says is fair game. Unless he knew I'd go for the forbidden stuff and therefore hid the smoking gun in plain sight. Unless he figured I'd figure that he'd figure I'd go for the forbidden stuff and hide the smoking gun in plain sight, so instead he put it in with the forbidden stuff. Ugh. Grifters. I may have to straight up ask him—pit my people-reading skills against his. I can't tell you how much I do not want to do that. Which circles me right back around to the file room and that pesky attendant.

When Scarlet pulls out her lunch bag to eat at her desk, I finally give up and go for plan B. I unlock my phone, dial the main NWI number, and ask to be transferred. Scarlet gives me a dirty look for talking on my phone, so I move into the hall where she won't hear me.

When the person at the other end picks up, I say, "Hi, it's Julep. How would you like to make another fifty bucks?"

Five minutes later, Aadila hobbles into the file room with a giant stack of folders that she can barely see over. A foot or so from the attendant's desk, she fakes a trip and spills the folders all over the floor, the desk, and the attendant. Scarlet scrambles to save the papers from her lunch, or her lunch from the papers, or both. Aadila floods Scarlet with apologies, straightening her hijab as she picks herself up from the floor. She's either a consummate stage performer or she really wants the money.

Attendant distracted: check. Locked file cabinets picked: check. I try to move as little and as quietly as possible to avoid attracting Scarlet's attention. I have minutes at most to work with, so I'll have to snap pictures of the names on the folder tabs and look them up later. Lucky for me, the folders are labeled with first, middle, and last names, as well as a thumbnail-sized picture of the initiate.

I'm working from the bottom of the file cabinet up to avoid being noticed as long as possible. I'll probably make it only about halfway or so before they're done refiling all the mixed-up paperwork, or Scarlet notices me, whichever comes first.

I've gotten entirely through the Rs when I hear renewed cursing from Scarlet and even more effusive apologies on Aadila's part. Something about a drink spill. Excellent. I may have to permanently recruit Aadila.

I'm just about to the Js, feeling the rush of getting so much classified information in one fell swoop, when I see a name that kicks the breath out of my lungs.

SAMUEL L. JACKSON

It's the alias I gave Sam when I made his fake ID last year. I look at the thumbnail picture, and it's Sam, all right. That *idiot*. What the hell is he doing? I filch his folder and slip it in my stack of random files. I slide the drawer shut and relock it. Then I gesture at Aadila to wrap it up as I walk out.

Time to torture my meddling ex–best friend.

• • •

I don't manage to sneak away from the intern pen again until after three. Joseph rounded us up after lunch for some weird "relaxation exercise" that only fueled my rage fire. Aadila fell asleep during the exercise, cushioned, no doubt, on the mattress of cash I'd had to cough up for her help this morning. Ackley was relaxing so hard that he probably gave himself a headache. The others followed the assignment correctly enough, though, that Joseph seemed satisfied.

The moment Joseph leaves our cubicle area, I slide Sam's file out from the middle of the stack and go through it. His application reads like a grifter's dream—executive vice president of a securities company with money to burn and connections that lead all the way to Capitol Hill. No matter what Salinger is looking for—money, secrets, blackmail fodder—Sam has built himself up to be able to deliver it. If Salinger is shady, he won't be able to resist trying to fleece Sam.

But how could Sam have even known about the NWI job? I sure as hell didn't tell him.

I'm torn between furious and impressed. This took planning. Not to mention, he has to pull off executive vice president. His height and confidence help, but he's still only seventeen. Even in an age full of Google and Facebook, it's hard to sell such power so young. And he's not selling it to just anyone. If Salinger takes one look at him, he'll see right through him.

I flip through a few more pages to get Sam's leadership workshop schedule. Five minutes later, I knock on a fifth-floor conference room door.

"Come in," says a lilting voice with a slight Indian accent.

I poke my head into the room. "Sorry to disturb you, Dr. Raktabija, but may I speak with Mr. Jackson for a minute? I need a little more information for his file."

"Of course," she says, nodding at an almost unrecognizable Sam. Tailored, pin-striped suit pants with a crisp white shirt, sleeves rolled up to midforearm. Glasses, dominating posture, the whole enchilada. He's a different person, even from the new Sam who came back from military school.

Sam smiles vaguely at me with not a spark of recognition. I don't know what happened to him the past six months, but he got good. Too good.

I barely keep it together long enough to round a corner before I haul him into a bathroom, slam the door, and lock it behind us. I crank up the water to drown out any yelling I might be tempted to indulge in.

"What the hell do you think you're doing?" I hiss at him as quietly as I can, considering.

He drops the persona like cutting away a curtain. His eyes snap to mine. "I'm helping. Like Murphy asked me to."

"*Murphy* asked you to?" That's it. I'm docking that boy's pay. Right after I deal with this boy. "Well, you can officially butt out, Sam. This is *my* job, not Murphy's."

"Well, maybe Murphy thinks you're in over your head."

"Oh, yeah? Murphy thinks that?" I'm glaring at the person who really thinks that. "I'll have to remind Murphy that I've been doing this for longer than all the rest of you put together."

"Murphy may believe that, but I know the truth. I've been doing this just as long as you have. Three-card monte, remember?"

Of course I remember. Sam and I made a bundle of cash fleecing our fourth-grade classmates with that old card trick before the principal cracked down on us. But it's not the same for him as it is for me. I've been steeped in grifting my whole life. He's had only his friendship with me as experience.

"So you just thought you'd show up and run your own con without telling me? Brilliant move, Samuel Jackson."

"I figured you'd find out eventually. I didn't think you'd be stupid enough to pull me into a bathroom and risk blowing my cover."

I point at myself. "This isn't stupidity; it's fury. Do you think I'd really let you stick around after crashing my con like this? You could have ruined my entire scam."

"What scam?" he asks, gesturing at the file in my hand. "You're digging through file cabinets like a damn cop. You stopped being the roper the second Salinger realized who you were. You're not the shill anymore, Julep. You can't be."

My angry retort dies in my throat, because as much as it kills me to admit it, he's right.

Sam's face softens as he sees the acknowledgment in mine. "It has to be me," he continues. "Salinger would have done his homework. I'm the only one who was never part of your investigation business. If there's anyone he wouldn't see coming, it would be me."

"I can't just sit on the sidelines, Sam. It's my *mom*."

He shakes his head. "I'm not suggesting you sit on the sidelines." Then his mouth quirks up in a smirk as familiar to me as my own.

"I'm listening."

• • •

"I still don't see how a card trick is going to convince Salinger to spill all his secrets," Murphy says, after I've soundly chastised him for bringing Sam into the picture.

"It's not the card trick, Murph. It's the principle behind it."

"Which is?"

Murphy takes the exit off the freeway toward the Ramirezes' house. Coaxing the van to slow down takes some careful pumping of the brakes so that the whole thing doesn't tip over. It perhaps wasn't the smartest purchase. But I have bigger problems than Bess—son of a muffler, now Murphy's got me calling it that. The *van*. Not Bessie—the *van*.

"The three-card monte is a scam where you fool the mark into thinking he can beat the dealer," I say. "With the cards, you plant a fake player who loses in a blindingly obvious way while the mark is watching. The mark thinks the planted player is an idiot and the dealer is giving away easy money. Then there's also a roper, or shill, who nudges the mark to play. If they're good, the mark can't resist placing a bet. As soon as he does, the dealer pulls the sleight of hand so that the mark guesses wrong. If you're lucky, the mark bets again a few times before giving up and you can empty his wallet when he's not looking.

"In this case, Salinger is the mark. He's expecting me to try to con him. What we're hoping is that he's not expecting me to turn over the real con to a new player."

"So you're the fake player who loses?"

I smile. "Yes and no. It's not a perfect analogy. I'm also the lady."

"What lady?"

"The 'lady' is the Queen of Hearts, the card that the mark is asked to pick out of a set of three. The fake player loses in an obvious way to make the mark believe he can easily win, but the lady is what truly distracts him. It's the thrill of the game. The competition of getting one up on the dealer. As long as I keep Salinger distracted, Sam can pick his proverbial pocket clean."

"You really think that will work?"

On the one hand, it's a brilliant plan. Use me to distract Salinger from the real mole. On the other hand, the role reversal is hard for me to get used to. I don't like being on the edge of the game. I prefer having my hands in the thick of it, knowing what there is to know immediately so I can deal with it on the fly if necessary. Sam's plan forces me to rely on him to make split-second decisions. If he makes a mistake, he could bring down the whole con. If I make a mistake, at least I'm the one who pays the price. I don't like the idea of Sam being closer to the line of fire.

Besides, I'm still not sure how much I can trust him. I know he'd never intentionally put me in harm's way, but his leaving hurt a lot, and his staying gone hurt even worse. What if trusting him again puts me right back in the same place?

"I'll be honest, I'm not used to Sam calling the shots. But the grifter in me senses that this plan is a good one. The right one," I say.

Murphy considers that for a moment and then says, "Good enough for me."

"I'll be sending you a list of names to start background checks on."

He groans. "Can't we get Lily to do it?"

"I think Lily's big memorial reveal was her way of tendering her resignation," I say. "The absolute radio silence from her since last Thursday is kind of a giveaway."

"Then why is she sitting on your doorstep?" Murphy says as he pulls Bess—the van—okay, fine, whatever—up to the curb.

Sure enough, Lily is sitting on the front stoop of the Ramirezes' house, scrolling through her phone.

Fabulous. The last thing I want to do right now is have a come-to-Jesus moment with a member of Tyler's family. My stomach is still grouchy from my confrontation with Sam. Now I'm about to have my nose rubbed in a big helping of Lily-guilt.

"I could keep driving," Murphy says.

"Such a gentleman."

"Or I could call Sam again."

I give him a look so dirty he'll need to shower with chlorine to wash it off. "And I could revoke your paycheck."

"Hey, you owe me. Where would your full-monty plan be if I hadn't looped Sam in?"

Sometimes I just can't even. "Three. Card. Monte," I say through gritted teeth.

"Whatever," he says.

"I'm getting out before I resort to violence."

"Sounds like a plan." He shoots me a goofy grin designed to make me smile. It almost works.

My corporate heels and I clack onto the sidewalk. Bessie rolls and coughs and sputters away, leaving me alone to face the aftermath of my transgressions.

Lily hears me coming and looks up from her phone. She doesn't smile, but she doesn't immediately try to knife me, either, so I'm calling it a win.

"Lily," I say. "How can I help you?"

She swishes her black hair over her narrow shoulders, pocketing her phone and getting to her feet.

"I want an explanation."

"Okay. Explanation for what?"

"For why you killed my brother," she says.

THE REPARATION

"I didn't mean to kill him," I say, though it sounds lame even to me. I'd like to say that I didn't kill him, that it wasn't me who pulled the trigger. But that would sound even lamer. "I was angry at him for betraying me, but I still . . ."

"You still what?" Lily asks.

I don't answer, because I can't sum up my feelings for Tyler in a single word. It's just not that simple.

She walks away. "This was a stupid idea. I don't know what I thought you could possibly say."

I grab her arm as she passes. "You wanted me to fix it, because that's what I do. I fix things. But I can't fix this."

She yanks her arm out of my grip. "I don't want you to *fix it*. I want it never to have happened in the first place!" Her face breaks and falls apart, though not a tear falls.

"If I could undo it, I would."

She laughs like porcelain shattering. "You're supposed to tell me that he didn't die in vain. That he died saving all those girls—the ones who idolize *you* now. You're supposed to say that his sacrifice had purpose, that he was a good person, that he'll never be forgotten."

"What good would telling you any of that do? He didn't die saving those girls. He died saving me. And I didn't deserve it. No one knows that better than I do."

She turns her back to me. Stiff, unyielding. I should let her go, but some part of me desperately wants to fix it for her. Or rather, for him. It's the least I can do for still being here when I shouldn't be.

"His sacrifice was senseless," I say. "But he *was* a good person. And I, for one, will never forget him."

"He was a jerk," she says, her voice shaking with anger. "A giant jerk. He ate all my Halloween candy. He teased me constantly about being short. He even tried to burn my hair with a lighter once."

She glares at me, daring me to contradict her, to force her to say only good about the dead. But I wouldn't do that.

"Did you know him at all?" she says. "His middle name? His favorite color? Did you know about the time he set a rubber tire on fire in the backyard and tried to put it out with a five-hundred-dollar bottle of wine?"

I shake my head. "I didn't. But I wanted to," I say.

She snorts and turns away again.

"Why are you here, Lily? What do you want from me?"

"I want you to give me my brother back."

"Okay," I say.

She blinks at me. "Okay?"

I nod and sit down on the patch of grass I was just standing on, about three feet from the stairs leading up to the Ramirezes' front door. Lily looks down at me, perplexed but with an edge of curiosity. Curiosity wins, and she plops down opposite me.

"Close your eyes," I say, nervous because this idea could go wrong in a hundred thousand ways.

She complies, her face shuttering as she prepares for what's coming.

"All right. Open them."

When she does, I contort my features into a ridiculous face, designed to make a child laugh. Tyler told me once that he did this to cheer his sister up when she was upset. It worked on me then. I'm hoping it works on Lily now.

A silent moment passes. Then her expression crumples completely, and she drops her head into her hands, sobbing. I know better than to offer her comfort. So I offer her memories instead.

"Your brother put a dead rat in my locker to get my attention. He spied on me for a gangster at your father's request. He lied to me about nearly everything. But he once offered to watch the world for me while I slept. And I still hear him saying that to me every night before I drift off."

Lily doesn't look at me. She weeps for several more minutes without so much as glancing up. Then she jumps to her feet, whirls toward the street, and takes off at a run.

I can't say I'm sorry to see her go. I have my own demons to bleed. I wipe my eyes and head into the house.

• • •

I spend all the next day trying to figure out a way past the locked door. I know I'm supposed to let Sam do the heavy lifting on this one, but getting on the other side of that door would be a coup. And it's what Salinger expects me to try to do. Otherwise, he wouldn't have put up giant neon Julep signs pointing straight to it.

I'm not even close to successful, though. I keep getting interrupted. Apparently, people actually expect me to *work* at this internship. If I have to staple one more initiate packet, I may stuff it down Joseph's throat.

The only time I get within a foot of that padlock is when Joseph leads me past it on our way to the second floor to clean up the ropes-challenge room. I glare at the door, at Joseph, even at innocent Brigitte as I walk by. I don't want to be here any longer than I have to. Having to wait on getting through that door is not going to make this process any faster.

"Everyone hates the ropes course at first," Joseph says as we're collecting the extra mats. "Though we don't usually start the initiates on the wall. You're special."

"I'm actually very ordinary." I fold up a few of the mats and carry them to the closet.

"That's initiate-level thinking," Joseph says as he stacks gym blocks. "The point of NWI's program is to break people out of the mind-set that underachieving is normal."

When I emerge from the closet, Joseph is standing by the doorway.

"What about the overachievers?" I ask.

"Overachievers tend to be underachievers in other areas of their lives. They burn themselves out and ruin their relationships because they never learned how to fail."

"So you teach people how to fail?" I say.

"We teach people that failure is just part of the process. That the end goal isn't perfection, it's adaptation."

I follow him down the ramp to the main level and back to the offices. I'm surprised, though, when we pass our cubicle and continue on to the back of the building.

"Where are we going?" I ask.

"I want to show you something," he says. For once, his easy smile is absent, his expression pensive. If I'm lucky, it means he'll finally reveal something I can use. If I'm not lucky, it means he's discovered my real reason for being here and is about to kick me to the curb, special dispensation from Salinger or no.

When he leads me to the mysterious locked door, my heart goes into adrenaline hyperdrive. I thought for sure I'd have to break in to get to the treasure trove of information I'm assuming is locked behind it. But Joseph is taking me right to it.

As he fishes out his keys, he says, "We have to keep the door locked for privacy reasons."

"Privacy reasons" could mean anything. Still, I have a range of expectations of what could be hiding behind that door—another room of tell-all files, a lab of wall-to-wall computers, a cache of nuclear weapons—but what I see is about as far from any of those as you can get.

A line of people in heavy overcoats, carrying plastic bags stuffed with filthy clothes and odds and ends, winds around the room. At one end of the line is a folding table with a clean-cut girl in wire-framed glasses sitting on the other side, taking notes. Standing next to her is Duke Salinger, wearing a light gray suit that stands out like a sore thumb in the warehouse full of itinerants. He's chatting with each person as they approach the table, shaking hands, patting shoulders, even offering a hug to a privileged few. Then he stows a few disposable plastic containers in a tote bag and hands one to each person with a warm smile before greeting the next person in line.

"A homeless shelter?" I say, stunned.

"Nothing that formal," Joseph answers. "Four years ago, when Duke first started outfitting the NWI building, he noticed the growing homeless population in this neighborhood. There had been a spate of homeless deaths from lack of services. So on a whim, he bought this building and had the door installed to connect it to the NWI building. He asked for volunteers from the staff to provide services to the homeless population."

"But why no publicity? There's nothing on the NWI website about a philanthropic arm of the company."

"It's not always about what you get out of it."

It isn't? First I'm hearing of it.

Joseph smiles at me as if he can sense my internal snark. "I know—it came as a shock to me, too." He gestures at Salinger. "But it's the reason I'm now on this side of the table."

It takes a moment for me to process what he's saying. "You were homeless?"

He nods. "I was sixteen when my dad disowned me for coming out. He told me I broke our family, though he was the one who threw me away."

"Wow, Joseph," I say. "That sucks."

He shrugs. "It gets better, right? Anyway, I migrated north to Chicago just after spring thaw. I heard about this place from a friend. After a few conversations, Duke took me under his wing. My NWI family supported me through getting my GED and eventually hired me. I literally owe them my life."

We're interrupted by a black guy in a calf-length, shiny pleather raincoat and stained purple bowler, holding a pug named Bill, apparently, as that's what Joseph says when he pats the dog. The intrusion gives me a few minutes to ponder this new development. Not just Joseph, but Duke and NWI as well. Grifters aren't typically known for their generosity. I can't think of a single con artist who works in a soup kitchen in his downtime.

So what am I going up against here? Did Salinger really go straight? If so, what happened to Mr. Antolini? How did he end up embezzling hundreds of thousands of dollars without so much as a blip of a prior criminal record? Something else must have triggered his descent into thievery. Organizations that secretly sponsor soup kitchens just don't have that evil tinge to them.

When Joseph finishes his conversation, he turns back to me. "Hungry?" he says.

I shake my head. "Why did you want to show me this?"

His expression morphs from inviting to empathetic. "Not every wall is as obvious as a twelve-foot wooden structure," he says gently. "Some walls are actually ruts—ways of being we've become entrenched in for one reason or another. But we don't have to stay there. I just wanted you to know that I know what I'm talking about. Personal experience."

As I'm absorbing this, Salinger approaches us, hand outstretched. "Ah, Julep. So you've discovered my big secret."

I take his hand. It's the polite thing to do, after all. "I had help," I say, nodding at Joseph.

"Remind me to keelhaul you later," Duke says to Joseph, winking.

"Yes, sir." Joseph's smile is easy and sincere, as if they've joked this way for years. "Mind if I take over for a while?"

"Not at all. I'd like the opportunity to get to know our new intern a little better." Then Duke turns to me. "Shall we go for a walk?"

I think about contract killers and calculate the number of daylight hours left. Luckily, the summer sun tends to stick around longer than it should. There's no guarantee an attack won't come in the middle of the afternoon, but it's a lot less likely. And I'd rather walk than sit still. I think better when I'm on the move.

I follow Salinger out onto the street, where the line of homeless people wraps around the corner of the building. The air is hot and humid, and I'm wishing I'd thought to wear sandals instead of dress shoes.

"So, how many skeletons have you found so far?"

I sigh heavily. "None," I admit. "I'm batting a thousand on this one."

"I won't ask why you're investigating me. I'm sure you need to keep your client's confidentiality."

"What makes you think I'm working for someone?"

"I looked you up. Fellow grifter, remember? The first Internet entry for you is for your private investigation firm. Since you and I have no personal history, I assume you're here on behalf of someone else."

No need to confirm or deny it. He'll draw whatever conclusions he wants to without my help. But it's a good opportunity to plant a little misinformation while trying to dig for information of my own.

"How do you know my mother?" I ask.

He smiles sadly. "I didn't know her well. The Morettis ruled the international criminal underworld. They probably still do. But in either case, you couldn't be a criminal twenty years ago *without* knowing Alessandra Moretti. She was destined to take over the family business when her mother retired."

Per mia fata turchina, A.N.M. For my blue fairy, Alessandra Nereza Moretti.

"I'm sorry. You must have my mother confused with someone else. She's not the criminal in my family."

"Maybe not anymore, but she was supposed to be."

I put one foot in front of the other, my mind whirling. *"Anything that scared your mother that much—your mother, who wasn't afraid of anything—should be avoided at all costs."*

Nope. I'm still not buying it. Heir to a criminal dynasty? That would make me the next in line, and growing up broke and family-less does not exactly fit that paradigm. Besides, nothing has ever happened to me to even remotely indicate that I'm on anyone's radar for induction into a criminal family cabal. Well, nothing but the strange note on the tuition check that mysteriously showed up for me last semester.

Travo la fata turchina. Find the blue fairy.

No. I still don't believe it. Too far-fetched. I'm not exactly normal, but I'm not criminal royalty, either.

"I respected your mother, even back then. But I respect her more for giving it up. I know what that's like."

"Do you?" I say, letting doubt color my tone.

We walk in silence for a few moments, navigating around the other pedestrians as we saunter upstream. Duke leads me off the beaten sidewalk into Ping Tom Memorial Park. The noise level falls dramatically, which will make his confession easier to hear. He sits at the first bench we come to.

"I didn't grow up like you or Joseph. I grew up privileged, entitled. But I was just as alone."

I think of Tyler and Lily and how growing up with all the money in the world doesn't guarantee you a carefree childhood. "Fleecing people doesn't win you any popularity contests."

"At the time, I didn't know that the great, gaping emptiness I wrestled with was isolation. I thought I could fill it with money and power. I didn't realize that prosperity couldn't love me back."

"Poor rich grifter," I can't help but say. "It must have been so hard for you, spending so much of other people's money."

He ignores my jab. "I fell into a deep depression. I wandered aimlessly, looking for something, *anything* to connect with. And then one day I thought, if no one sees me, maybe I'm not worth being seen. It was the darkest moment of my life.

"I happened to be out walking when I passed a woman struggling to get her belongings and her young child off a bus. The passenger behind her was badgering her to hurry up. She looked stressed and miserable, so I picked up the bags she'd dropped and offered her my hand. She took it and smiled at me gratefully.

"The moment her eyes met mine . . . the closest I can come to describing it is getting struck by a train, but in a good way. I'd never felt anything like it before. She adjusted her burdens and walked away. But that single moment changed my life, because I did the reaching.

"I thought about that exchange all the rest of the day and into the night, trying to figure out why such a tiny act had felt so significant. After hours of racking my brain, I finally realized that my interaction with the woman from the bus showed me that I wasn't the only one alone, and isn't that just a half step away from not being alone? More importantly, I realized I could do something about it, something that would finally fill the emptiness I'd struggled with my whole life.

"I gave back the money I stole, where I could. The rest I donated to any charity I came across. I served my time in prison. And when I was released, I founded the New World Initiative."

"Why are you telling me all this?"

"Because I see the same signs of alienation and isolation in you. I want to help you the way that woman from the bus helped me."

I drop my gaze to my hands, swallowing. "I tried connecting with people. It didn't work out so well."

"Keeping yourself at a distance isn't going to work out, either."

"What kind of a grifter tells his mark that he's a grifter to earn her trust?"

He smiles and pats my hand. "A reformed one." He gets to his feet, smoothing the front of his suit jacket. "If you ever want to talk, my door is always open." Then he walks away, leaving me on the bench trying to reconcile this kindly mentor version of Duke with Mrs. Antolini's insistence that NWI is responsible for her husband's incarceration.

Oddly, the exchange reminds me of Ralph. It was probably the fatherly hand-patting. Ralph used to do that to me, too. As I realize that, I suddenly yearn for nothing more than to be that young girl again, exploring Ralph's trinket shop for the first time. He may have been my dad's bookie, but he was a good friend. And right now, his shop seems like the safest, sanest place I've ever set foot in. But then, as always happens when I think about Ralph too long, my guilt engulfs me and shuts me down. No one knows what happened to him, not even Petrov. Which means I'll never know, either.

My phone buzzes in my pocket. I pull it out and check the number. It's Mrs. Antolini.

"Hello?"

Her voice on the other end is garbled and hysterical, the signal cutting in and out.

"Slow down," I say, cupping the phone closer to my ear to hear better. "Take a breath. What's going on?"

"It's my husband. The warden just called. Gerald t-tried to k-k—"

"Tried to what?" I say, walking back toward the NWI building.

"They found him in his cell. Unconscious."

My chest tightens. "Mrs. Antolini—"

"He tried to kill himself!" She breaks down completely. "He tried to hang himself in his cell."

THE QUARRY

"This is twice to a prison now," Dani grouses as she makes a U-turn with the newly returned Chevelle to reach an exit on the opposite side of the road. "Just because no one has tried to kill you in a week does not mean the contract has been canceled."

"I need to talk to this guy. I can't find anything at NWI that leads me to Bar63 or the blue fairy. There's nothing that indicates NWI is shady. The only thing off is Mr. Antolini. If everything keeps leading back to him, I have to find out what he knows."

"And the uniform will get you into a maximum-security facility's hospital wing?"

I tug at the cuff of my tab-collar clerical shirt. The sleeves are slightly too long, which makes me crazy. Nothing gives away a disguise quicker than a poor fit. But there's no hope for it. Clerical shirts aren't exactly easy to find. At least the matching pants fit well. And by "well," I mean "like a pair of stovepipes." As disguises go, this is the least fashionable one I've worn in years. I guess it could be worse—I could be dressing up as an inmate. Actually, I might be dressing up as an inmate, if I get caught.

"I want to see him. But he's on constant visual observation in a safe cell. Impersonating a priest is the best I could come up with on short notice."

"I find it amusing that you happen to have a priest's garb in your closet."

"'Be prepared.' It's the grifter's motto."

"I thought that was the Girl Scouts' motto."

"It's a popular motto."

"Do you think it is wise to talk to him after he tried to commit suicide?"

That's Dani for you. She's not really of the beating-around-the-bush school of thought.

"It's the best chance a fake clergywoman has to interview a high-risk prisoner. Besides, he's vulnerable. I might get more out of him while his guard is down."

Dani nods. She doesn't grimace or look offended that I'd take advantage of a person like that. She just nods. More than anyone, she accepts me completely for who I am. I don't know whether to love her for it or judge her.

"After this, no more errands. You take too many chances as it is. You are still in danger."

"I know, but it's not like we have any leads on the person

who ordered the hit. Maybe drawing the hit man out will help us."

She takes her eyes off the road to shoot me a glare. "No, it will not help us. I have ideas of how to get information. But I cannot pursue them if you insist on behaving like no one is trying to kill you."

"Understood," I say, more to appease her than because I believe I'll do anything differently. "I do try to keep myself on lockdown as much as possible."

"Do you," she says flatly, her glare receding from pointed to merely grouchy.

We spend the rest of the drive to the detention facility picking apart my conversation with Duke.

"You think he is telling the truth?" she asks.

"I don't know. He's a grifter with a lot more years of experience than me. He could easily be conning me, because he knows how to hide his tells."

Dani pauses, processing. "But you *want* to believe him."

I pull my collar to loosen it. I don't want to admit that she can read me, especially when I've been lousy at reading myself lately. But she's not wrong.

"I want to believe a person can earn absolution," I say.

She rubs her neck, touching the spires of her cathedral tattoo poking out from under her shirt. "Only a person who believes in absolution can earn it."

I shake my head. "So you're saying absolution is subjective? Isn't that the same as saying it's imaginary? That any idiot who decides they're forgiven automatically is? I don't buy that. Either you can make up for your sins or you can't."

"I am saying that it is a path, not a state of being. The first step on the path is believing it can be done."

I stare out the window at the mix of countryside and suburbia we're passing on the way to the max-security prison. Unfortunately, they don't tend to put those sorts of places near cities. Gives me plenty of time to brood about impossible things.

"Do you ever worry about earning forgiveness?" I say as we turn onto the winding road leading from the freeway to the prison parking lot.

"I do not worry about it, no," she says quietly.

"Because you believe you can earn absolution?"

She doesn't answer for several long moments. "Because I know I cannot," she says as she pulls up to the curb to drop me off.

"Dani—"

"I will park under the nearest floodlight. Find me when you are finished."

And the conversation is over. Dani has an irritating habit of turning herself on and off around me. I prefer to be the person controlling the flow of information. But I'll let it go for now, because I need to get my head in the game.

I slide out of the car and make my way up the long walk to the front door. Once inside, I approach the glassed-in guard gate. The prison lobby has a completely different vibe from the medium-security facility my dad's in. For one thing, the word *lobby* is not remotely appropriate for the empty, cement-floor vestibule that leads to the gate.

"Can I help you, Reverend?" says the security guard behind the bulletproof glass.

"Yes," I say, adjusting my spectacles. The white and gray face makeup that I sponged into my hair at the temples lends credibility to my disguise, as does my severe posture and air of superiority. "I'm here to visit an inmate. One of my constituents requested I pray with him for healing. He's gravely ill, and I'm to intercede on his behalf."

The guard looks bored, which is a good sign my disguise is holding up. He sets a clipboard and pen in a metal tray on his side of the glass and pushes a lever. The tray slides out on my side, and I pick up the contents. I fill out the register with my name, the inmate's name, and time in.

I put the clipboard and my minister's license (yes, I have a forged minister's license—it's a long story) in the tray, and the guard reels it in. He checks my license and sends it back with a visitor's badge to clip to my shirt pocket. He buzzes me in, and I push through the scary, spiky-looking turnstile into the institutional hallway leading in one of two directions. The signage is less than helpful, so another passing guard, taking pity on me, points the way to the hospital cells. I thank him and head down the hall.

When I get to the next checkpoint, a guard escorts me to the bank of cells housing the inmates under observation. The guard leading me is a beefy Latino who could give Mike a run for his money. The cells themselves are overly bright, far too much fluorescence to be healthy. The furniture in the cells is not what you see on TV. It looks more like something from an Ikea catalog—smooth plastic supports, rounded edges, padded futons for mattresses. I suppose it's to keep inmates from hurting themselves, but it makes the rooms look futuristic.

Most of the cells are empty, but a few are occupied. I follow the guard to the end of the row. I'm not sure what I expected to see when I looked through the bars, but the man sitting on the Ikea futon was not it. His hair is stringy, his cheeks hollow, and his eyes stare straight ahead at nothing.

This isn't normal. He shouldn't have deteriorated this drastically. Prison's rough, sure, but this is . . . this is weird.

"Mr. Antolini?" I say, revising my game plan. I expected him to be hostile, or at least withholding. I don't have a contingency for him being mentally incapable of answering.

"You'll have to sit out here," says the guard, pointing to a chair adjacent to the cell.

"I thought members of the clergy were allowed to see the prisoners without supervision."

"I'll be at my station if you need me."

I mumble a quick thanks and turn my attention to the catatonic inmate. He hasn't even looked at me. This is going to be harder than I thought.

"Mr. Antolini, your wife sent me to talk with you. She wants you to know that she is worried about you and would like to see you as soon as possible. Do you have a message you'd like me to take back to her?"

He looks at me blankly, then returns to his scrutiny of the concrete wall. So much for the gentle approach.

"She thinks you're here because NWI brainwashed you into stealing money. Do you think that's true?"

He doesn't look at me this time, but he starts to rock back and forth. He's mumbling something, which I can't quite make out.

"Mr. Antolini—"

Before I get out the next question, he stands and shuffles over to the wall. The collar of his too-big shirt shifts down, revealing an angry welt on his neck. I flinch, but force myself to watch. He draws on the wall with his finger. His mumbling increases in volume, so I can just make out what he's saying.

". . . eight two one two eight four nine five seven zero nine eight six three NWI three six eight nine zero seven five nine four eight two one two eight four nine five seven zero nine eight six three NWI three six eight nine zero seven five nine four . . ."

By about the third repetition, I catch on that he's reciting a pattern. I pull a receipt out of my wallet and borrow a pen from the guard's desk. The guard doesn't look happy about me asking, but I give him a certified clergy glare, and he hands me one. I thank him and head back to Mr. Antolini's cell. I hold my breath as I draw close, afraid that he's reverted to his catatonic state. But my luck seems to be holding thus far—he's still repeating the numbers.

I write down the sequence and stow it in my pocket for Sam and Murphy to analyze later. But a random string of numbers is not exactly what I came here for. I'll try one more time to break through before giving up.

"Mr. Antolini," I say, standing close to the bars of his cell. "My name is Julep and I'm trying to get you out of here. Is there anything you can tell me about NWI or the blue fairy—"

Suddenly, Mr. Antolini grabs his head and starts howling. The sound is earsplitting and awful, and the other inmates on the cellblock are getting agitated. I stumble back from the bars, hands over my ears. What did I say? The blue fairy? What the hell happened to this guy?

A couple of guards and a medical technician rush in and take over. My escort guard firmly ushers me out.

"I didn't mean—"

"Remember to sign out when you get to the front desk," he says curtly before abandoning me on the other side of his checkpoint.

There's nothing I can do but follow his orders. I walk swiftly back the way I came, fighting guilt as a madman's cries chase me down the halls.

As I near the front desk, I pull out my phone and call Mrs. Antolini.

"The number you have reached is no longer in service."

I check the number and try again, but I get the same recording. Something's not right.

When I go through the turnstile, I take a chance and ask the new security guard manning the desk if he has Mrs. Antolini's contact information. He seems greener than the last guy, more nervous but also more pliable.

"We're not supposed to give out personal information, Reverend," he says, looking distressed. I bet he's a believer.

"I have her number, my son, but my phone ran out of battery power. I'd like to discuss her husband's situation as soon as possible. You would be doing your inmate and his grieving family a kind service."

He's waffling. One more solid nudge and I've got him.

"I will pray for you, my son," I say coolly, bowing my head slightly at him and turning to walk away.

"Wait, Reverend."

Slam, and dunk.

I hear typing behind me. I turn back, giving him a benevolent smile and Mr. Antolini's name.

His typing slows. "Um, Reverend," he says, sounding confused. "According to our records, Gerald Antolini has no family."

• • •

"Dani!" I yell as I rush up to the passenger's-side door of the Chevelle. "We've got—"

I pull the handle, but the door is locked. I knock on the black-tinted window but nothing happens. I cup my hand to block rays from the setting sun and peer through. No Dani.

I look frantically around the parking lot for any sign of her. The killer didn't get her, did he? My heart lurches at the thought.

Then she emerges from the interior of the prison. She must

have been looking for me, though I wasn't gone that long. Then she touches her face gingerly.

I rein myself in from running up to her and demanding to know what the hell she was thinking, going anywhere near that prison without me. I meet her halfway, keeping my pace to a brisk walk, and only then do I see the cut on her cheek, the swelling under her eye.

"What happened?" I say, trying to modulate my anger.

"It is nothing. A conversation with an inmate."

"A conversation involving assault?"

She shrugs.

"What was it about?" I reach out to touch her injured cheek.

She pulls her head away, which causes a strange and painful tightening in my chest. I let my hand fall, but the urge to reach out again is strong—like I won't know for sure she's okay without the tactile input corroborating the visual and auditory. But I know better than to push it. What I don't know is where all this feeling is coming from. Her being hurt bothers me a lot more than it should.

"You," she answers, as if she hadn't pulled away from me, as if she hasn't just scraped my heart the way someone cut her cheek. "I interrogated Petrov. I believed his contacts in Chicago might know something about your contract. He landed a punch before the guards restrained him, that is all."

"You did *what*? He's *here*? At this prison?"

"This is the closest maximum-security prison."

For some reason, the idea had never occurred to me.

The thought of how close he is—just beyond a few feet of concrete—gives me the heebie-jeebies. I fold my arms to keep my hands from trembling.

"Petrov knew who put the hit out on me?" I shiver anyway.

"No. But he had heard of it. Not who ordered the hit, but who took the contract. Now that I know a name, I can find him and extract more information about his employer."

I don't really want to dwell on what she means by *extract*, but knowing we have a lead is somewhat comforting. Except . . .

"Why would Petrov tell you the hit man's name? Why would he help me?"

Dani looks away, her jaw clenching. "It is unimportant."

"Tell me you didn't make a deal with him," I say, ten degrees colder than I was a moment ago.

She doesn't answer, but her expression confirms it.

"Damn it, Dani! You should have talked to me first."

She's still not saying anything, which makes me nervous that the hit man's name wasn't the only favor she was granted. But there's nothing I can do about it now. Petrov is still behind bars, and will be for some time, so whatever Dani promised is not going to come due for a while. Long enough for me to figure out how to get her out of it.

"We should go," she says, eyeing the parking lot like I did a few minutes ago. "It is not as safe here as I would like."

I follow her to the Chevelle and get in. "We would have noticed if we'd been followed," I say.

"Better to not take chances." She exits back onto the freeway in the direction of Chicago, flipping the Chevelle's lights on against the darkening sky.

"I'm not going to just let you go after a contract killer on your own."

She arches an eyebrow at me. "You do know what I do, right?"

"That doesn't mean it isn't dangerous. Besides, you're just an enforcer. You're not a professional killer."

"But I have killed people. My job is to enforce the rules of the organization. I do what it takes to gain compliance."

I shiver again. "Look, I know that you can take care of yourself. But you're not invincible. And I don't want you going after this guy without someone having your back."

She snorts. "Fine. I won't go after him alone. . . ."

"Good."

"On the condition that you call Ramirez and tell him what's going on."

Son of a— "You think putting me in a government safe house is the answer? Why not just leave me back there at the prison? It amounts to the same thing."

"It is not the same thing at all! Why are you being so stubborn? I am just trying to keep you s—"

A loud pop interrupts our argument and the Chevelle starts listing to the side.

Dani starts swearing in Ukrainian.

"Flat tire?" I say as she swerves onto the shoulder.

"Stay in the car," she barks at me as she kills the engine and gets out. She opens the trunk.

"I'm not staying in here while you jack up the Chevelle," I say, and follow her out. I pull my phone from my pocket and tap to open the browser. "Crap. There's no signal out here."

"Just . . ." Dani flows into Ukrainian again for a sentence or two. "Keep your head down and stay close to the car." Then she disappears under the car to look for a place to set the jack.

I sneak a few feet away to find a signal. There has to be one. We're not *that* far from Chicago. We're close to Joliet. I think. We're on the edge of a quarry, and the only quarry I know about in this direction is the Joliet quarry. I guess I'd better find a mile marker so I can tell the towing company where to pick us up. I walk a few more feet to the mile marker, note the number, and then veer off into the grass, still looking for a signal.

My life was a whole lot simpler before I met these freaking Ukrainians. Dad was free, I didn't have an arrest on my record, and Dani hadn't pried open the cage around my heart and muscled her way in.

Ugh, why did I just think that? I was arguing with her not five minutes ago and now I've got this unacceptable warmth spreading through my chest. I can't give in to it. The last time I felt all skittery and strange about someone, I got him killed. I will not allow that to happen again. Dani is still Dani, and I'm still trouble.

The trees around me darken the blue of twilight to black shadow. It's not pitch-black, but it's darker than it was even a minute ago. I must have wandered farther than I meant to.

Dani's going to be pissed if I don't get back before she notices I'm not right by the car. I wave my phone a final time, knowing it's futile but trying anyway.

Then something crunches behind me—a footfall where no footfall should be. I whirl just in time to hear the gunshot.

THE OLD MAN

The bark on the tree next to me splinters and flies apart. I can't tell where the shot came from, but I can still hear it ringing in my ears, silencer or not. I duck behind a different tree, praying my attacker isn't hiding behind it.

Another shot blasts through a bunch of leaves to my right, and I veer in the other direction. Is he trying to kill me or herd me? It doesn't matter. I can't lead him back to Dani. There's no cover on the open road. I just have to hope she's heard the shot and will come to us. Or maybe I shouldn't hope that. All I can see in my mind's eye is Tyler's face. Alive one minute, covered in blood the next.

The crunch of running steps behind me speeds up in time with my heart. I tear my hair and hands on oak and switch-grass. But better that than the alternative. My thoughts distill to run, cover, duck, and darkness. And pulse-pounding *fear*. I keep stumbling forward, getting slower and slower in my desperation to escape.

My ankle turns on a loose rock, and I collapse in a quivering heap. I crawl a few more feet, but a throat clears behind me, and I know that I am about to die.

Click. A round goes in the chamber.

"Sorry, kid. A paycheck's a paycheck."

But instead of a gunshot, I hear a dull thud and squelch behind me. I muster enough courage to roll over, then hiss in terror and scramble backward into a tree.

The hit man's body lies limp on the ground, the point of a long sword sticking out of his chest.

"Are you all right, *jang mi?*"

No! I want to scream. *No, I'm not all—* Wait. I know that voice.

I jump up. "Ralph?"

"I'm afraid it is," he says, his voice the same but his accent different. Instead of Korean, it's British. He bows to me, the palms of his black-gloved hands pressed together. "I'm sorry for the dramatic entrance, but I'm glad I arrived in time."

Ralph? A sword? A *British accent?*

"What the hell is going on?"

He smiles, but his expression is regretful. "I've been ordered to keep an eye on you."

"Why?"

"Because you are in danger," he says.

"That is not an answer. Who *are* you?"

"I am Ralph Chen—"

"The hell you are. Ralph Chen could not have done that."

He stands still as I skirt around him and the body.

"Perhaps it's more accurate to say I am *also* Ralph Chen."

"What is *that* supposed to mean?" I'm more afraid than angry, but if I cling to angry, maybe I'll get through this. Where the hell is Dani? The killer didn't take her out first, did he? I shudder in dread at the possibility.

"Ralph Chen is one of many names I have legally, and not-so-legally, adopted over the years. It's the one you know me by, so it's a fair answer to your question."

"This is insane! Who are you really?"

He leans down to wipe his sword on his victim's camo shirt. Then he sheathes the sword and clasps his hands behind his back, probably to appear less frightening. It helps, but not a lot.

"Maybe it would be more instructive for you to ask whom I work for," he says.

"Fine, who do you work for?"

He doesn't move, though I'm behind him now. "I can't tell you that," he says.

"Then why did you tell me to ask!"

"Knowing that my employer is significant is helpful, is it not?"

I growl in frustration. He's right, but that doesn't make me want to punch him any less. "This is ridiculous! Why are you even here?"

"You were in danger."

"And before? When you worked at the shop? Was I in danger then, too?"

"My orders were different then—just watch and report. I set myself up as a confidant to your father, though it wasn't easy. Your father has few exploitable weaknesses and he's smart enough to know a con when he sees one."

"Well, he certainly didn't see through you."

"It is impossible to suspect everyone all the time. And you must admit, I played a pretty believable harmless old man."

He certainly did sell harmless. So well that he fooled not one grifter but two.

"But *why?*"

He doesn't answer. I've circled him almost all the way around again. I stop when I realize it. I don't want to be trapped between him and the body and the tree. I want a clear path out of here.

"So your orders change then?" I ask. "Will they change to a kill order at some point?"

"Doubtful," he says. But he doesn't smile when he says it, so I don't think he's joking. "I'm not going to kill you right now."

"Well, that's *so* comforting. Thanks for that."

"I have a message for you."

"What is it?"

"Be careful."

"Okay, great. That's super helpful, Ralph. Thanks."

He bows again and walks away. I'd follow him and demand more answers, but by the time I decide to do so, he has disappeared. In an instant. Just gone. Which probably means he's some sort of British spy with ninja training, and isn't it just wonderful that I now have to worry about *that* on top of everything else. At least he's not dead. Or maybe that's a bad thing. I don't freaking know anymore. I mean, what the hell am I going to tell my dad?

And then I remember I'm standing in the woods at night with a dead body.

I hustle to where I think the Chevelle is, but I get turned around a time or two. When I break through the trees and back into the quarry, I just about melt down. I want to go *home*. To my apartment with my dad. To a time before I was lost and confused. I hurt, and I'm pissed, and I'm scared, and the damned trembling has started again. And I *hate everything*.

But when I turn to head back into the trees, I see Dani running toward me. Before I even think about it, I throw myself into her arms, spewing everything about Ralph and the hit man. She pushes me to arm's length, looking me over for injuries, but after hearing that Ralph has already dispatched my would-be assassin, she crushes me close again.

"I *told* you to stay in the car."

"I know," I whisper into her shoulder.

"But there is time now. It will take time to hire someone new."

I nod, wishing she'd stop talking about it. She must read my mind, because she goes quiet. After a moment or two, she leads me back through the trees to the Chevelle. I sink into the passenger's-side seat sideways with my feet still outside the car, finally feeling the night chill settle into my skin. Dani rummages in the trunk again, and then slams the lid shut.

Crouching in front of me, she opens the world's smallest first-aid kit and takes out a couple of Band-Aids.

I lay my hands palm up in my lap so she can assess the damage. Nothing too deep, thankfully. Just scraped and bloody and stinging like hell, now that I'm paying attention to it. Dani clenches her teeth but doesn't say anything as she digs through the first-aid kit for a sample-sized envelope of antibiotic ointment. There isn't much in the envelope, but it's enough for her to spread a thin smear over each hand. Then she abandons the Band-Aids for a tiny roll of gauze. She wraps each hand in a single layer before running out.

"The tire . . . ," I say, noticing the cut on her cheek again when she tilts her face up to answer.

"I finished before I noticed you were missing. Then I heard the shot. . . ." Her voice breaks, and she pushes herself to her feet. "It was not an accident. Someone cut the tire enough that it blew as soon as we accelerated to freeway speed."

"I'm sorry. I was looking for a phone signal. I didn't realize I'd wandered so far."

She leans against the roof of the car, so I can't see her face. "When I heard the shots, I thought—" She pauses. "I thought I was too late. I saw your trail. You led him *away* from me. Why? Do you want to die?"

"Of course not," I say, catching her hand in my bandaged ones. "I thought it would be better to lead him deeper in so you'd have cover. I *will* put you in danger to save myself, just not a stupid amount of danger." I rest my forehead against the back of her hand, hating myself for using her, for continually throwing her into harm's way. "If you were smart, you'd get away from me. As far away as you can."

She squeezes my hands gently. "I will not leave willingly," she says, which is both what I wanted to hear and, at the same time, not. Because not only is she risking her life by staying, she's also implying that she might have to leave *unwillingly*. And the last thing I want to contemplate right now is the myriad of ways in which that might happen.

Part of me wants to snap at her; the rest of me wants to wrap myself up in her coat and cry. Instead of indulging in either, I pull my feet into the car and fasten my seat belt. Dani shuts my door and walks around to her side.

I gaze through the window at the quarry as she drives us back onto the freeway. I never want to see these bone-colored cliffs ever again. But right now I'd rather stare out into the inky depths than see Dani's tortured expression, knowing that I'm responsible for it and that there's nothing I can do to fix it.

"I don't know what would happen to me if I lost you on top of everything else," I say without looking at her. "Lost you and it was my fault, I mean. Because I'm going to lose you one way or another, aren't I?"

She doesn't answer, and I don't pursue it. I've said what needed saying, and she wouldn't tell me anyway.

The next thing I know, she's shaking me awake. I straighten in my seat and look blearily around, disoriented. We're parked in front of Mike and Angela's house. Crap. I must have fallen asleep. Oh, god, did I snore? I blush, actually *blush* at the thought. *Come on, Julep. Get it together.* And then memory comes crashing back.

Ouch. I look at my bandaged hands, wincing at how much they hurt when I move them.

"How do I look?" I say. Well, *croak* is probably more accurate.

She frowns. "Like a demon just dragged you out of hell."

"Fantastic," I say sourly. "What time is it?"

"Nine o'clock. But I am not taking you anywhere else. It is not safe."

"Just to the 7-Eleven. If I can get a brush through my hair, I can hide everything else. Please, Dani?"

"You should not be hiding anything."

I give her my biggest, saddest puppy-dog eyes.

"Fine," she says. "Just stop looking at me like that."

When we get to the 7-Eleven, she goes into the store for me. When she comes back, she hands me a bag with a brush, baby wipes, more gauze, and a tube of antibiotic ointment.

"Thanks," I say as she rips the brush out of its packaging. I gingerly pull its bristles through my rat's-nest hair, squashing any feelings of awkwardness I have about doing this in front of Dani.

By the time my hair is under control, she's pulling the Chevelle up to the Ramirezes' house again. Dani gets out and walks me to the door, looking in every direction but mine.

When we get to the door, she says, "If you want to go anywhere tomorrow, call me and I will take you."

"I'll lay low from now on, I promise. I don't want a repeat of today." I look her directly in the eye as I say it, no matter how uncomfortable it makes me.

She nods and leaves without offering a good-bye. I carefully open the door and let myself in. Angela is in the living room watching baseball.

"Hey," I say wearily.

Angela looks at me sharply. I must not be hiding my distress terribly well. Her eyes flick to my bandaged hands and then back to my face.

"What happened?" she says, jumping up and coming over to hug me. "And what are you wearing?"

I manage to tamp down my fear enough to keep my voice from shaking. "Priest costume. Just some scrapes. I fell. Dani patched me up."

"Fell off what? The back of a moving truck? Let me take a look at that."

She is a nurse, so I willingly follow her into the bathroom. It feels nice, actually—letting her mother me. Normally, I'd hate it. I often yelled at Sam for being too much of a nagging busybody. But the gentle touch of her hands unwrapping the gauze and washing my skin with antibacterial soap is soothing even as it stings. She doesn't ask me questions, she just carefully wipes away the water and wraps my hands with fresh gauze. It makes me want to confide in her, which is kind of an odd feeling for me.

I'm not sure how to start, though. I'm so not good at this revealing-myself crap. But I need to talk about *something*. Even if I can't tell Angela the big stuff, maybe I can tell her something else and get some small measure of catharsis. I don't even know what I've decided to say until it pops out.

"How do you stop liking someone? Like, *liking* liking." Oh, my god. Did that really just come out of my mouth?

To her credit, Angela takes the stupid question in stride. "Does this have something to do with what happened to your hands?" she says deceptively mildly.

"What? No. Well, maybe the part after what happened to my hands has something to do with it. Or rather it made me realize some things. I don't even know. Forget I said anything."

She shakes her head, smiling. "Oh, no, you don't. You opened this can of worms—there's no closing it now. What do you mean 'stop liking someone'? You're having feelings for someone and you don't want to?"

I nod.

"You can't stop, Julep. That's kind of the point."

"But I'm a con artist. A: I shouldn't have feelings like this in the first place. B: I can make other people feel anything I want them to. Why can't I do that to myself, too?"

Angela grimaces. "Okay, that's not exactly normal. You don't really think that, do you?"

I don't know. Do I think that? "I don't know what I think anymore," I finally admit.

She sighs and leans back against the shower door. "Is it a crush, or are you actually in love with her?"

Wow. I guess I'm not as good at hiding my dysfunction as I think I am. "I . . . don't know. How did you know I was talking about Dani? Is it that obvious?"

"It's obvious that she'd crawl over broken glass for you. What's less obvious is how you feel. Sometimes I think you return her feelings, but other times . . . ? It's hard to get inside your head. Your reactions to things—it's like you calculate everything before you say it. Dani's the only one I've ever seen throw you off your game." She shrugs. "I guess that's telling."

Well, that's not true. People throw me off my game all the time. The measure of a good grifter is how fast we compensate. Maybe that's what she means. Maybe I can't adapt with Dani.

"Why do you want to stop, if I may ask? Is it because she's a girl?"

I blink, surprised. "What does that have to do with anything?"

A smile plays at Angela's lips. "It matters to some people sometimes. I just wondered if that was what was bothering you."

"It hadn't even crossed my mind," I say truthfully. She's just Dani. Like Tyler was Tyler. "Honestly, I have so much crazy in my life right now that I can't even care about that."

"Some people will care about it. You could lose a few friends over it."

"I don't have friends. I have associates. Besides, nothing's going to happen. Nothing can happen."

"Why not? What's holding you back? Is it that she's older?"

I roll my eyes. "She's only three years older than me. She's already bossy enough without anyone else reminding her of that, so please keep that observation to yourself."

"Then why?"

I think about Tyler. About how I was the death of him. About how much his loss hurt me, how much it still hurts me. About how he deserves better than for me to get any kind of happiness in love, even with a stubborn mob enforcer with enough baggage to swamp Atlantis. And then there's Sam . . .

Angela must read something in my face, because she tips my chin up until I look at her. "Being in your company is not an automatic death sentence, you know. Even for Dani, who would happily take a bullet for you. You need to accept that."

"I can't," I say, my voice getting wobbly all of a sudden. "Tyler—I can't be responsible for another—" I take a breath and blow it out. "I just have to stop feeling, and it'll all go back to the way it was."

"Oh, Julep . . . ," Angela says, touching my arm. "I'll admit, I'm not wild about you hanging out with, much less dating, anyone who does what she does for the kinds of people she does it for. But the way she looks at you—like you're her center. I couldn't wish much better for you than that."

I shudder, some scab inside I've been jealously guarding finally breaking off and crumbling to dust, revealing the pink healing cardiac tissue beneath. Hope is a heady thing. I'm not sure it's something I should be imbibing while trying so hard just to survive. I do feel about ten pounds lighter in the shoulders, even if my pestiferous, inappropriate heart is the least of my problems.

"But how—?"

The sound of the front door opening and closing puts me on instant alert. Angela and I are both here. Mike isn't due back for days yet. I jump to my feet, moving in front of Angela and fumbling with my phone. Dani's still close. My heart is pounding as I clumsily unlock the screen to dial her number. Heavy footsteps round the wall separating the foyer from the hallway. I was supposed to have time, damn it!

I press Call, praying I can keep us alive long enough for Dani to return.

"Julep Dupree!" Mike's voice booms. "What the hell is this I hear about a *contract*?"

THE NEGOTIATION

"That's all I know, Mike, I swear. Can I please go to bed now?" I cast a pointed glance at the clock; it's three a.m.

Mike paces to the other side of the living room and back again. "Someone shot at you in an empty quarry on the way back from a prison. Then Ralph Chen came back from the dead with a samurai sword to defend you."

"For the eighty-bajillionth time, yes. That is what happened."

"And the shooting near Loyola? What can you tell me about the truck?"

I go from slumped to full-out prone on the couch and close my eyes. If he wants to keep on talking, he can go right ahead. If he wants me to stay awake just to watch him pace, he can kiss my—

"Wake up, Julep. You can sleep all you want in WITSEC."

That pops my eyes open. "I'm not a witness to anything that I haven't already testified for, G-man. Witness Protection doesn't apply to me. Even you can't pull that many strings."

"Watch me," he says.

"Whoa. This is not my fault," I object, sitting up again.

"The fact that I had to find out about it from a phoned-in anonymous tip is *most definitely* your fault. You should have called me after Dani's car was vandalized."

"So that you could come back and lock me in your guest room for the next two years? I think I'll pass."

"You should have trusted me!"

"Like you trust *me?*" I yell back.

He scrubs a hand over his bald head. "Look, we're both tired. We can yell at each other tomorrow. Tonight, let's just make a plan."

I eye him warily, arms crossed. "Okay."

"There's an FBI safe house available. I checked with dispatch on my way—"

"No!" I say, pushing myself off the couch. "If you lock me up, I will get out and you'll never see me again. Is that what you want?"

"Julep, be reasonable."

"I've done everything you've asked me to since you arrested me. Well, except for a couple of missed curfews. But everything else, I've done. Court, community service, even *therapy,* for Pete's sake. I've kept my end of the bargain. You owe me my freedom. If you won't give it to me, I'll take it. And I'll never forgive you."

"This isn't some kind of *deal*, Julep. My responsibility as your foster father is to keep you healthy and relatively happy and, above all things, *alive*. Freedom doesn't enter into it until you're eighteen."

"You are my *handler*, not my father!"

"You are a *kid*, not a criminal informant!"

"Hey." Angela comes shuffling out of the back of the house in her pajamas. "What is all this yelling? It's three in the morning."

My eyes fill with water from frustration and embarrassment. The truth is, I don't have much choice if Mike decides to push his solution on me. He's ruining my life. Again.

"Both of you. Sit," Angela says.

My knees fold under me, but I stay perched on the edge of the couch, ready to bolt to Dani's if I need to. Mike sits, too, but he's about as relaxed as I am.

"There has to be some kind of compromise we can agree to," she continues. "Julep, you can't possibly think we'd be okay with you wandering off in your usual way while someone's out to kill you."

I open my mouth to retort, but she holds up a hand.

"Mike, you can't possibly expect someone like Julep to submit to incarceration. It would kill her."

Mike grinds his teeth. "It's not incarceration if it's for her own safety."

Angela gives him a sour look. "It would feel like it to her. Stop being so pigheaded." Then she turns to me. "Julep, what would be an acceptable concession on your part?"

"I could agree to a five p.m. curfew. And I would stick to it. Both attacks happened after dark. Most attacks do."

"That's not—"

Angela gives Mike a withering glare. "Agent Ramirez," she says, ice in her voice. "Your counteroffer?"

He sits silent for a moment, clenching his jaw against his nearly uncontrollable urge to take charge. I know him too well. We're too much alike.

"Home by five p.m. on weekdays, twenty-four seven on weekends, and mandatory security detail at all times."

"No way!" I shout, standing again.

Angela's superior glare turns on me. I deflate under it and collapse back onto the sofa.

"Your turn," Angela says to me.

I chew my lip, thinking. "Home by five p.m. on weekdays, twenty-four seven on weekends, and Dani is my security detail. My *only* security detail."

"Dani is only one person, and she's not trained—"

"I can't have suits following me around everywhere I go, they'll ruin—"

"Hold it!" Angela says, and Mike and I fall silent again. "It's like refereeing a boxing match with you two. Here's what's going to happen. Five p.m. curfew on weekdays, home twenty-four seven on weekends. Dani will escort you everywhere, and I mean *everywhere*. And when you're here, a team of agents will monitor the house."

I exhale a shaky breath. It sucks, but it's not a safe house. "Okay," I say.

"Mike?" Angela says.

"Fine," he growls. "I'll set it up."

"Good. Now, can we all please get some sleep? My shift starts in three hours."

"God, yes," I say, getting up again. I drag my sorry self to the guest room and collapse onto the bed, still in my priest disguise, hands bound in gauze. I'm asleep before my face hits the pillow.

• • •

Six a.m. comes awfully quickly when one is up until three a.m. the night before arguing with recalcitrant parental types. And I'm made even grumpier by the fact that it's summer and gloves covering up my damaged hands will stand out more than my hands would. I finally settle on a light jacket with sleeves that have holes for my thumbs. The sleeves cover only half the scratches on each palm, but it'll do.

Dani picks me up on time, like a total jerk, looking fresh as a daisy. I want to punch her and eviscerate Mike by the time I shamble into the NWI office. Coffee. I need coffee.

Five minutes later, I'm at my desk, sipping my coffee like it's the only thing keeping me sane, when I get a text from Sam's untraceable burner phone.

Saw you hobbling in the front door this morning. Fun party last night?

I tap back:

You have no idea.

I'll fill him in on Ralph and the hit attempt, but not over text.

As I'm putting my phone away, Joseph walks in. He looks casually gorgeous, as always.

"Oliver and Sally, I have a new project for you. I put some time on your calendars to meet the project lead later this morning. Aadila, you'll be taking over Julep's project for today. Julep, you'll be working with Duke on developing initiate training. Jane, I have some data entry. . . ."

I tune out the rest of his project assignments. Duke? Why is Duke still singling me out? Is he trying to distance me from the other interns? Is he trying to con out of me what I've discovered so far? There isn't much, to be honest. He probably knows everything I know. Ugh, I do not have enough brain for this today.

And honestly, I'm nervous to see him after my interview with Mr. Antolini, which until this very moment I'd completely forgotten about. I left the number Mr. Antolini had been repeating in my priest pants back at the Ramirezes'. I need to have Sam analyze it. I would have brought it with me, but with everything that happened with the hit attempt and Mike coming home, I just didn't think of it.

In any case, I can't imagine what could have happened to turn Mr. Antolini into the bombed-out shell of a man I saw, but it can't have been good. And Mrs. Antolini being a fraud is almost as frightening. Who the hell was I working for? Part of me is screaming that I should ditch this hot mess of a job immediately. Like, walk right out the door without laying eyes on Duke Salinger again. But my mom is still somehow connected. The blue fairy, the bar. She's *missing*. I can't abandon the job without knowing with absolute certainty that NWI has no connection to her disappearance.

"Julep?" Joseph is looking at me expectantly. Crap. What did I miss?

"Yes?"

"Are you going to go meet Duke in his office, or just sit there staring off into space?"

"Heading up now," I say, jumping to my feet and grabbing a spiral notebook.

Hurrying up the curling ramp, I branch off onto the executive floor and hustle to Duke's office.

"Ah, Julep. So glad you're here. Come in, come in," Duke says from the sofa area. He shuffles some papers out of the way so I'll have room to sit.

"I'm not sure how I can help. I don't know the first thing about inspiring people."

"That's why you're here, isn't it? To learn."

I smile. "Right."

"We're not going to do much in the way of design anyway. It's more of a brainstorming session. I find I develop my method best when I have a fresh mind as a sounding board—the fresher, the better."

"Well, not to toot my own horn, but I can get pretty fresh when the situation calls for it."

Duke chuckles, deep and rumbly. "Fair enough. So let me start by asking you, why do you think people come to NWI?"

"Because they're lonely and confused?"

"That's part of it," he says. "But why are they lonely and confused?"

I think back to what Duke said yesterday afternoon. "Because they're trying to fill their emptiness with the wrong things?"

"Yes, exactly. This workshop I'm building now is about developing a life purpose, because dedicating your life to a purpose is a healthy and effective way of filling the emptiness. What do you think of that?"

Even my thoughts feel heavy, that's how tired I am. But I do my best to rally. Duke is likely testing me. I have to pass if I want to earn any useful information.

"I think 'purpose' is too broad. Making millions of dollars is a purpose. But I don't think that's what you're going for."

He smiles. "Excellent point. What would you call it, then?"

I think for a long moment, turning ideas over in my head and then discarding them. Though sluggish, the grifter part of me is starting to juice up at Duke's line of questioning. It's interesting, thinking about people like puzzles you can coax into putting themselves back together again.

"How about 'aspiration'?" I say finally.

"I like it," he says, and writes it down on a notepad. "I like the double meaning—hope and breath. Two things we can center the workshop around. I like to include movement when I can. People seem to retain the lesson better when kinesthetic exercises are involved. But what about the hope part? What does hope symbolize to you?"

. . .

Two hours fly by in what feels like minutes. Duke really gets into the discussion, gesticulating, striding around the office, lighting up like a crystal chandelier whenever something I've said sparks an idea he hadn't thought of. And I'm caught up in his vision. I can't seem to help myself. His charisma is irresistible even for me, another grifter expecting the sting at any moment. I'm falling for his game, chomping at the line and welcoming the hook, because the payout—peace, self-acceptance, happiness—is *that* tempting.

"Fabulous idea," he says after my last suggestion. "I may have to cite you as a resource on this, with all you've contributed." He looks at his watch. "But on that note, it's time for lunch, and Joseph will have my hide if I keep you away from your regular duties too long."

"Sure thing," I say, my stomach growling at the mention of lunch.

I make my way to the door, but before I leave, I turn back to watch Duke shuffling thoughtfully through the papers on the table. "You know, you're not what I expected," I say before I think better of it.

He looks back at me. "*I'm* not what you expected, or NWI isn't what you expected?"

I think about it before answering. "Actually, it's my reaction I wasn't expecting," I say.

He studies me for a moment. I can see him weighing the

wisdom of saying something. I wait him out. Either he'll say it or he won't.

"I know you're running from something, Julep. All grifters are. I just want you to know that when you're ready to run *to* something, I'm here to help you do that."

"I—" I swallow hard, thinking of Yale and dreams lost and wish that I'd met this man a year ago. "Okay. Thanks."

On the way back down the ramp, I try valiantly to force my objectivity back into place. Unfortunately, it's like trying to fit a round peg into a cocktail dress. You could do it, but do you really want to? I hope Sam is having better luck on his end. I can't seem to gain any traction with Duke directly. It's like he's exactly who he says he is or something.

By the time I get to the first floor, I'm settling into a nice funk over my ineptitude. But then I catch sight of the reception desk, or more specifically, the person standing in front of the reception desk. I casually turn around, avoiding sudden movement, and hide behind a giant ficus.

"Yes. I'm here to see Mr. Salinger," says Victoria Febbi.

THE STAKEOUT

I stay out of sight just long enough for Tori to walk up the first bend in the ramp to the next level. Then I spring out from behind the plant and start to follow her. I make it all of three steps before I hear Joseph calling me.

"Where do you think you're going? We have another team-building activity after lunch."

I groan inwardly. Why did he have to catch me *now*? Now when I'm so close to figuring out the connection between Bar63 and NWI. Although, if it's another relaxation exercise, maybe I'll get a nap out of it.

"I left my phone in Duke's office." He might buy it.

"The phone that's there in your pocket, you mean?" he says, smirking at me.

"Oh," I say, mentally cursing his advanced powers of obser-vation. "I must have put it in my pocket without noticing."

"Great, then there's nothing preventing you from building some team with the rest of us."

"You know, there is such a thing as being too enthusiastic." I give up and walk over to him. I've lost Tori. For now. But at least I saw her. That confirms there's a connection.

"It's still your first week, grasshopper. You're supposed to respect me or something."

"I *know* that wasn't in the job description. I'd have noticed that."

We bat mild insults back and forth all the way to the intern pen. He's a good guy, Joseph. I really hope he's not evil.

Sadly for me, today's team-building activity requires actual teamwork. I let Ackley take over, because that's what everyone expects, and rule number 783 of grifting is, when you're trying to blend in, never do what people least expect. It's kind of an obvious rule, but you'd be surprised how many amateurs break it. I think it has something to do with the Texas-sized egos con artists are born with.

In any case, after Joseph calls time on the activity, I plead raging headache, which, sadly, is not entirely fictitious, and knock off early. I text Dani to come pick me up. As it turns out, she never left the neighborhood.

"You hung out in the pool hall across the street the whole day?" I ask when she opens the Chevelle's passenger-side door for me.

"I am used to waiting for you," she says, smiling. And is it my imagination, or are her eyes lingering on mine just a minute longer than usual? "If you moved any slower, I would have to get you a walker." Definitely my imagination.

"Whatever, grandma. You're the one who's three whole years older. Practically Jurassic."

"Where to today, Miss Daisy?" she asks.

"Oh, come on. How could you possibly know that reference?"

"I told you. I am used to waiting for you. You would not believe the movies I have seen on grainy televisions while sitting on uncomfortable barstools."

I smile at her. I love the way she says *televisions* like that's a thing anyone ever says anymore. "Can we go to your place?"

She stiffens slightly, her easy smile fading at the edges. "Why?"

I try to ignore that I noticed, because it's easier to ignore that than to ignore that noticing it hurt. I look out the window and keep my voice neutral and disinterested. "It's the only place you'll take me that's not Mike's or NWI, and I need to talk to Sam and Murphy without Mike or Duke overhearing."

"Oh," she says. "All right."

And now we're back to awkward. Whatever. I refuse to participate in that. I pull my phone out and text Dani's address to both Sam and Murphy. Murphy's not doing anything but working for me this summer, and Sam has a break between afternoon and evening sessions.

"You are irritated with me," she says. "Why?"

I sigh. "I'm not irritated with you. I have a headache." I text

Mike and Angela to let them know where I'm going, more because I want something to do that's not talking to Dani than because I really feel the need to clue them in. It's only two o'clock. I have hours before my five p.m. curfew. I can't believe I have a five p.m. curfew.

Mercifully, it takes only about ten minutes to get to Dani's apartment complex. I follow her up the stairs and wait, as told, on the landing while she inspects the nooks and crannies for bogeymen.

"All right," she calls from the back.

I'm curious to see what her place is like. For grifters, scoping out someone's living space is almost as good as reading their diary. Unfortunately for me, Dani's apartment is depressingly impersonal. No art on the walls. Mismatched furniture. A couple of lamps. Empty pantry, with the exception of some condiments and a box of—gag—chamomile tea. Everything neat, despite the small space, mostly because she doesn't have much to fill it. For her, it's clearly just a place to sleep. Well, sleep and clean guns. There's a dismantled Magnum on her kitchen table, which she'd probably been in the middle of cleaning before coming to get me this morning.

"Got any aspirin?" I ask as I tour the kitchen, opening the fridge to confirm that, yes, Dani pretty much survives on ketchup and iron will.

She brings me two white pills, and I chase them with a glass of tap water.

Sam and Murphy show up a minute or two later, Murphy carting both Bryn and Lily with him. I'm not surprised to see

Bryn, but I'm shocked to see Lily. This is the second time I thought I'd chased her off for good only to have her reappear unexpectedly.

"What's this about?" Sam asks.

"Ralph's back," I say, easing them all into the story.

"What?" Sam says, eyes wide. Of all of them, he's the only one who ever actually met Ralph. "Is he okay? Where's he been this whole time?"

"I'd like to say Tijuana, but I really have no idea."

"How did you find him?" Murphy asks. "We've been looking for months without a blip."

"He found me, actually." Then I launch into the whole sordid tale. Bryn gasps and Lily visibly pales when I get to the part about the quarry. Sam doesn't say anything, but his expression isn't something I'd want to face alone in an alley at night.

"Jesus, Julep," Murphy says. "What are we even doing here? You should be at Agent Ramirez's house on lockdown until he finds this guy."

"See?" Dani says to me. "Everyone thinks it."

"I don't think it," Sam says, his voice low and grave. "It's pretty unlikely Mike will find whoever's behind this when you couldn't," he says to Dani. "The best way to resolve this is to use Julep as bait. Just like the NWI scam."

I beam at him. He gets it. He knows what it takes and he's willing to make the hard choices. I'm going to have to double his salary. I can afford it, too, since his salary is zero and zero doubled is still zero.

"You are both insane," Dani says. "Thank god Ramirez is on my side."

So then I tell them about my stupid new schedule.

"I guess that means you're out for the party at Val's house this weekend," Bryn says. "And I was so looking forward to watching you swindle her drunken jerk of an older brother again."

"Yeah, I probably wasn't going to that party anyway," I say.

"So no one's found the person who put the contract out on you yet?" Lily asks.

"Not yet," I say. "Dani even asked Petrov. He knew something, but it's irrelevant now. We're back to square one."

"No other leads?" Lily says.

I'm about to answer in the negative, when Dani interrupts me. "I have an idea of someone else to ask," she says. At my questioning look, she continues, "An old friend with more connections than me."

I file that little tidbit away for later delving. But first, I need reports.

"Sam, any luck from the initiate side of things?"

He studies me for a moment before answering. "Nothing yet."

"Well, I saw our old friend Victoria Febbi today at the NWI reception desk, asking to see Duke. Maybe you could find out what that was about?"

"I'll try," he says. "I don't have nearly as much access to Salinger as you do, though. It'll take me a little time."

"What about you, Murphy? Anything new?"

"Nothing on the Bar63 angle. I couldn't find anything in relation to Victoria Febbi besides what I found for the Italian actress. It's like she didn't exist until she started working at the bar."

"That's telling in its own way. Keep digging for now. Lily, do you even still work for me?"

She hesitates for a split second, then nods.

"I'm putting you on Sister Rasmussen detail. See if you can find out why she was trying so hard to steer me away from NWI. She may know something useful."

"Okay," she says. "I'll work on it."

I regard the group as a whole. "So no one has anything? Really?"

"You say that like you've found anything," Murphy points out.

"Actually, I may have." I tell them the details of my visit to Mr. Antolini.

"Numbers?" Sam says. "Did you write them down?"

"Yeah, but I don't have them on me. I'll text them to you when I get back to the Ramirezes'. Anything you guys find out, anything you think of, even if you think it's nothing, call me immediately—I don't care what time of day or night it is. We need to end this sooner rather than later."

"Don't say, 'Because there might not be a later,'" Murphy says, and Bryn heaves an exaggerated sigh. "I'm just saying it would be really cheesy."

I massage my aching temples. "All right, class dismissed." Everyone gets up to leave. "Except you, Dani. I want to hear more about this lead."

• • •

"I can't believe I actually suggested a five p.m. curfew. What the hell was I thinking?" I check my phone again to make sure there's still time. We have about forty-five minutes before I'm officially late.

Dani doesn't say anything, but she gives me that fond, re-signed smile she reserves only for me.

"Corn nut?" I say, offering her the bag.

She shakes her head. I pop another couple in my mouth and crush them between my molars. I sometimes pretend they're the bones of my enemies. That's not weird, is it?

"What are you going to do about the bartender?" Dani asks.

"Finally, she talks."

She gives me a sour look, but we've been staking out this Chinese restaurant for the last half hour, and she's said maybe five words to me.

"I cannot talk and listen at the same time," she says.

"Wow, Dani. Was that a subtle dig at my verbosity? I must say I'm impressed."

"Take your feet off the dashboard of my car. I just washed it."

I pat the Chevelle's door. "It loves when I put my feet up. It wants me to be comfortable."

Dani sighs. "Well, I want you to be paying attention. We are not sitting here for our health."

"You're sure this guy you're looking for eats here?"

"Yes."

"What's his name again?"

"*Her* name is Han."

I put my feet down. "You didn't say your friend was a woman."

"Does it matter?"

"No." Maybe. "How do you know her?"

Dani arches an eyebrow. "Enforcers Anonymous. Stop asking questions."

"Well, if you're such great friends, why are we stalking her instead of just calling her?"

"We had a falling out."

"About what?"

Dani rubs her forehead. "You are like a puppy. An annoying, yappy puppy."

"Would it really kill you to just tell me stuff I want to know?"

"Fine. What 'stuff' do you want to know?"

"Were you dating Han?"

She hesitates. "Yes."

"Ha!" I crow in triumph that I don't really feel. "And it ended badly?" I'm hoping it ended badly.

Dani sighs heavily. "Yes. It ended badly."

"Why?"

She's not looking at me directly, and she's fidgeting. "She asked me if I loved her, and I said no."

Ouch. I suddenly don't envy the woman so much. "How long were you together?"

"Almost two years."

"Jeez," I say, aghast. "And you didn't love her at all?"

Dani's hands go still on the wheel. "I thought I did, but then I realized I did not. Is it really necessary for you to know all this?"

I purse my lips. "Just one more question."

"What?" Dani says, impatiently.

"Is she unattractive? Maybe a little troll-like? Unusually hairy or something?"

"What?" she asks, her expression half amused, half appalled. "Why are you asking—? Never mind. No, she is actually very beautiful."

All the wind flutters out of my sails. I'm suddenly over the conversation, so I change tack.

"You really think she knows who's behind the contract?"

"Maybe. Maybe not," Dani says, her smile fading. "But her network is more extensive than mine, and I have run out of people to ask."

Then it occurs to me that Dani is really sticking her neck out for me this time. She's asking an ex-girlfriend for information that can help me. That can't be comfortable. Especially when that girlfriend is a criminal and would probably shoot Dani as soon as look at her.

"Dani, we don't have to do this," I say. "Mike—"

"Has no more information than I do," Dani interrupts. "We cannot wait on this, *milaya*. Not this."

She has a point. Contract killers are so far beyond my experience as to be in another stratosphere. The truth is, I'm scared. I want Dani to fix it, because I don't want to die.

So instead of something useful, I say, "What does *milaya* mean?"

The assessing look she gives me makes my heart trip all over its shoelaces. "It means 'pest.'"

"Really," I say, doubtful.

She smiles and goes back to casing the restaurant.

"I actually don't know much Ukrainian," I say.

"I am so surprised by that." She's still a bit challenged when it comes to contractions, but her sarcasm is spot-on.

"Teach me something." What? It'll pass the time.

She's silent for long enough that I assume she's ignoring my request. But then she murmurs something that sounds like all the melancholy in the world wrapped up in a single sentence: *"Hoÿda, hoÿda-hoÿ, nichenќa ide, Ditochok malykh spatonќy klade."*

"Wow," I say. "What was that?"

"It's a lullaby Tatyana used to sing," she says softly.

"Oh," I say. I'm almost afraid to ask, but I do anyway. "Where is she now?"

"I don't know," Dani answers. And somehow the not knowing sounds worse than any fate could have been.

Hurt for her fills my chest, making my ribs ache. I want to touch her. To give the minimal, hopelessly inadequate measure of comfort I am capable of giving. But things have changed since the quarry. I've acknowledged things I can't take back. So I keep my hands folded safely in my lap.

And then Han finally appears. Naturally, she is drop-dead gorgeous. Long, rippling curtain of glossy black hair. Perfect figure, strong but curved. Facial features that would make angels cry. Because, of course.

"She is here," Dani says, as if I couldn't see that appallingly well on my own. Dani gets out of the car, seeming to forget my presence altogether. She only has eyes for Han. I sigh and get out of the car a few beats behind her.

When Han spots Dani, she crosses her arms and glares at her. "I'm not talking to you."

"Please, Han. I need your help."

The note of pleading in Dani's voice is not something I've ever heard before. It hurts me. She shouldn't have to ask for anything from this woman.

"Why should—" Han starts, but then stops when she sees me. "You brought *her* here? How dare you?"

"She is just a child, Han."

Oh . . . *ouch.*

"She needs our protection," Dani continues. "Like your cousin Lydia, remember?"

I can't believe I got out of the car for this. I could be eating corn nuts right now, instead of feeling marginalized and pathetic.

"Except, unlike my cousin, she's a traitor to our kind."

Our kind? Seriously? "If you're referring to me taking down Petrov, you'd have done the same thing if he were going to kill you and everyone you ever loved," I snarl, ignoring Dani's quelling gesture. "And yeah, I *did* take him down. The leader of a major Ukrainian crime syndicate. You should show me more respect."

Han's face twists in fury, and she lunges at me.

Dani intercepts her, holding her back. "We are in the open. This is not the place."

"On the contrary, I think this is the perfect place," Han says. Then she draws a gun from an underarm holster and aims it directly at my heart.

THE BLUE FAIRY

Dani moves so fast she blurs, twisting the gun out of Han's hand and wrestling her to her knees. I feel light-headed and sick. No matter how many times someone points a gun at me, I'm never going to get used to it.

"Don't be stupid, Han. We are on a busy street in broad daylight."

"What the hell do you care?" Han says bitterly.

"I do care." Dani glares intensely at Han for several moments before gradually letting her up.

Han tosses her perfectly mussed hair over her shoulder in a haughty gesture, as if she'd planned for it to go that way all along. Then she stalks into the restaurant without a backward glance.

I notice that Dani still has Han's gun, which makes me feel

a little better. Not much, but a little. Dani doesn't even bother to look at me before following Han into the restaurant. I debate between going in and taking off. On the one hand, I feel like someone's been carving a thousand cuts into my heart. On the other, I'm *not* "just a child," and I'm not proving Dani right by acting like one. I need answers, and if this woman has them, well, I can live with a lot of cuts.

It takes a few seconds for my eyes to adjust when I enter the darkened restaurant. But I spot Han sitting at a table just behind a giant saltwater fish tank. Dani is pulling out a chair across from her. I feel like a third wheel, but it's my life that hangs in the balance, so I walk up and take the chair sticking out into the aisle. Which means I'm sitting between Han and Dani like some kind of mediator or marriage counselor or something.

"I wasn't really going to shoot her," Han says without preamble. "Even though I have every reason to."

Dani slouches back in her chair, her posture deceptively relaxed. But her expression is hard.

"Do you know who put the contract out on me?" I ask. I'm done letting Dani take the lead.

"Stay out of this, little girl," Han snaps at me. "The grown-ups are talking."

Okay, putting up with Dani calling me a kid is one thing. Letting this chick get away with it is something else entirely. So I get up and deliberately push my chair to the table across the aisle from us. Then I slide into Dani's lap like I've done it a million times.

"Needed a booster seat," I explain. "You were saying?"

Dani's hands press into my hips as she pushes me gently but firmly off her lap. "You are not helping," she says reprovingly.

And she's right. I shouldn't be antagonizing our source. I should be manipulating her. Time to get my head back in the game.

"We don't need her," I say, crossing my arms and sniffing disdainfully. "She probably doesn't know anything anyway. Let's just go." Then I make a determined move in the direction of the door.

Jilted lovers are ridiculously suggestible. The one thing better than getting back an ex you didn't want to lose is proving to that ex in whatever way possible that she made a huge mistake in dumping you. Han wants Dani to be indebted to her. Plus, she wants to one-up me. There's no way she'd let me be the one to end the conversation.

Sure enough, Han's hand snakes out and grabs my arm before I can go two steps.

"You want what I know? It's going to cost you," she says.

"*I* am asking, so I will pay your fee," Dani says.

I could kick Dani. She's going to drive the price through the roof if she doesn't shut the hell up.

Han narrows her eyes, conflicting thoughts flashing through them. "A life for a life," she says.

Dani's expression goes dark. I recognize it. She had the same look just before she shot Petrov.

"Done," she says.

"No," I say. Screw negotiations. I won't be responsible for this. "No more deals, Dani."

She ignores me, which makes me want to strangle her. It's like we're on totally different sides.

Han's gaze is fixed on Dani. "I don't know who the source is, but the contract is active. There's a call up on the message board. Several of my associates have expressed interest in it, though none have officially engaged, as far as I know."

"What are the specs?" Dani asks.

"Kill order, but there are special instructions. Whoever it is wants to torture the child before killing her, which says personal vendetta to me. I try to stay away from those—too messy. But I was tempted this time."

"The rate is that good?" Dani asks, her tone suggesting deepening worry.

"Quarter-of-a-mil good."

Dani falls silent, a muscle popping in her jaw as she thinks. "When was it posted?"

"Yesterday."

"Dani, don't even think it," I say, knowing already she won't listen.

"What are the contact instructions?"

"A list of references messaged directly to the poster."

"Can you send the message for me?" Dani asks.

"I said *no*." I slam my hand down on the table between them. The other patrons scattered throughout the dining area shoot me disapproving glares. "I'm not letting this happen."

Han laughs at me. "You're wasting your breath, grifter. The deal is struck. Besides, that look on her face?" She points at Dani. "Nothing changes her mind once she gets that look. Consider it carved in stone."

"We'll see about that," I say, though the last thing I want is to be fighting Dani along with everyone else.

Wrapping up the conversation took way more words and longing looks than I'd have liked. Han still has it bad for Dani, and Dani certainly still cares about Han. It's revolting, really.

The car ride back to Mike's involves considerably less prattling on my part and no corn-nut crunching whatsoever. I'm not feeling terribly confident in the enemy-bone-crushing department right now.

I can tell Dani doesn't know what to say to me. She doesn't get why I'm so moody. It's both hilarious and depressing. Our whole relationship is textbook transference. She's using me as a Tatyana stand-in. I should have known from the beginning she thought of me that way. And it *absolutely* should not hurt this much.

"I'm sorry I called you a yappy puppy," Dani says as we pull to a stop.

I unbuckle my seat belt. "I am a yappy puppy," I say, getting out and walking away without looking back. Her door creaks open, and her footsteps echo on the pavement behind me. I can feel her standing at the end of the walk, uncertain about whether to guard me or give me space. She must decide on space, because I get to the door and through it without another word to or from her.

This time, I sail right past the living room and collapse on the guest bed fully clothed. I press my stupid face into the stupid pillow and think about how stupid life is. So. Stupid.

"Tough day at the office?" Angela says from the doorway.

I groan into the pillow. I'd never let anyone else see me at this level of wretchedness, but for some reason, Angela's the exception that proves the rule.

"Seriously, what's going on?" Angela sits on the corner of bed not taken up by my sprawled limbs. I wish she'd stroke my hair like my mom used to, but then I chew myself out for the thought. What is up with my rampaging emotions lately?

"She thinks of me as a helpless child who needs protecting. Nothing more."

"She actually said that?" Angela says.

I shrug, because I don't want to admit that she pretty much did. "This is why I wanted to get rid of these stupid feelings. This right here. How'm I supposed to even look at her tomorrow?"

Angela doesn't stroke my hair, but she does lay a hand gently on my back. She stays silent. Because what is there to say? I appreciate that she doesn't try to cajole me or cheer me up or offer me useless platitudes. It is what it is.

Finally, she says, "Can I get you some coffee?"

"With chocolate? And marshmallows?"

"Sure," she says, and leaves.

• • •

To: Julep Dupree
From: Duke Salinger
Subject: Busy?

Hi, Julep.

Could you come up to my office just before you leave today? I'd like to discuss something with you.

Duke

"We're all going out to Freddie's for happy hour. Want to come?" Sally asks as I close the email.

"Can't today," I say. "I have to go up and see Duke. Next time?"

"All right," she says, and grabs her purse. The others, even Aadila, gather up their stuff and head for the entrance.

"You could meet us after," Aadila says. She's eyeing me as if she suspects I'm lying.

"Yeah, maybe," I say. I can't, of course, because of my curfew, but I'm not telling her that.

She leaves and I turn back to my computer feeling sorry for myself. Not about missing happy hour, but about pretty much everything else. Dani was awkward and distant this morning, which is her go-to whenever she doesn't know what's going on in my head. It was actually kind of comforting, because as long as she doesn't know what I'm thinking, then I don't have to be embarrassed about it.

I'm also chafing under the new rules. I wasn't meant to spend long hours trapped in a house. TV isn't often fun for me, because I find it too predictable. Books are better, but my attention keeps wandering. I wish I could see a way through this, but until the person who wants me dead is out of the picture, I'm stuck. What I try to not let myself think about too carefully is that I might be stuck for a long time. Indefinitely, even.

And of course, as soon as I think that, I feel the walls closing in. I start breathing faster.

"Julep, what's wrong?"

The voice, warm and familiar, pulls me back from the edge. I look up to see Sam walking into the intern pen. He crouches low next to me, taking my hands.

"It's nothing," I say, letting out a shaky breath. I shouldn't let him see me vulnerable, nerves too close to the skin. I used to tell him everything, but now I'm wary of him, too raw from his leaving to trust him again.

"It doesn't look like nothing—it looks like you're deciding between throwing up and passing out." He goes from crouch to seated on the floor, pulling me with him. I leave my hands in his as I follow him down.

"I feel like I'm a fish and someone's aiming a missile launcher at the barrel I'm swimming in." I bow my head, letting my hair fall to block my face. "You shouldn't be here, Sam. You'll blow your cover."

He brushes a lock away from my face, his fingers gentle. "Remember the time we snuck into that construction site, and you talked me into traipsing out onto the steel girders twelve stories above the ground?"

I nod slowly, pensive. I'm not in the mood for a history lesson.

"I was freaking terrified," he continues. "But I was more afraid that you'd go out there without me than that we'd both plummet to our deaths. I didn't want you leaving me behind—then or ever."

"I remember your eyes," I say, smiling. "They were huge."

"Do you remember taking my hand?" He turns my hands palm up in his.

I nod. I remember losing my equilibrium for a split second and grabbing Sam to steady myself.

"You took my hand and you looked at me, and suddenly I knew how to fly."

The intensity of his gaze sends a bolt of electricity through my chest. My skin burns hot and cold at the same time.

"Letting go of your hand was the hardest thing I've ever done, and I swear to you I will never do it again. But I had to find my own way, to make you believe in me the way I believe in you."

I blink, breaking the connection. I let go of his hands and draw my knees under my chin, wrapping my arms around my legs. "I do believe in you, Sam. I always have. But right now I have to concentrate on not dying."

"That's why I brought it up," he says. "To remind you that you can show people how to fly, and that no matter what happens, you'll never again have to face anything alone."

I shiver. "What am I gonna do, Sam?" I whisper.

"We'll get through this, Julep. We always do."

I rest my head on his shoulder. "I miss you."

"I'm right here," he says.

I clear my throat to try to dislodge the boulder blocking it. "You shouldn't be here, though. I don't want to have to explain to Joseph why I'm fraternizing with an initiate."

"I was trying to find Joseph, actually."

"Why?"

"He's supposed to lead our evening session tonight, but he's late. I thought it might be significant, so I started looking for him. I found you instead."

Honestly, I can't say I'm sad he did. I actually feel like I can breathe somewhat normally again since the Han debacle. Risk to the con aside, I really needed the pep talk, and he said pretty much everything I needed to hear. He's always known me better than I know myself. Apparently, that hasn't changed, despite his dressing like a fed and pulling cons like a kingpin. The part of me that wants to trust him, to tell him everything, edges one degree past the part that's afraid he'll leave again. Maybe there's hope for our battered friendship yet.

"Hey," he says, ducking so our eyes are on a level. "Are you sure you're okay?"

I unwrap myself and push up to standing. "Yeah," I say, brushing the wrinkles out of my pants. "Oh, *crap*. What time is it?"

"Four-thirty-five," he says, looking at his watch. "Why?"

"I need to see Duke before I can leave."

"Can it wait?"

"I don't want to miss the opportunity to snoop," I say, grabbing my phone and keys from my desk.

"Okay, but be careful," Sam says, stepping aside to let me pass. His expression is suddenly sad, unsure.

I pause long enough to squeeze his hand, smiling up at him. "See you later, partner."

He squeezes back. Then I move past him into the hall.

When I get to Duke's door, I knock. No answer, though, which could be a problem. I try the door, and it cracks open. Not locked.

"Hello? Duke?" I ask. Still no answer.

I pull the door open and step inside. And the second my foot lands beyond the threshold, I know something's wrong. Really wrong. Not a trap. Something else. I stick to the perimeter of the room, keeping my back close to the wall and my hands close to my body so I won't accidentally brush anything.

When I get to the sitting area, I have to loop away from the wall to go around the couches. Doing so puts me closer to the center of the room and alters the angle of my view. Just past the edge of the couch, I stop abruptly, terror rooting me to the carpet.

A long, thick smear of blood leads from a pool of it next to the couches to behind Duke's desk.

"No," I whisper. "Nonononono." I run to the desk, jumping over the trail of blood to keep from tracking any with my shoes. Images of Tyler's body flood my brain, but I force them back. I can't deal with the past. Not right now.

I hesitate for a split second before looking behind the desk. Duke lies curled on his side, unmoving. I fall to my knees next to him, looking at my hands as if doing so would magically wrap them in gloves. But I give myself a mental shake and reach for his suit jacket, which is draped over the back of his chair. I wrap it around my hands and turn him onto his back.

"Duke! Duke!" I wheeze past the fear stopping my breath. "Duke!" I grab his shoulder and shake it hard. But as soon as I see his face, I know he's dead.

I gasp into Duke's jacket, shaking and trying desperately to stifle the urge to scream. The first thing I allow myself to do when I calm down enough to think rationally is back slowly away from the widening pool of blood. As I move, my eyes fall onto Duke's hand, half clenched around a small blue object.

I crawl around the blood and reach for his hand. Uncurling his fingers with my jacket-covered hands, I pull out a three-inch figurine. It's dressed in a sparkly blue, sleeveless dress, blond hair shorn in a pixie cut. Its expression is mischievous, and it can't weigh more than a few ounces.

But then the feeling of long, thin ridges pushing out of its back and into my palm shakes me to my core. I turn the figurine over to confirm my suspicions: delicate, translucent wings.

I'm holding the blue fairy.

THE DOUBLE DOWN

I burst through the door to the pool hall across the street from NWI. I spot Dani immediately, hands in her pockets, leaning against a pool table next to a propped-up pool cue. Her eyes lock on mine and she ditches the man with the mustache she'd been chatting with.

"What is it?" she asks, her expression fierce.

"Duke—" I swallow, eyeing the curious onlookers. I should be more careful. "I need to talk to you. All of you."

"Ramirez, too?"

I shake my head. I can't tell Mike. The authorities can't know my family is involved with this until I know what *this* even is. Who killed Duke and why? Was it for the blue fairy? Was it the contract killer? If I tell Mike, there will be no more compromises, no more second chances. I'm on my own. Well, almost.

"The Ballou. It's the closest," I say.

"It is not secure." She glares at me, though the heat of it is tempered with concern. She must see I've been crying.

"No place is secure, Dani. The safest thing to do is to end this as soon as possible."

She breaks eye contact to stare stonily out the window. After a moment, she caves. "Half hour. At most."

Meet me at the Ballou.

I group text it to Murphy, Sam, Bryn, and Lily. I don't specify a time, which means I expect them to drop everything and go there.

"What is this about?" Dani asks, drawing close enough to whisper.

"Not here," I answer. She opens her mouth to argue, but I silently plead for her not to push. She must read it in my face, because she changes her mind, leading the way to the Chevelle rather than interrogating me.

I get a few return texts.

Sam:

On my way.

Murphy:

What? Why? I'm going to dinner with Bryn's parents.

Bryn:

Who is this?

I don't hear anything from Lily, but that's not terribly surprising. If she shows, fine. If not, she's probably better off.

When we get to the Ballou, I bypass the coffee bar (a first

for me) and climb the stairs to my office. Dani precedes me and scouts the room as usual.

She lowers the blinds, which is fine, whatever. I push the plastic slats at eye level down an inch to see if anyone else is here yet. Looks like Sam is parking. Murphy and Bryn will take a few more minutes to get here from her parents' house.

"*Milaya*," Dani says softly as she comes up behind me.

"Don't," I say, putting distance between us. I can't let myself be discombobulated by her right now. I can't let myself worry about putting her in harm's way, because that's exactly where I need to put her.

"I—"

Sam's timely arrival interrupts whatever statement she was about to melt me with.

"What happened?" he says.

"Duke Salinger is dead," I say without preamble. "Someone shot him."

That jolts him into silence long enough for Murphy and Bryn to join us.

"Did I hear that right?" Murphy asks, shutting the door behind them. "Salinger got shot?"

"Who shot him? When?" Dani says.

"How do you know?" Murphy says.

I tell them about going up to Duke's office and finding him on the floor. As I'm nearing the part about the blue fairy, Lily joins us.

"What did I miss?" she says.

"Salinger got shot," Murphy says from his corner of the office.

"What? Is he all right?" she asks.

"He's dead," I say. "I found him in his office."

She shivers and pulls her jacket closer around her.

"Do you still think NWI's legit?" Murphy asks.

"I don't know. Mrs. Antolini is a liar, but maybe she didn't lie about NWI. Or maybe she did. I haven't seen any signs of shadiness. But there's still the connection with the bartender, the numbers I texted you this morning, and the blue fairy."

"What blue fairy?" Sam asks.

I show it to them. "Duke was holding this when I found him."

"Do you think it's why he was killed?" Murphy asks.

"Possibly. I think so."

"Wouldn't the killer have taken it if it were?" Bryn asks.

"I found him behind his desk, but he wasn't shot there," I say, pushing myself through my answer. "There was a trail of blood from the center of the room to where I found him, which means he probably didn't die right away. He knew I was coming up to see him after my shift. He waited for the killer to leave and then took the fairy from its hiding place so I'd find it."

"How do you know all this?" Dani asks.

"I don't. It's an educated guess. The killer could have planted it on him for all I know."

"Are you going to call the police?" Bryn asks.

"I can't. Not directly. But I called in an anonymous tip on our way here, like I did when Ralph's shop was Molotoved."

"So now what?" Bryn says. "You can't really expect us to do anything about this. We're high school students. Not vampire slayers."

"I know, I know. I just need more information."

"It's too late," Murphy says, swiping through his phone. "A news story from the AP wire just went viral." He pulls the article up on his phone's browser and shows it to us.

Duke Salinger, founder and CEO of leadership organization New World Initiative, found shot dead in his office earlier this evening, sources say. Investigation under way. No comment yet from authorities.

A sharp pang slices through me. I ignore it.

"Gets worse," Murphy says, showing us another article.

Devi Raktabija, vice president of New World Initiative, released a statement earlier this evening. "We are in mourning, bereft," says Dr. Raktabija. "But we will not let Duke Salinger's death distract us from our mission. We soldier on in our efforts to bring life fulfillment and leadership to those who need it. Duke would have expected nothing less from us."

In response to questions about the investigation into Salinger's murder, Dr. Raktabija said that local police were pursuing all leads, and that NWI was cooperating fully with the investigation. "We will be providing police with full access to our facility, to our membership files as relevant to the case, and to the security footage from around the time of the incident."

Security footage. *Crap.*

"Can I see the fairy?" Sam asks, his expression guarded. I hand it to him, and he turns it over carefully.

"Doesn't look like any of the fairies I've seen at the hobby store or in any of the D&D games I've played," Murphy says. "Do you recognize it, Bryn?"

Bryn budges in between Murphy and Sam, examining the blue fairy critically. "Looks a bit like Amalthea from the *World of Darkness* LARP last month."

All of us but Murphy turn stunned stares on Bryn.

"What?" Bryn says. "I LARP."

"You should see her with a *plançon*," Murphy says, chest puffed with pride.

"What's a LARP?" Lily asks.

"Live-action role-play," Sam says. "Nerds at their nerdiest."

"You say that like you've never cosplayed." Bryn pokes him in the chest. "I happen to know you have a Captain America outfit in your—"

I can't even with this right now. "Focus, people. Sam, what do you think?"

Sam holds the top and bottom of the fairy in each hand and pulls sharply, separating it into halves.

"What are you—?" I say, reaching for it.

But then I see. One half of the blue fairy is a cap. The other half . . .

"It's a flash drive," Lily says. "How did you know?" she asks Sam.

Sam holds my gaze as he says, "Because I've seen it before."

"Where?" I say, fists clenched.

"I stole it. From a bank vault in New York."

"You *what*? Why would you do something so insane? Why would you—? Wait a minute." My stomach sinks to my shoes. "Mike was investigating a bank robbery in New York. Was Mike investigating *your bank robbery*?"

Sam straightens. "I haven't had any conversations with Mike since I've been back, so I wouldn't know."

"Ugh, I am going to *strangle* you. Why would you do it? What could possibly be worth the risk?"

"A woman called me a few months ago. She needed my help stealing the contents of a safe-deposit box."

"And you just *agreed*? For some strange woman you didn't even—?" And then I figure it out. Suddenly. Like a Taser to the brain. I sag backward, catching myself on my desk. "Oh."

"What?" Murphy asks, as Dani puts an arm around my shoulders. "What 'oh'?"

Sam is waiting for me to say it, enduring my look of hurt and betrayal stoically.

"Why didn't you say something?" I say.

"She gave me a good reason not to."

"There are still a few of us on the slow track," Murphy says. "Will someone please enlighten the rest of us as to what the hell the two of you are talking about?"

I break my gaze away from Sam's, squashing my fury into a tiny, heavy box in my chest. I straighten up, pulling away from Dani.

"He stole the blue-fairy flash drive for my mother."

Everyone's incredulous stares go to Sam this time. "For real?" Lily says. "That's messed up."

Sam doesn't answer.

"How did you even get into a bank vault to steal it?" I say, but then I think better of the question. "You know what? Never mind. We'll deal with the fallout from that after we figure out what happened to Duke, what the hell is on this flash drive, and what any of it has to do with my mother."

"How will we?" Bryn says. "What exactly do you suggest we do?"

Instead of answering, I boot up my desktop computer and plug in the flash drive. The computer's hum is the only sound in the room as the flash drive's file folder opens on the screen. There seems to be a single file in it, but when I click on it, a new window pops up requiring a password.

"It's encrypted," Sam says. "Don't you think I'd have tried opening it after I stole it? I am a hacker, you know."

"Well, did you hack it?" I ask, clicking the window closed angrily.

"You can't hack encryption. You need a supercomputer, and even then it could take months if not years to break it."

"So it's essentially worthless," I say.

"Your mom wanted it, so it must be valuable to her at least."

"Speaking of that, if you gave this drive to my mother, how did Duke end up with it?"

"I don't know," Sam says. "It's a one-way stream of information with your mom. I haven't even seen her. She arranged a drop for the drive. And she called me from a burner phone that doesn't accept return calls."

"So you have no idea what she wanted with it."

He shakes his head. "I'm sorry, Julep. I wanted to tell you." His tone is resigned with an undercurrent of pleading. I give him a withering glare in response.

"Now what?" Murphy asks.

I turn an assessing look on Bryn. LARPing, huh? I can work with that.

"Now it's time to storm the castle," I say.

• • •

Dani drives me to the Ramirezes' house, and we miss the five o'clock cutoff by about twenty minutes. Luckily for me, Angela's on a twelve-hour shift rotation today, and Mike is still at work. If a girl misses curfew and no one's around to see it, did it really happen? No. No, it didn't.

"Do you want me to stay until the FBI arrives?" Dani asks, looking at the floor.

I nod and take a half breath, steeling myself with it. She's not going to like what I'm about to say.

"What is it?" she says, eyeing me suspiciously as I get us Cokes from the fridge. She's getting too good at reading me.

"I need you to let Mike help you find the person conspiring

to kill me. Han's given you access by setting up the meeting for you. But I need you to let Mike go with you."

Dani makes an irritated noise. "If you put cops on his trail, you will scare him off. It is safer to let me go alone."

"By 'safer,' you mean 'more effective.' Effective's not enough for me. It's safer if Mike goes with you. And by 'safer,' I mean 'less likely I'll end up at your funeral.'"

Dani mutters something in Ukrainian under her breath. I don't catch the words, but I'll bet none of them are *milaya*.

"It is safer for *Ramirez* if I go alone," she tries again.

She may be right. What do I know about clandestine meetings with murderers? But I can't send her in by herself. It's too much to ask.

"I'm sorry, Dani. I told you before. I can't let you go alone."

"Why?" she asks. "Something is different. I can tell."

I close my eyes, trying to grift up an answer that will satisfy her. But in this case, the truth has the best chance of getting me what I'm asking for.

"Knowing Mike is watching your back makes it possible for me to think about other things. It may be a false sense of security, but it's all I have."

"It really means that much to you?"

"You mean that much to me," I whisper past the knives in my throat. I've never wanted to tell a truth so badly and keep it hidden at the same time. "I knew Tyler for only a few weeks and his death crippled me. What would happen to me if something happened to you?"

She's silent, because she knows she can't guarantee something won't happen to her. "You should not feel that way," she says instead.

I laugh, hearing the echo of my own words to Angela from just a week ago. "I don't have any control over that."

"I wish things—I cannot give you what you deserve."

God, could my cheeks get hotter? My whole body is on fire.

"I know." I take a deep breath. "I know you think of me as a child. And that's—"

"What makes you think that?" Dani says, surprised.

"It doesn't matter. I'm trying to—"

"It does matter," she says. "I do not think of you as a child."

"You told Han—"

Dani sets her Coke on the table. "I needed Han's cooperation. I would have told her anything."

"You don't see me as a child?" I say like an idiot.

"No," she says, running a hand through her hair. "I should. But my feelings are more . . . complicated than that."

"Complicated how?"

She pushes away from the table and takes a step closer to me, capturing my gaze with hers. My breath catches.

"You make me want things I can never have," she says, murmuring something in Ukrainian. "You are precious to me."

Our noses are almost touching. "You're precious to me," I say, light-headed.

But then she pulls away. "This cannot be, *milaya*."

"Why not?"

"I am nineteen. You are only sixteen," she says.

I laugh in disbelief. "Between the two of us, we've broken almost every law there is, and you're hung up on a technicality? Three years is not as much as you think it is."

"I am decades older than you in experience. Besides, it's not the only reason."

I hear Angela in my head. *"I'm not wild about you hanging out with, much less dating, anyone who does what she does for the kinds of people she does it for."*

"You have no idea of all the things I have done," she says. "I am a criminal."

"So am I," I say defensively. "I'm tired of everyone making me into some kind of white knight. I'm just another grifter trying to survive."

"Your concept of good and evil is so skewed as to be almost worthless. Your hands are clean, and whether you believe it or not, you are a good person."

"Then so are you. You've been right next to me all these months, helping me help people, helping me heal from Tyler's death. If you say I'm a good person, then you have to believe you're good, too."

"It is different for me," she says, her eyes blue oceans of regret. "I am a bad person who has done good things. You are fundamentally a good person. You care about people. I only care about you."

"If that were true, you wouldn't have helped my dad." I want desperately to touch her, but I know reaching out would just

225

scare her off. "Give me any other reason, Dani, and I'll drop it. If you don't . . . want this, I'll respect that. But don't tell me you're not good enough. Because you are the only person who has never left me, betrayed me, or tried to change me. For me, you're the only one who *is* good enough."

I press my hands together to hide the fact that they're trembling. On top of everything else that's happened tonight, I'm not sure I can handle where this conversation is going. But I can't back out of it now, not without sending the wrong message. God, my timing is just the worst.

"I cannot protect you from your enemies and myself at the same time. *Please* do not ask me to."

"I'm not asking you to."

"I—" She reaches up, bridges the distance between us, brushes my cheek. I lean into the touch, feeling the warmth of it like electricity lighting me up.

The unmistakable sound of a car parking outside the house breaks the spell into pieces. Dani jerks back as if stung.

"I cannot," she says, shaking her head. "I . . ."

"Dani—"

I try to take her hand, but she rushes out of the house, and in a blink, she's gone. The roar of the Chevelle leaping away from the curb is the only sign she was here at all—other than the sleepless night ahead of me, that is.

A few minutes later, Mike walks in the door that Dani just slammed her way through.

"Must have been one hell of an argument," Mike says cautiously, gauging my emotional state. "She stormed out of here like she was going to set the world on fire."

"No," I say, the memory of her touch branded into my skin. "Just me."

THE LARP

"I'm having second thoughts about this plan," I say as I adjust Sam's black hoodie. "Pull your pants down more. You should have gotten a bigger size."

Lily, Murphy, and Bryn are spread throughout the Ramirezes' living room, prepping for today's infiltration of the company that processes security footage for NWI. They're not paying attention to me and Sam, so I'm not worried about throwing them off their game. Sam is different. He can handle my doubts.

He gives me a flat look. "My pants size is not going to prevent this from working."

"It's not that I think it won't work. I just . . . Are you sure you're okay with this?"

"Julep, we've done this a million times. What's the problem?"

I hesitate, which isn't like me. Once I decide on a con, I don't second-guess myself. But Sam is leading the charge on this one, since I'm stuck at the Ramirezes' under FBI guard. I'll be going along for the ride virtually, but it's not the same as being there. And Mike and Dani are off trying to make contact with the person who put a hit out on me, so Sam will have only Murphy for backup. Just then, I happen to catch Murphy moving a pair of glasses close to his face and then out to arm's length again, multiple times. Maybe *backup* isn't the right word.

"You just look more dangerous than you used to," I say, tousling his hair.

He laughs, ruining the thug effect entirely. "I'll take that as a compliment."

I keep fussing with his hoodie to hide my lack of confidence. It's one thing to have a half-grown kid traipsing by someplace he's not supposed to be. It's entirely another for a six-foot, well-muscled young man to be doing so.

I may still be mad, still *furious* with him for doing something as reckless as robbing a bank, not to mention hiding my mother's resurfacing from me. But that doesn't mean I want him in danger, especially without me there to pull him out.

He grabs my hands to get my attention. "I'll be fine. You have the harder job this time. Are you sure Bryn's up for this?"

Bryn is wearing one of my work outfits plus a chic fedora for camera-evading purposes. She's a bit tall for my pants, but not so much that it's noticeable. Murphy hands her the glasses he'd just been playing with. She slides the chunky frames awkwardly over her nose. They have a camera built into them so she can be my eyes for this operation. And my hands.

"If she can hang with Murphy's larpers, she can do this. We need to get that footage before the security company has a chance to turn it over to the cops. This is our best play."

Sam nods, dropping my hands as Murphy comes over with our communicators.

"All right, I calibrated these to access a secure channel through Bessie's network," Murphy says, handing us the tiny tan earpieces. "They're wireless, though, so there may be static from time to time. We'll all be able to hear each other as long as we talk loud enough. Whispering won't cut it."

"Explain to me why we're doing this again?" Bryn says, sliding her earpiece in.

"Because if the camera caught me near Duke's office, I'll either become a murder suspect or I'll be arrested outright for removing evidence."

"Or both," Sam puts in helpfully.

"Besides," I continue, ignoring him, "if we get the footage first, we may be able to track down Duke's killer."

"And we would want to do that because . . . ?"

"Because we're the ones with the best hope of figuring out what's really going on."

"Can't we just tell the cops what we know?"

"Not without implicating me and my entire family," I say. "Look, if any of you want out, I'll understand. I can do it myself."

"No, you can't," Sam says just as Bryn says, "I didn't say that." Bryn takes a breath and continues, "I just want to be sure we're all on the same page."

I nod, sticking my earpiece in. It feels like an earbud except a little bigger and without a cord. Weird.

"How will I ask questions when I'm in the building?" Bryn says.

"That's what the glasses are for," I say. "I should be able to anticipate your needs if I can see what you're seeing."

"This is crazy," Lily says, putting her earpiece in. "I can't believe this is actually happening. I feel like I'm a movie extra."

Murphy snorts. "Get used to it. Working for Julep Dupree is like flinging yourself off a skyscraper without a parachute."

Sam fist-bumps him.

"Hey, I resent that," I say. "I provide parachutes."

Bryn looks at her watch. "Are we doing this? I have a manicure at five."

"Suit up!" Murphy says.

"Murphy, really?" I say, pained.

He shrugs. "I've always wanted to say that."

I sigh. "Just try not to do anything stupid. If you get caught, I'm denying everything." Then I turn to fuss with Sam's hoodie a final time and say under my breath so the others can't hear, "Take care of them, all right?"

"I will," he says with a small smile.

"Seriously, you guys, come on," Bryn says. "It's like herding cats."

My band of unlikely criminals piles into our crappy van,

which then putters off down the street. I watch them through the window until they round the corner, and then slouch my way into the guest-room desk chair. I open my laptop and start the camera-feed app. It's jarring at first, seeing Bryn's surroundings through her perspective. For one thing, she plays with her hair a lot.

I flip the On switch for my earpiece. "Can you guys hear me?"

"Yep," I hear Sam say in my ear. Bryn looks at him, and I see him sitting hunched on the floor of the van, looking thoroughly gangster for such a privileged rich kid. I'm nervous for him. This is a lot to ask.

Fifteen minutes and a few jokes about Bessie's backfiring later, Murphy pulls the van into the back of the parking lot for Allied Security Systems, Inc. I'm pretty sure the *Inc.* was added for the sake of the acronym. There may have been a few jokes about that as well.

"All right, pull it together," I say. "Bryn, the glasses are crooked. Could you—?" The camera angle tilts crazily for a few seconds before righting itself into the exact same crooked angle as before. "Never mind. Sam, you're up."

The first phase of Operation Peeping Tom (Murphy's name, not mine) is for Sam to distract the security guards using our time-tested, highly effective walk-by-dressed-like-a-hoodlum method. It's not the classiest of grifter tools, perhaps, but it works.

Sam gets out of the van, pulling up his hood and adopting the trademark slump characteristic to most boys in our age group. He swaggers past the security guards, casting them a quick, guilt-laden glance and then looking away. He's playing it casual, but in a trying-to-cover-up-anxiety way. And he's nailing it.

Both security guards covering the side entrance peel off after Sam, calling out to question his presence. Bryn sneaks around to the building wall, carefully skirting the security cameras' field of vision while Sam gives the guards just enough attitude to keep them occupied.

Phase two is a little trickier. Sam and Murphy spent the morning figuring out how to hack into the building's fire alarm system. Bryn waits between a bush and the back door for Murphy to fake an alarm.

"She's in position. Now, Murph," I say.

A few seconds later, the alarm sounds, automatically unlocking the external doors for firefighters to enter. Bryn slips in, taking me with her.

"We're in," I say to the team. "Sam, get out of there. Murphy, kill the alarm. If we're lucky, they'll think it was a short."

"They'll still have to come check it out, so you have ten minutes, tops." Murphy says.

Bryn walks us down a darkened hallway. It's the weekend, so she shouldn't run into anyone in this wing of the building. Most of the Saturday shift works in the annex. It's amazing what you can learn about people's work habits on their Facebook pages.

"Keep your hat low over your face," I say to Bryn. "Just in case."

"I know, I know," she says.

"Wait," I say as she passes an office directory affixed to the wall. "Look at the directory."

I'd called the company earlier today, first posing as a potential client and getting the rundown of the process for collecting and storing security footage. The second time I called, I posed as an OkCupid date for "George" and gotten all kinds of information out of the well-intentioned, if airheaded receptionist.

Now to match up the cube number with the directory, and . . . "Bingo—three rows to the left, five rows back."

When Bryn gets to the server room, she walks up to the nearest terminal computer and, gloves on, presses the power button.

"Five minutes," Murphy says into our ears. The door to the van slides open and closed in our ears as well.

"Is that Sam?" I ask.

"I'm here. What are you seeing?" Sam says.

"Windows log-in screen," Bryn says. "It was off."

"Okay," Sam says. "Press F8 a bunch of times until you get the command screen."

Bryn follows his instructions, and the screen goes dark. White text appears.

"Check," I say. "What next?"

"Click Safe Mode and wait for the administrator log-on screen to pop up."

"It's up."

"I know," Sam says. "I'm looking at the camera feed. Now, open the Control Panel and click User Accounts. Okay, click

George's user account and then Remove Password. Now restart the computer and log in with the new credentials."

Bryn logs in successfully and opens the aptly named Security Footage Database.

"There doesn't seem to be a browsing function, only a search function. What do I search for? Cult leader killing?" Bryn hisses as quietly as possible.

"Search by date and time. Anything we can do to winnow down the results."

Bryn complies. The results do winnow down, but there are still far too many files.

"Add NWI as a search parameter," Sam says.

Bryn does so and the files winnow further, but still not enough.

"I don't have time to look at every single one to find the right room," Bryn says. "I have to be gone before the cops get here."

"Okay, okay," I say. "Open just the ones that say 'hallway.' There are fewer of those, and one of them has to be the hallway outside of Duke's office."

The first four video files Bryn opens are elsewhere in the NWI building. But the fifth file is the one we want.

"That's it!" I say. "Email it to Sam, quick."

Bryn opens a browser window and puts in the URL for Sam's email. "Why can't I just use Gmail?"

"Video file size is too large," Murphy says. "Gmail won't let you send it unless it's a link to somewhere else, like YouTube. Sam's email is set up for emailing larger files."

Bryn heaves a sigh and attaches the file to a hastily composed email. "This better be worth it."

"We're over the time cutoff by three minutes," Murphy says. "Hurry up."

"I'm hurrying," she says, just as we all hear sirens rapidly approaching the building's parking lot. "Okay, hurrying faster."

After the email sends, Bryn closes down the browser, wiping the browser history as she goes.

"Now, delete all the files on the hard drive for that date and time," I say. "The cops can't know about the blue-fairy flash drive."

Bryn highlights all the files in the folder and presses Delete. "There better not be anything else—"

"No. Go!" I say.

But just as she reaches the door, it opens of its own accord, admitting a security guard and the fire chief.

"Bryn!" Murphy shouts in my ear.

"Calm down, everybody," I say. "Bryn, listen to me, we can still salvage this. Just don't say anything."

"What are you doing here?" asks the security guard. "Didn't you hear the fire alarm? Protocol states that you are required to evacuate when the fire alarm goes off."

"Okay, Bryn," I say. "Start signing."

She doesn't move.

"Like, with your hands. It's okay if you don't know sign language. Odds are they don't, either. But you have to be confident. Pretend you're onstage. Pretend you're angry. Now. Do it now."

Bryn obeys, though I see only the tips of her fingers as they flick into her line of sight. I can't be sure, but it looks like she gestures to her ear a few times as well.

"Good," I say, studying the security guard's expression. "He's buying it. Mimic writing something."

The security guard startles and pulls a small notebook and pen out of his pocket. He hands it to her, sheepishly.

"Now write 'I'm deaf, you idiot.'"

"Is the 'you idiot' necessary?" Murphy asks.

"Yes," I say. "Write it."

Bryn complies and shoves the notebook at the guard. Nice touch.

"Sorry, m-ma'am," the guard stutters. "But the alarm has flashing lights, too."

"The alarm cut off after less than a few seconds," the fire chief points out. "She might not have seen it."

The security guard nods. "Well, protocol still states that everyone must evacuate the building until the alarm is confirmed false."

"Nod and follow them out," I say.

Bryn does as told and follows them to the door. The security guard swipes his employee badge at the card reader, looking at Bryn expectantly.

Crap. They must require employees to badge in and out at every checkpoint.

"Murphy, pull the alarm again."

Earsplitting noise erupts through my communicator. I wince and try to ignore it. "Go, Bryn. Just go."

The security guard and fire chief are so distracted by the renewed alarm that Bryn is able to push her way past them without further objection.

"Don't stop until you're out of the building and back in the van," I say, leaning back in relief.

"Jesus, that was close," Bryn says shakily when the van's doors close behind her.

"Get out of there, Murphy. You're not safe until you're back here."

"Are you sure nobody caught us on camera?" Sam says.

"Well, if they did, we now know how to get rid of the evidence," Lily says.

None of us laugh.

"Too soon?" she says.

"I'll drive," Sam says, slipping into the driver's seat.

Then my camera feed cants crazily as Bryn throws the glasses onto the dash and throws herself into Murphy's arms. I get an up-close-and-personal, if upside-down, view of Murphy's sweater-vest pocket as he holds her close.

"You were amazing," he says to her, which of course, all of us hear.

"Yeah, you were," I say, feeling beyond tired all of a sudden. It's a lot harder talking someone through a job than just pulling it myself.

"This better be worth it," Bryn mumbles into Murphy's chest.

"It will be," I say.

• • •

Two hours later, Sam downloads the footage and remotes me in so I can watch it from the Ramirezes' guest room.

"You could have stayed," I say to him over the phone.

Sam fiddles with the window size and screen resolution on his laptop. "Last time I had dinner with you, you kicked me out."

"True. And I might have kicked you out again. I'm still furious that you kept the fact that you were working for my mom a secret. I'm not letting that go, by the way. We will be talking about that as soon as I put out all these fires. There will probably be torture. You may want to bring Band-Aids."

"I'd laugh, but I think you're being serious."

"Like a prison sentence," I say. "Are you done messing around? How long does it take to load a video?"

He must have moved the phone closer to his mouth, because his voice sounds clearer and closer now. "Julep. Are you sure you want to watch it?"

"It's not the actual murder," I say. "It's just the hallway after. We'll find out the killer without having to . . . watch."

"All right," Sam says. "Video playing in three . . . two . . ."

It's a long, silent wait, because each video segment is broken into twenty-minute chunks. The first thirteen minutes show a lot of nothing. Then there's me, walking up to the door and knocking. It's surreal watching myself through the silent feed.

"This can't be right. It doesn't show anyone else leaving before I got there."

"Maybe he was dead for longer than twenty minutes?" Sam says. "The killer could have left—"

But then something moves at the bottom of the screen, emerging from behind a potted plant and skulking along the wall. Someone was obviously trying to evade the cameras in the hallway—someone with a hipster haircut and glasses. Someone who looks an awful lot like . . .

"Ackley."

"Ackley?" Sam says.

"He's one of the interns."

"Do you think he did it?"

"Why else would he be trying to evade the cameras?"

"The same reason you would have tried to evade the cameras if you'd known Duke was dead?"

"Okay, but how did he know Duke was dead if he didn't kill him?"

"I don't know, Julep. The evidence seems pretty flimsy."

"I can get better proof. We'll need to anyway, since we erased the other video feeds and compromised the chain of custody for the video we have. The police might still accept it as evidence, but you're right—we need something more substantial than grainy hallway footage."

"Just be careful. If this guy is the killer, he won't have any issue taking you out for suspecting him."

I hang up with Sam and shut down my computer. I don't want to think about Duke's murder any more tonight. Especially when my own potential murder keeps hovering at the back of my brain. The darker the sky gets, the more I worry that Mike and Dani aren't back yet. I spin in the chair, trying to rid myself of images of gun battles and blood.

After a few minutes, I wander out to the kitchen.

"Have you heard from Mike?" I ask Angela as I pick an apple from the basket on the counter.

"Not yet," Angela says, doing just as poor a job as I am of hiding her concern.

"Do you suppose they went out for burgers afterward?" I ask.

"It's possible." She taps her pencil on her mostly empty crossword puzzle.

We sit in silence for several more minutes as I pretend that I have any intention of eating the apple and Angela pretends that she's working on her crossword.

"I could call FBI headquarters," I say. "See if they've heard anything."

"You could," Angela agrees. "But they probably wouldn't tell you anything."

"Speaking from experience?"

"Maybe."

We wait another few minutes with nothing disturbing the silence but the ticking cuckoo clock Angela's mother got her during a trip to Switzerland a couple of years back.

"Waiting sucks." I suddenly feel bad for anyone I've ever made wait for me.

"Yes, it does."

"Does it get any easier?"

"Nope," Angela says, finally giving up on the crossword and coming over to sit next to me. "Want to make brownies and watch silly kung fu movies?"

I smile. "Sure."

We're halfway through *Project Ninja Daredevils* when Mike and Dani finally show up. It takes everything I have not to jump up and hug them.

"Brownie?" Angela says, holding up the plate to Mike. He leans in for a kiss first, then snags the biggest brownie from the middle of the pile. "How'd it go?"

Dani walks by, passing up the brownies and the seat next to me on the couch. She sits on the other couch instead.

"No-show," Mike says, sitting on the other half of Dani's couch. There's something between Dani and Mike, some kind of understanding that neither of them is sharing.

"What does this mean?" Angela asks. "If the person didn't show up, does that mean they know you weren't on the level?"

"That was always a risk," Dani says, speaking for the first time.

"Do you think Han—"

"No," she says.

"It could also be that whoever it was gave up, changed his mind," Angela says. But even she doesn't sound like she believes it.

"Dani, can we talk privately for a sec?" I say.

She looks questioningly at Mike first, which irritates the hell out of me. He nods, and she follows me into the guest room. I try to shut the door after us, but she stops it with her hand. The warning look she gives me is enough to convey her meaning. I relent and leave it open.

"I was worried about you," I say without meaning to.

"I am always worried about you," she says back.

"Tell me really. What do you think happened tonight?"

She sighs and leans against the doorjamb. "I think someone informed the client. Not Han," she says as I open my mouth to ask. "Someone else. But I do not know who."

"Who else is there? Nobody knows but us."

"The FBI knew. We have no way of knowing how many people were aware of the operation."

"Speaking of operation . . ." I fill her in on Operation Peeping Tom.

"Are you planning to tell Ramirez?"

"No. I'm trying to keep things uncomplicated." It's the best way I can think of to put it.

"Uncomplicated. I see," she says.

I fidget with the hem of my shirt, feeling uneasy. "Are you in danger now?" I ask, my question trembling embarrassingly at the end. "Because of me?"

"*Milaya*," she says, wrapping me in a rare hug. "I am always in danger."

I laugh bitterly, my head tucked between her ear and shoulder. "That's supposed to make me feel better?"

"It is supposed to make you laugh," she says.

I hate that I'm falling in love with you. I hate that you won't love me back. I don't say it out loud, though. It would ruin the moment, and I'd rather chew off my own arm than do that. But the moment is shattered anyway when my phone buzzes in my pocket. I sigh and pull away.

"Hello?" I say with perhaps a slight hint of irritation.

"Julep? It's Lily," she stage-whispers. "I broke into Sister Rasmussen's office."

"You did what?" I say. "Why?"

Instead of answering, she says. "You're not going to believe what I found."

THE INTERN

"Back up. What are you doing at St. Agatha's?"

"You put me on Rasmussen detail, remember? Besides, I couldn't sleep. Figured I might as well be productive."

"How did you even get in?"

"I told the security guard I'd left my purse in my locker and only just realized it—wallet, keys, phone, everything. He agreed to let me in when I slipped him a hundred."

"You can't just decide to do this stuff on your own! What if I already had plans?"

"Did you already have plans?"

"No, but I could have." This is why I prefer working alone whenever possible. When minions start thinking independently, it's time to kick them to the curb. "And just because you bribed the security guard doesn't mean he isn't going to rat you out. It's your word against his, unless you made a recording of the bribe." The silence on the other end of the line isn't reassuring. "Look, I'm sending Dani to get you."

"Wait! Don't you want to hear what I found?"

I do, but I'm not sure I should reward her behavior. I pull the phone from my ear and cover the mike.

"Lily is at St. Agatha's administration building. Would you mind bringing her back here? I'm afraid she's going to get caught, or worse."

Dani nods and squeezes my hand before heading out. I put the phone back up to my ear as I watch her go.

"Dani's coming to get you. When she texts you, you'd better be outside waiting for her, or I will send her in to pull you out by your hair. Understood?"

"Do you want to hear what I found or not?"

I sigh heavily. "Fine. Tell me."

"At first, I—"

"And take pictures of everything while you're talking," I say.

"Okay." She switches me to speakerphone. I hear the snap-shot noise of her phone taking a picture. "At first, I didn't think anything of it. I figured if it was out on her desk, it wouldn't be anything useful. So I dug through her file cabinet and drawers before looking in the most obvious place in the room."

"Lily, speed it up. I want you out of the building ASAP."

She takes another picture. "I'm taking shots of it now, by the way. I can't believe she just left it out."

Now I'm starting to believe she *didn't* just leave it out. It could easily be a trap.

"Lily, really. Get out of there. You can tell me all about it when Dani picks you up."

"Not yet. Listen, it's a bank notice. Notifying the recipient that her safe-deposit box was broken into."

"What?"

"Yeah. The address in the letterhead says the bank's located in New York."

"Is the letter addressed to Sister Rasmussen?"

"Nope. It's—"

My heart jumps as Lily cuts herself off. "Lily? What happened?"

"I just heard something," she whispers.

It's been only five minutes since Dani left. It can't be her.

"Hide!" I say. "Take me off speaker. Whatever you do, don't hang up. Even if you get caught, try to hide the phone on you somewhere and keep the line open as long as possible."

Then I freeze as I hear the office door creaking open. Lily whimpers softly in my ear.

I shush her and whisper, "Stay with me. You can do this."

She goes silent. It's only a matter of moments before whoever it is spots her. Even if she's hiding under the desk, a determined searcher will find her in seconds. It's not that large an office.

"You still have surprise on your side. Get ready to run. As soon as the person gets close to where you're hiding, jump out and push them hard, then run for all you're worth."

Lily's breathing speeds up, which I take to mean that the

person is closing in on her location. Then I hear a shout and some muffled swearing and, finally, words.

"Whoa, whoa, whoa, it's just me," says Murphy's voice through the line. "What are you doing here?"

"What are *you* doing here?" Lily hisses.

"Ow," he says. I smile at the mental image of Lily throwing her shoe at him. "Same as you, obviously. Thought I'd take a look around Sister Rasmussen's office while Bryn's at Val's party. Holy crap! Did you see the letter from the bank?"

"Hit him again, Lily," I say.

"Ow!" he says as she complies.

"Hey, guys. Find anything?" I hear Sam's voice through the phone and pinch the bridge of my nose. "I'd be happy to smack Murphy upside the head if that's the price of admission," he says.

"What the hell?" I yell into the phone. "Lily, put me back on speaker." I wait a few seconds for her to comply before continuing my tirade. "Why are all three of you there?"

"I came with Murphy," Sam says. "You know, backup. Why'd you send Lily alone?"

"I didn't send Lily. I didn't send any of you!"

"Initiative is a good thing in an employee," Lily says.

"It didn't occur to any of you to clue me in to this little adventure?"

"It's not like you could have come," Murphy says. "Besides, it was a spontaneous, carpe diem kind of thing. Masters of our own—"

"Shut up, Murphy," I say. "Sam, you at least should have known better."

"I didn't think we'd find anything, so I didn't want to worry you with it. Breaking into the school is kid stuff anyway."

"Hey," Lily says, offended. "I bribed a guard."

"All three of you are going to be on crap admin duty for the next six months," I say.

"There's not enough to keep all three of us busy," Murphy points out.

I hear the rustling of paper and assume Murphy or Lily is passing the letter to Sam.

"Oh, my god," Sam says. "Julep. You're not going to believe this."

"So everyone keeps saying. Just tell me already."

"This letter is addressed to Lucrezia Moretti."

Of course it is.

"Who's Lucrezia Moretti?" Lily asks.

"She's my grandmother."

• • •

"They say too many cups of coffee will stunt your growth," Mike says from his place at the kitchen table as I pour the last dregs of the coffee into my mug.

I wave off his comment. "You're just saying that because you want another cup. It's not hard to make more, you know."

"Maybe. But still, this is your third cup in under an hour. That seems like a lot, even for you and especially on a Sunday morning. Everything okay?"

I hide a jaw-cracking yawn behind my hand. "Long night punishing minions," I say. "Worth it, though."

He chuckles. "Anything I should know about?"

The look in his eyes is half joking, half cagey. He's hoping he'll get something out of me. Which means he probably suspects something and he's not telling me. Great. Now I have to waste time worrying that he's on to Sam for the New York bank robbery. The bank robbery that resulted in the theft of the blue-fairy flash drive. The blue-fairy flash drive that, apparently, belonged to my grandmother Lucrezia Moretti. As if I didn't have enough problems trying to figure out who killed Duke and who is trying to kill me.

"Oh, you know. Bribery, some light B&E. The usual."

"Why do I feel like you're telling me the truth in such a way that I'll think it's a joke?"

"Because I do it all the time."

He sighs. "Walked right into that one, didn't I?"

"Most people do. So when are you going to tell me about your trip to New York?"

"Empire State Building was nice. Statue of Liberty was a bit overrated, though," he says. "Hey, this truth thing is fun."

"I'm just offering to give you my professional opinion on the case. I'm stuck here till tomorrow morning, after all. I have to keep myself entertained somehow."

"I appreciate that, but my team has a lead or two we're following up on. No grifter input needed."

Fabulous. Just freaking fantastic. I'm going to have to find a way to sabotage that investigation or Sam's going to end up with a one-way ticket to serious jail time.

"Well, if you change your mind, you know where to find me."

"Thanks," he says, gulping the last of his coffee in one swallow. "So. You and Dani, huh? Can't say I saw that one coming."

My face heats up. "There's no me and Dani. There's no me and anybody."

Mike scratches his stubbly cheek. The man shaves, I swear, but he always has stubble. It's, like, an immutable tough-guy law. "Funny, she said the same thing when I talked to her."

"Oh, my god, Mike, you didn't." For a second, I seriously consider smothering him in his sleep. "I hope you know this is a spike-your-coffee-with-Drano offense. Not a single person would blame me. Not even Angela."

"Not even Angela what?" says a sleepy Angela as she shuffles into the kitchen.

"Your rube of a husband asked Dani what her intentions were regarding me."

Angela gasps. "You didn't." She sounds almost as horrified as I feel. "The Drano's under the sink. Do you need me to get it?" she says to me.

"Hey, I'm in charge of your emotional as well as your physical well-being," Mike says. "Dani is, no offense, the *last* person I'd feel good about you dating. I was completely justified in my actions."

"No, honey. I'm sorry, but no. Just no." Angela is totally my hero. "Besides, I already talked to Dani."

"Are you both on *drugs?*"

Angela pats my head. "It's adorable how sincerely you believe you don't need parents," she says. "But you do, whether you like it or not."

I'm not big on embarrassment. I don't generally dwell on it. I feel it and let it go. But this is a whole new realm of mortification.

"What did she say?" I ask, not sure I want to hear the answer.

Mike and Angela share a look, but it's Angela who answers. "She's in denial. Not of her feelings, but of any ability to act on them." She squeezes my shoulder. "I don't think she's going to budge, sweetie."

Well, that's not surprising. The depth to which my heart plummets is new, though.

"I think I'll go back to bed," I say, pouring my coffee into the sink. "If anyone needs me, tell them to get lost."

"Julep, about New York," Mike says, leaning back in his chair. "I'd hate to find out that you or any of your friends were involved in that robbery. I don't want to arrest you."

"Then don't," I say, and leave.

•   •   •

"Crap. Are you sure?" Sam says.

"Pretty damn sure, Sam," I say into the phone. "He knows something or he wouldn't have brought up the bit about not wanting to arrest us."

Some muffled swearing follows. Sam's picked up a few new phrases in military school. "I'll handle it."

"No. No, you will not *handle it*. No more solo missions, remember? All three of you swore blood oaths to me after the bank letter debacle."

"Quit being melodramatic. It wasn't a debacle. A mild catastrophe, at most."

I roll my eyes, though only Dani can see since she's driving me and Sam's just on the phone.

"Listen, *I* will handle Mike. *You* keep digging at NWI. Ackley probably had an accomplice. Somebody higher up."

"Gotta go. The other initiates are arriving for the big meeting. Are you going to get here in time?"

"I wouldn't miss it," I say, and hang up.

Dani seems extra broody this morning. I remember my conversation with the Ramirezes and my cheeks heat again.

"What's the stony face for? Not enough barbed wire for breakfast this morning?"

It's a measure of her mood that she ignores my playful jab. Instead, she says, "I know you think this Ackley person is harmless. But if he did kill Salinger, he is deadly. You should avoid confronting him."

"Come on, you know me. Or you should by now. I don't confront people directly."

She arches an eyebrow.

"Okay, I sometimes confront people directly. But you can stop worrying. I've got this."

She's still looking at me dubiously when she drops me off at the front door. I hustle in because I'm just short of late for Dr. Raktabija's big speech to the entire organization. It's apparently being recorded for the website. I don't want to be the jerk disrupting it with a squeaky door.

I manage to make it in just before the auditorium doors shut, sliding into a seat Aadila saved for me in the interns' row.

"You're late," Aadila says, cutting her eyes over to where Ackley is sitting, quietly seething. "His panties are screwed on far too tight."

I swallow a laugh as the lights dim and a spotlight illuminates the podium onstage. Dr. Raktabija strides purposefully up to it, her face drawn and puffy from crying, and I suddenly don't feel like laughing anymore.

I have a weird moment of almost déjà vu seeing another woman standing on another stage about to give another eulogy. The place and circumstances may be different, but the end is the same. Someone was taken from a community that loved him with a single, well-aimed bullet. But there the similarities end. Dr. Raktabija, the future leader of NWI, is nothing like Sister Rasmussen. Where Sister Rasmussen is a pasty white woman in her sixties with gray hair, Dr. Raktabija is an Indian woman in her late thirties, with long, black-brown curls framing a heart-shaped face. The few times I've seen her in passing, she wore bright colors, but today, she's swathed in deep black.

"Duke Salinger was like a father to me. He brought me out of a darkness so expansive that I could not even see it until he let in a small ray of light. The longer I followed him, the more light surrounded me, until I floated in a sea of light every day. I know many of you feel the same. That was Duke's gift to the world, to each of us.

"But Duke did not teach us to lean on *his* light. He taught us to nurture and harness and fight for the light within ourselves. It is only by adhering to this teaching that we will regenerate the light we lost. We owe it to ourselves, to each other, and to Duke to continue perfecting the skills he taught us.

"How we react to this tragedy will define us as an organization. We can either come together and build the New World Initiative into an even stronger entity, or we can let everything Duke lived and died for crumble into dust. The choice is made here in this room, in this moment, in each of our hearts."

There's no applause at the end of Dr. Raktabija's speech, but a pervasive and profound feeling of respect and resolve moves through the room. Joseph leans forward in his seat, trying to control an overflow of emotion. Even Ackley seems affected, though he could easily be putting on a front to throw me off.

After the meeting, I corner Ackley outside the men's room. "How are you holding up?" I ask.

"At least I can use this travesty for my college essays."

I fake-smile. "Always thinking, aren't you? Awesome. I was wondering whether they'll be continuing our summer internships after all this?"

"Why wouldn't they? Joseph needs us even more now. He's been promoted to Dr. Raktabija's second-in-command."

"Really? I hadn't heard that. Interesting. That's quite the jump from internship coordinator, isn't it?"

Ackley shrugs. "If you're valuable, you get promoted. That's how it works in business."

Okay, Ackley, are you just a naive, arrogant douche bag, or are you trying to play me into believing you're a naive, arrogant douche bag when really you're a conniving murderer?

Adding an undercurrent of melancholy to my voice, I say, "Did you get to see Duke? You know, that last day?"

"On Friday?" Ackley asks, barely managing to keep his voice neutral. Beads of sweat appear on his upper lip. "No," he lies. "I meant to go up and ask him a question. He said we could. But I didn't get around to it before we left for happy hour."

Ah, yes. Happy hour. How did you get out of that? Make some excuse about leaving something at the office? Your gun, perhaps?

"Oh, well. It's probably for the best," I say, dropping my gaze. "It's harder now without him." That part is less a lie than I'd like it to be. I gesture in the direction of the intern pen. "I guess I'd better get back there. See you in a few."

"Wait," Ackley says as I move away. His eyes flick nervously around the hallway. "I heard something was taken. From Duke, I mean."

"Really?" I say, freezing midstep. Could it really be this easy?

"Yeah." He drops his voice a few decibels. "A blue pixie . . . or something? Out of curiosity, did you ever see him with it? You were in his office for that workshop development project."

Now, I could do a number of things at this stage of the game. I could tell Ackley I didn't see it, keep him at a distance, delaying the inevitable in a "did she or didn't she?" dance. Or I could tell him I have it and see what he does. But Dani would have a conniption if I do, and besides, I'm not quite ready for the fallout from that yet. I need to know who he's working for and why. So I go for option number three: Show him a glimpse of the lady, then make him work to find it—the three-card monte.

"I did see it," I say. "Or at least, I think so. He had something like that on his desk when I was there. I noticed it because he kept looking at it."

"Oh. Maybe it's just in a drawer somewhere, then."

"Yeah, maybe," I say, letting my voice hang a little heavy with significance. If Ackley is crooked, he'll hear it and make a play. "Though if I were Duke, I'd keep it on me." *Telling the truth like it's a lie.*

He licks his lips. "Are you going to the wake tomorrow?"

"I didn't know about it," I say.

It's almost too easy. I can see my suggestion taking root in his mind. . . . *I'd keep it on me.* If he has half a brain, he'll try to steal the blue fairy from me at the wake. Too bad for him I'll be leaving it at the Ramirezes'. Meanwhile, he makes any kind of move on me at the wake, and I'll have him.

"Right, you were late," Ackley says. "Joseph told us about his promotion and the wake before we went to the auditorium for Dr. Raktabija's speech."

"Oh, okay, I'll be there," I say. "Thanks for letting me know."

He nods an awkward thank-you and turns toward the men's room.

"Hey, Ackley. Where is the wake going to be?"

"Bar63," he says, and then steps through the door.

THE WAKE

"You sure you don't want more, Sam?" Angela says, offering him the plate of empanadas.

Sam holds up a hand, warding them off. "No, thanks. I think I had my share, plus half of Mike's."

"I heard that!" Mike yells from the kitchen.

We're sitting on the Ramirezes' back deck, enjoying the coolness of the evening. Or rather, Angela, Mike, and Sam are enjoying the coolness of the evening. I'm obsessing about the connection between NWI and Bar63.

"Julep?" Angela says, turning the plate in my direction and not quite hiding the worry in her eyes. I feel guilty, because I barely managed to choke down one empanada. And not for lack of deliciousness on the part of Angela's cooking.

"I'm good, thanks," I say.

"You seem sort of distracted, actually," she says.

"I'm just struggling with something work-related. I'm okay."

"Anything we can help with?"

I carefully avoid looking at Sam. "I don't think so. Thanks, though."

"All right," she says, touching my shoulder. "I'll just take these in before the flies carry them off."

Sam nudges my chair leg with his foot. "What's eating you? I haven't heard you this quiet since that time Jimmy Kendricks bet you five dollars you couldn't shut up for five minutes."

I glare at him. "It was thirty minutes, jerk."

"Okay, thirty minutes," he says, smiling. "The question still stands."

"I'm just so frustrated. It doesn't make any sense. Nothing fits. I'm not a detective, Sam. And I'm missing stuff because of it. I can feel it."

He leans forward, toward me. "So hand it over to the people who actually are detectives, who have the resources to figure it all out for you."

"If I do that, I risk you going to prison. They can't find out about your role in all this."

"That's my problem, Julep. I made the choice I did for a reason, and I'm not sorry I did."

I shake my head. "You're a sentimental idiot, but I won't have you going to prison for it. No cops." We fall silent for a few seconds before I get up the nerve to ask, "What did she say to you? What did she sound like? Why didn't she come to me?" About fifteen other questions crowd my brain, but I force them back. I know that letting myself care is a recipe for disaster, but I can't help it.

Sam looks down at his hands. "She sounded scared. She said she needed my help. That *you* needed my help. I couldn't say no."

"Probably because you have no common sense whatsoever."

He chuckles ruefully. "Yeah, you're right about that."

"But why did she insist you keep it a secret from me?"

"She didn't have to give me a reason. I would have kept you out of it anyway."

"It's *my* family, Sam. My responsibility."

Sam frowns. "It's technically your parents' responsibility. But I'll overlook that and go straight to we've been friends since the fourth grade. We've been there for each other since before either of us even knew what that meant. So the last thing I'm going to do is let you shoulder this thing by yourself."

I do know that, and despite him leaving me last year when I really needed him, I'd do the same for him.

"I get what you're saying," I say. "But still, she gave you a reason not to tell me. I need to know what it is."

He pauses for a long moment. "She said if you found her, you would lose your father."

I sigh. "Shows what she knows. I've already lost my father."

The sound of the Chevelle's engine grows in the distance, which means Dani is getting close. I hadn't expected to see her tonight, so either she couldn't stay away from me, or, and more likely, she has bad news. But I've had so much bad news lately that a little more won't hurt, and the thought that I get to see her makes my heart flip. Queen of messed-up priorities— that's me.

"You're into her, aren't you?" Sam asks.

I don't answer because I don't need to. If he's asking, he already knows, and me answering will just open the door for him to get all judgy about it. And in any case, it's none of his business.

"You're a total moron, you know that, right?" he says.

"Yep. I am well aware."

"She's a *mob enforcer.*"

I'm starting to get exceptionally tired of having this conversation. "I'm a criminal, too, Sam. We're all criminals, remember?"

"You are a fixer. I am a hacker. We skirt the law. We don't *obliterate* it by murdering people."

"I know what she does, but it's not who she is. And it won't change how I feel anyway. I'm too far gone for that."

Only I know him well enough to see the slight tightening in his features that says he's fighting a wince. Seeing it makes me both sad and angry.

"It's impossible, Julep. You have to see that. Tell me you see that."

"It doesn't matter," I grumble, annoyed that I have to say this out loud. "She won't let anything happen."

"Thank god," he says, relieved.

I glower at him. "Don't get too comfy in your moral superiority, there, Sam. At least she stayed."

"Julep—" He tries to touch me, but I stand up and out of reach.

"Just do your job, Sam, and I'll do mine." Then I turn to march inside, but Dani is there before I have the chance.

"Get in the house," she says. "Both of you."

Sam and I head straight for the house without question. Dani scans the fence line as she waits for us to cross the threshold. Then she slams and locks the door behind her, drawing the curtains.

"What's going on?" Mike says, taking out his phone.

Dani pulls me to the center of the room, away from all the windows. "Someone has picked up the contract."

Angela's face turns a few shades paler. I'm sure mine is a match. I think about my close call at the quarry and start trembling again, damn it.

"Do you know who?" Mike asks.

"Yes," Dani says, as she closes the blinds in the living room. "His name is Spade. He is not just a professional. He is *the* professional you call if you are not getting results."

Mike rubs his face. "I've heard of him. From D.C., right?"

"D.C., Los Angeles, Istanbul. He is a force of nature."

"Fabulous," I say, hugging my soon-to-be-dead self. "Do you suppose it's too late to take out a life insurance policy?"

• • •

"Really, Dani, you don't need to come in with me," I say as we troop up the sidewalk toward Bar63. "There'll be a huge crowd. It's not like Ackley's going to pull a gun on me or anything."

263

"It is not Ackley I am worried about. Crowds can be just as much cover as darkness if used correctly," she says. "I am not letting you out of my sight."

"I suppose I can live with that," I say, smiling. "This disability has interesting side effects."

She growls at me. "This is not a joke."

"I know," I say, laying a hand on her arm. "And I'm grateful for your help. I am. But lighten up a little, all right?" Urban streets give way to neck-craning skyscrapers and when we get to Bar63, we bump right into Aadila.

"Who's this?" Aadila asks, gesturing to Dani.

I loop my arm through Dani's. "This is my girlfriend, Dani." Then I beam up at her to see her reaction. She turns eight shades of red and glares at me when Aadila turns to the bar to get us a couple of glasses of something sparkling.

"Nice to meet you, Dani," Aadila says vaguely, her attention already elsewhere. She gestures at the mike set up in the corner. "They're doing these lame toasts to Duke. Anyone can jump in, so feel free."

"I think I'll pass," I say. "Where is everybody?"

Aadila gestures with her chin to where Joseph is sitting in shadow, nursing a glass of water. He looks listless and rough. Duke's death is hitting him particularly hard.

"I should go over and check on him," I say to Dani. "Keep Aadila company for a minute?"

Her glare sharpens for a second, but then she nods. It's not like she can't see me from the bar.

"This seat taken?" I ask as I slide in next to Joseph.

He shakes his head. He glances at me briefly but then goes back to staring at his water glass, looking for answers that I know from experience aren't there.

"I lost a friend once," I say. "A good friend. It almost wrecked me." For once I allow the full feeling of those months after Tyler's death to infuse my voice. "I have to admit, Dr. Raktabija's theory about the light never really worked for me."

"What did work for you?" Joseph asks.

I meet his eyes, letting mine tell the truth. "I'll let you know when I find out."

He swallows hard. I put my hand on his arm—it's all I can do. And it's not nearly enough, because if I'm right about Ackley, then it's my family's fault Duke is dead. Whatever's on that flash drive has to do with my family, and Duke could still be alive if he hadn't gotten involved.

"I need to go." Joseph gets up quickly and walks to the other room. I don't follow. Instead, I go back to where Dani is sitting with Aadila, who is apparently chattering her head off about Dani's Chevelle.

"Having fun?" I ask her.

"You are the luckiest— How did you not tell me that you get to ride in a 1969 mint-condition Chevelle on a daily basis? Do you have any idea how *cool* that car is? You don't, do you? Oh, the waste!"

"Well, I know how cool it is *now*. Besides, the Chevelle and I have a terrific relationship based on mutual respect and understanding."

Aadila rolls her eyes at me. "You are so weird sometimes."

"That is an understatement," Dani pipes up. I elbow her in the ribs for her trouble.

"Speaking of things that are beautiful, have you seen that guy before?" Aadila asks, pointing surreptitiously at Sam.

I'd laugh, but then I'd have to explain myself. "Um, he's an initiate, I think. A new one."

"Weren't you working on the initiate files?" she asks, raising an eyebrow. She's referring to the files I rifled through in the document room.

"His wasn't in there, I don't think. Not that I remember anyway. Why? Are you interested?" I ask, starting to feel annoyed. I'm not here to facilitate Sam's love life.

"He's too old for me, I'm sure. I was just curious if you knew him. Maybe he has a younger brother."

Nope. Just Sam. No siblings. Tough luck. "Why don't you ask him?"

Aadila makes a face. "No way. I don't really care about this internship, but I don't want to lose it in disgrace for hitting on an initiate. Even if I'm not really hitting on him."

Okay, this conversation is officially getting weird. Time to redirect. "Who else is here?" I ask.

Aadila shrugs. "Everybody. Ackley's coming late. Something about a doctor's appointment. Whatever."

"Wait, what?" I say, heart suddenly pounding. "Ackley's not here?"

"Nope, and I can't say I'm super sorry to be missing his smug . . . What's wrong? You look like you've seen a ghost."

"Oh, nothing. Just got a little dizzy. I'm going to go sit down for a minute."

I grab Dani's arm and tow her over to the bench Joseph vacated. My fingers fly over my phone screen as I text Sam to meet us outside immediately.

"Change of plan," I say to Dani, trying to keep my voice as low as possible in the din. "We have to get out of here."

Dani, bless her, isn't a question asker. She swings immediately into action, threading through the crowd to the door.

"Ackley's craftier than I thought," I say when we catch up with Sam. "He never showed. He must have figured out I was playing him."

"How do you know?" Sam asks as we head to our cars. "Maybe he just ditched the wake."

"I can't take that risk. I have to assume he's searching the Ramirezes' house," I say, sending a text to Angela.

"Why there? Why not Salinger's office?"

"Because the flash drive isn't at the office. I have to act on the possibility he's anticipated me and . . ." I dial Angela's cell—no answer. "That's not the worst of it. God, I am such an idiot." I dial the house phone—still no answer. "Angela's there by herself. Mike's working late tonight."

My phone pings with a text from Lily. *I need to talk to you.* I dismiss it.

"What about the FBI detail?" Sam yanks open the driver's-side door of his Volvo.

I rush past him toward the Chevelle. "The FBI is there only when I am—after five and on weekends."

Once we're in and buckled up, Dani floors it. The Chevelle's tires squeal as we swerve into traffic, cutting off a BMW SUV. Sam's Volvo weaves into the lane right behind us. The roar from the Chevelle's engine does little to calm my racing heart. If anything happens to Angela, I'll never forgive myself.

Sam and Dani slice through the tail end of rush-hour traffic on 290, driving on the shoulder when necessary. It must look like we're in a race against each other, when really we're racing the clock. If Ackley gets to the blue-fairy flash drive before we do, we'll lose what little upper hand we have. Plus, there's no telling what could happen to Angela if she tries to interfere.

Ackley didn't seem that dangerous, not really, but I know nothing about the people he's working for. And if he *is* searching the Ramirezes' for the blue fairy, then I've already gravely underestimated him. I am such an *idiot*. I thought going up against Duke was the challenge. But Duke was never the problem. I've been looking in the wrong place the whole time.

Dani swerves to avoid a semi, then shifts into fifth again. "Five more minutes."

Sam maneuvers ahead of us and switches lanes, slowing down to let us in just before we reach the off-ramp that leads to Mike and Angela's. We speed through the red light, taking the corners fast enough to make even the Volvo sweat.

When we skid to a stop in front of the house, there's a gray van out front that I've never seen before. I throw open my door and run toward the house. Sam grabs my arm, holding me back long enough to let Dani pass me. Dani barges through the front door, gun drawn.

I hear someone shout "What the—?" as I rush in behind Dani, who has a portly man I don't recognize pushed against the wall, her gun to his forehead.

"What the hell is going on?" Angela yells. "Dani, unhand my plumber!"

"Are you sure he's a plumber?" I ask, drawing Angela to the opposite end of the room.

Sam darts into the kitchen. "Clear!" he shouts as he abandons it to check the other rooms.

"Yes, I'm sure!" Angela says, tugging her arm out of my grip. "I've known him for eight years!"

Sam comes back, nodding to Dani. Dani slowly releases her grip on the plumber, holstering her gun without taking her eyes off him. The plumber, his small eyes open as wide as they go, wipes the sweat pouring from his forehead.

"Will someone please tell me what's happening?" Angela says, her nurse's no-nonsense tone getting more pronounced with every word.

I leave it to Sam to explain as I run back to the guest room to check for the flash drive. The room feels eerie, too quiet after the rush and noise of racing to get here and confronting the plumber. But nothing is even a hair out of place. My schoolbag is still slumped half open in the desk chair. Yesterday's clothes are still in a pile on the floor. My notebooks are still stacked haphazardly, just the way I left them. I allow myself a brief flicker of hope before pulling open the desk drawer I stowed the flash drive in last night.

But my stomach sinks to the floor when I discover that the drawer is empty.

The blue-fairy flash drive is gone.

THE PHONY

"Do you have the blue-fairy flash drive?" Joseph asks me.

Startled, I look up from staring unseeing at my computer. "What did you say?"

"The asset backup drive," he says. "I can't find it."

I blink, shaking my head. Of course, he wouldn't say blue-fairy flash drive. It's just my distracted brain filling in the blanks when I'm not listening.

"I think Sally had it last," I say. "She was backing up some files from the marketing video project."

Joseph sighs, but smiles at me. "Okay, I'll check with her. Everything okay? You seem distracted today."

"Yes, fine. I'm just—" I make a vague wavy gesture that encompasses all the chaos in my life without explicitly referring to anything.

"Me too," he says, his guard slipping to show the pain beneath.

My phone buzzes. I pull it out to see a text from Lily. *I really need to talk to you.*

I completely forgot her text from yesterday in all the craziness. I dismiss the new text. I'll call her after work.

Speaking of, Ackley never showed for work today. It's as good a smoking gun as I'm going to get without being able to track him down. I tried emailing, texting, calling. I even had Dani drive me to Ackley's house this morning. The place was a dump that has been on the market for years. All of which points to him as Duke's killer, and a damn smart one at that. Which makes his getting caught on security camera that much more odd. If he's really that smart, how did he get caught on video?

In any case, the only way I'm going to get the blue-fairy flash drive back is if I can lure him out of hiding.

"*Julep.*"

I jump for the second time in ten minutes. Aadila is standing just behind me, an annoyed look on her face.

"I said your name, like, five times," she says, setting some folders down on my desk. "Are you okay?"

"Yes, sorry. What's up?" I give her a sheepish smile.

"Nothing. You're just staring off into space like a vegetable. It's weird." She leans against the desk. "You got dizzy and took off like a shot last night, and now you're practically catatonic. Do you have a brain tumor or something?"

If only. "No, I'm fine. Just crappy family stuff. What's up with the folders?"

"The police wanted files on all us NWI chickens. They have some lame theory that Duke's death was an inside job. Something about security footage going missing. As if any of these zealots would ever consider offing their beloved leader."

"Interns, too?" I ask.

"Yeah, why?"

"Just curious what's in my file," I lie. "You taking these up to Dr. Raktabija's office?"

"That was the plan," she says, eyeing me conspiratorially.

"I'm headed up there to get some sales data from her assistant. I could drop them off for you."

"Well, it is a pretty long hike up to the fourth floor," she says, smirking, and then heads back to her desk sans folders.

I riffle through them, looking for Ackley's. It's fourth from the bottom, which makes sense, since Scarlet, the document coordinator, probably pulled them in alphabetical order. I slide it out and flip it open, scanning the contents for anything that might help me contact him.

A frustrating ten minutes later, I close the folder, no closer to finding Ackley than I was before. And now I have to lug all these folders up to Dr. Raktabija's office for no good reason. Ugh.

But as I slide the folder back into its place in the stack, I notice a thin slice of yellow peeking out from the top of another folder higher up in the stack than Ackley's. On a hunch, I pull out the folder in question.

DUPREE, J.—INTERN

I open the folder and flip to where the Post-it is affixed. In Ackley's handwriting is a simple note.

PHONY.

It's followed by a phone number. I peel off the Post-it and slip it into my pocket. Fantastic. Now I'm the one following the lady. Not the best position to be in, but I can turn it around again.

I just have to find the one thing Ackley still needs: the encryption key.

• • •

Dani's waiting for me in the lobby when I get back from dropping off the folders. She's actually reading, which is the first time I've ever seen *that*.

"I read," she says when I question her about it. "How do you think I learned English?"

"You learned English from *Car and Driver?*"

"I bought it for the articles."

I laugh loudly at that.

"What?" she says, puzzled.

"Never mind."

We get to the Chevelle without incident, but I can tell

Dani's nervous. This Spade guy really has her on edge, which puts me on edge. I've never heard of him, so I don't know what to fear. But when Dani's this tense, I'd be a fool not to be worried.

"We've got some time before curfew."

She gives me a calculating look. "What do you propose?"

"I'm craving a club soda."

• • •

Twenty minutes later, we walk from the bright sunshine of Broadway into the dark shadows of Bar63. The place is nearly empty at four-ish in the afternoon, but there are a few patrons taking advantage of happy hour. Tori is behind the bar, expertly brandishing a martini shaker. She doesn't notice me right away. Dani waits by the door. I slide onto what I've come to think of as my stool and wait.

It's a hell of a long shot, pumping Tori for the encryption key. If she does have it, she's not likely to give it to me. Or admit that she even knows what I'm talking about.

The truth is, I have precious little else to go on for finding the encryption key. No one remotely associated with the flash drive has even mentioned it was encrypted, much less how to go about getting the key. Duke was dead before I even knew the flash drive existed. Sam knew it was encrypted but not why or how to decipher it. My mom is in the wind. She could be anywhere doing anything right now. Not to mention it's possible the woman who called Sam wasn't even my mother. It's not like he ever saw her.

"Kennedy, right?" Tori says as she plops a club soda in front of me. No twist.

It takes me a minute to figure out what she's talking about. Kennedy Fairchild is the name on the fake ID I gave her on my first trip to the bar.

"That's right," I say. "I'm impressed you recognized me without the Catholic schoolgirl costume."

"I never forget a face." She smiles at me, the skin at the corners of her eyes branching into the beginnings of crow's-feet. She hands a round of tequila shots to a group of college students that just came in.

I wipe a finger through the condensation on my glass, leaving a spiral pattern of clarity through the mist. "You know, I saw you the other day. At the New World Initiative office. I'm an intern at NWI. Small world, huh?"

"Yes," she says, not meeting my eyes as she scrubs the bar with a towel.

"Tragedy about the founder, isn't it? I got to work with him pretty closely before everything happened," I say, my own voice not as neutral as I'd like it to be. "He showed me this really cool statue of a pink fairy—"

"Blue fairy," Tori corrects me automatically before thinking. Then she stops wiping and closes her eyes. "What do you want?"

"The encryption key," I say. Might as well put it out there. I almost add that I want an explanation as to what the hell is going on, but it's never a good idea to admit to a hostile witness that you don't know as much as they think you do.

She comes over to me and lowers her voice. "I don't have it. I don't have the drive, either, if that's what you're going to ask next. Though if you're asking for the key, then I'm guessing you already have the drive."

"You work for my grandmother, don't you?"

She takes a deep breath, bracing herself against the bar. "I'm not telling you anything."

"It's too much of a coincidence. Victoria Febbi. The blue-fairy flash drive. The bank letter confirming that the safe-deposit box the blue fairy was taken from belonged to my grandmother. It's the only thing that makes sense."

She glares at me, lips pressed together in a line. Looks like it's time to play hardball. I slide off the stool and take out my phone. I pull up Mike's mobile number and show it to her. I press Send and put the phone up to my ear.

As it rings, I say to Tori, "You know my foster father is an FBI agent, right? I think he'd be very interested to know that you're part of the Moretti crime family. Very. Interested."

She dithers for a second or two before finally breaking. "Okay, okay! Stop the call. I'll tell you what you want to know."

"Hi, Mike," I say when he answers.

"Make it quick, kid, I'm in a meeting."

"I was wondering: What's the mandatory minimum sentencing for involvement in organized crime?" I smirk at Tori.

He sighs heavily. "You're trying to get the bartender to talk, aren't you? Fine. But you better fill me in when I get there." Then he hangs up. I'm impressed he already knew the bartender was my target.

I cover the receiver with my hand and say to Tori, "Start talking."

"I'm not talking with him on the phone!" she says.

"And I'm not taking your word for it that you'll tell me everything when I hang up. Start talking or I do." Then I uncover the receiver and pretend to keep talking to Mike. "What was that, Mike? Sorry, my phone cut out for a second." I pause. "Oh, no, just a friend and I debating the subject." I pause again. "Twenty years is the minimum?" I whistle low. "Wow. I'd hate to be the criminal who gets charged with that."

"You're right, okay?" Tori all but whispers. "I work for your grandmother. We didn't know the blue fairy had any value until it was stolen. When we heard the rumors that it was actually a flash drive and that Salinger had it, I was sent to infiltrate his company and get it back."

I pocket my phone, dropping the act. "Did you kill him?" I say, leaning so far over the bar that I'm almost nose to nose with her.

"No. I hadn't found the blue fairy yet. I needed more time. I assumed *they* found it and then killed Salinger. Where do *you* fit into all this?"

"Uh-uh. I'm the one with the FBI on speed dial. You do the talking."

"Well, I'm not answering anything else out here in the open."

That's fair. I signal to Dani, who follows us through the door marked OFFICE. Tori eyes Dani askance but doesn't object. She shuts the door and gestures for us to sit on the well-worn sofa along the wood-paneled wall, then leans against the desk in the middle of the room, crossing her arms.

"Who the hell is 'they'?" I ask.

"Traitors trying to take over the organization."

"If you know they exist, why do you not just eliminate them?" Dani asks.

"We've tried. Obviously, it's complicated."

"And I should care about that because . . . ," I say.

"Because it's your family, too. Your mother may have left us, but she's up to her neck in this. It's not a coincidence that the flash drive is shaped like a blue fairy."

"Who are you?" I ask.

"I'm your second cousin once removed," she says flippantly. She could be lying or she could be telling the truth. I'll likely never know.

"Is Tori your real name?" I ask.

"Of course not. You think 'infiltrate' means handing over my pedigree and résumé and saying, 'If it's all right, can I have the blue-fairy flash drive, please?' Don't be ridiculous."

"Then why *that* name? Didn't you think someone would figure it out?"

"That was the point. We were hoping to draw your mother from hiding without giving away who I was. It didn't work."

"What's your real name?"

"Why do you care? I'm a Moretti. That's all you need to know."

"All right, then, what now? If you don't have the flash drive, and I don't have the flash drive, then who has it?"

"I don't know who else would know its value."

"What *is* its value? What's on it?" Dani asks.

"We don't know. But it's a good bet it's something bad for us. Why else steal it from us?"

"It could be a treasure map."

Tori snorts. "Then it's bad for us that someone else could get to it first."

"Do you know where my mother is?" I ask.

"If we did, we'd just wait until she got the drive back from Salinger and then get it from her."

"And you have no idea what the encryption key is?"

"It doesn't matter, because if I knew, I wouldn't tell you."

"What is Sister Rasmussen's role in all this?"

Tori blinks, surprised. "How did you—?" She shakes her head. "She's your grandmother."

THE HIT

As I push open the door to leave Bar63, I run smack into Mike. Dani slinks out behind me into the light.

"Well?" Mike says.

"I didn't get much," I say. "Mostly conspiracy theories. How'd you figure out I was confronting her?"

"Because I know you well enough by now to guess what you'll do at least about fifty percent of the time," he says. "I was coming to question her myself, actually, but you beat me to it. I still expect you to tell me everything she said."

"All right, but let's grab a latte. All this crazy is making me thirsty."

We head to a diner a few blocks over and order a round of coffees.

"Okay, spill," Mike says. So I do. Partially. I fill him in on the missing blue-fairy flash drive (though I leave out the part about how it was stolen from his house); I tell him about the Moretti angle (minus the bit where my friends broke into Sister Rasmussen's office); and I tell him about suspecting Ackley of being involved (failing to mention our theft of the video footage, of course).

"Why am I just now hearing about this? You should have told me days ago."

"You were too busy investigating the contract out on me. Which I greatly appreciate, by the way." I have been known to throw out some gratitude now and then. You'd be amazed how much a well-placed thank-you redirects people's actions. "How did you know about the bartender? I never told you about her."

He frowns. "Sam confessed to the bank robbery this morning."

"He did *what*?" I gasp. "He's lying! It was me!"

Mike gives me a flat look. "Nice try, Julep. He did the right thing, and you mucking it up by trying to get him out of it will only make things worse for him."

"He doesn't belong in prison, Mike. You know that." My heart is pounding hard. I can't let Mike arrest Sam again. I can't.

"The owner of the safe-deposit box, not to mention the bank, not to mention the NYPD, would beg to differ with you. But I'll do what I can for him. Which is quite a lot, considering he's still a minor and he came forward on his own. Just please, for once, let me handle it."

I take a deep, shuddering breath. "I'll try."

He sighs. "Look, I don't think you should worry about any of this right now. It's enough just trying to keep you alive. The rest can wait." He gives Dani a knowing look over my head. There's definitely something they're not telling me, and whatever it is, I'm pretty sure I'm going to hate it.

I need to get that blue-fairy flash drive back, and fast, before whatever it is they're plotting gets in my way. Duke died for whatever is on that drive, and for all I know, my mom could be next. I'm the only one who knows how to reach the person who has it. So, yeah, it's a trap. But it's my trap, damn it, and only I can spring it.

• • •

"*Milaya*," Dani says reprovingly after I roll down my window to enjoy the early-summer breeze whipping past us. It felt weird at first, actually rolling down a window, but I've gotten used to it over the past few months.

"Oh, come on. It's just a window."

She raises an eyebrow at me, and I roll the window back up again, watching as the world turns a muted gray from the overkill window tint.

"It is for your protection."

I snort my opinion of that reasoning. I do appreciate that Dani decided to take us back to Mike and Angela's the long way—down Sheridan to Lake Shore Drive. Seeing glimpses of the water glittering in the sunlight counteracts some of the weirdness I've felt since the confessions in the windowless bar.

"And speaking of protection," she continues, shifting down to accommodate the slower speed limit along Lake Shore. "I talked with Ramirez while you were in the shower last night, about an FBI safe house. . . ."

Well, that shoe dropped quickly. I thought I'd at least have another day before Mike and Dani's plot began to play out.

"Let me stop you right there," I say. "Before you waste your breath trying to convince me to ship myself off to some undisclosed location to rot, tell me if this place you're talking about is even in Illinois."

Her silence is deep and profound. No, then.

"Is it even in this time zone?" I press.

Dani frowns at the windshield. "A contract out on you is one thing. Spade is something else entirely. He is ex-military, an assassin. Neither Ramirez nor I is equipped to protect you from that. An entire police precinct is not equipped."

"It's like Petrov, Dani. I can fix it if I can face it."

"Not this time."

There's no reasoning with her when she sets her mind on something—Han was right about that.

"Are you coming with me to this safe house in wherever?"

Silence again.

"Then I'm not going."

"I must help find Spade so you can come back."

"Running never works, Dani. You said that to me once, remember?"

"Circumstances change. We have to adapt."

"Stop making boneheaded decisions. Adapt."

Tyler. The memory is so strong, it takes me a minute to remember where I am, and when. I shake my head to clear it.

"This is not a choice I am offering you," Dani says. "I am explaining what will happen. Ramirez and I agreed that my telling you would be best, but it has been decided."

"That is just crap. This is *my* job. My life. I'm not sitting by, buffing my nails, while other people handle it. It's not like I'm helpless. I have a superpower, too."

She sighs. "Your 'superpower' is worse than useless against someone like Spade. If you ever get close enough to use it, you will be dead before you open your mouth."

"That was true of you, too, and now look at us."

A ghost of a smile crosses her lips and is gone again. "I was never trying to kill you. If I were, you would be dead."

That comment sends a chill down my spine.

"I am doing the best I can," she continues, the edge in her voice softening. "And that means getting you as far away from here as possible."

"Dani." I reach across the gearshift and curl my hand around hers. "Please don't do this. Don't send me away. I would sooner have this guy put a bullet in my brain than let you go up against him alone, which is what you're planning, isn't it? I'm a lot of things, but I'm not an idiot."

She doesn't answer. Of course.

It's time to have The Talk again. But how do I tell her what I need to in a way so that she won't immediately shut me down? My grifter abilities are failing me here.

"Listen. I know I'm crap at talking about my feelings. But if

285

there's one thing I figured out from Tyler's death, it's that you get lots of chances to lie and only one chance to tell the truth. So here it goes.

"I know what it's like to think you don't deserve happiness. I've felt that way since the night Tyler died. But all of this is what we choose, what we make of the consequences of those choices. And yeah, we've both made some poor decisions, but that's not all we are."

"It is not the s—"

"I'm not finished yet," I say, squeezing her hand hard. I need to get through all of it now before I chicken out. "The choices you've made whenever I'm around have led to the consequence that I've fallen in love with you." I register her wince when I say that, but I keep going. "You talk about me enacting miracles, but to me, that's the miracle. You made me believe in love after living with a guilt that nearly destroyed me. All your effort at keeping your distance is not going to make that less true. And sacrificing yourself for me is just going to wreck me again."

Her jaw clenches as she stares through the windshield. She's thinking. I can almost hear the wheels turning in her head.

She opens her mouth to speak, but my phone rings. She changes tack and says, "Answer it."

I sigh. "Okay, but we're not done with this conversation."

I look at the caller ID, remembering suddenly that I still haven't called Lily back. But it's not Lily, it's Sam. Maybe he finally found something useful. I press Answer.

"Drugs," Sam says, sounding breathless.

"Drugs?"

"Drugs. Hypnosis. NWI *is* manipulating people, Julep. Fake Mrs. Antolini was right."

"*What?* No way. Duke wouldn't do that." I couldn't be that wrong about everything.

"Not Duke. Devi."

"Dr. Raktabija?" I say, floored. "But *Ackley* killed Duke. Not Dr. Raktabija."

"I'm not saying she killed Duke. I'm saying she's drugging the initiates."

"Start over. What makes you think she's drugging people?"

"She asked a few of the other initiates to stay after the workshop last week. I didn't think anything of it at the time, but then I happened to ask one of the initiates what the extra session was about and *she couldn't remember.* Then Devi asked the same people to stay after today, and I managed to get myself invited. All I remember is it started as a relaxation exercise, and then nothing. Julep, I don't even know if I kept your secret. You could be in danger."

I laugh. "Well, that's not new. But how do you know it wasn't just some sort of deep meditation?"

"Hypnosis doesn't work like that. You may not have full control of your actions, but you remember. Which is where the drugs come in."

"*You* were drugged?" I say.

"Brigitte brought in a snack tray and bottled water. Devi

told each of us to drink, saying that we'd be more relaxed if we were well hydrated. When I finally woke up a few minutes ago, I felt hung over and had a funny, fuzzy taste in my mouth. Julep, I literally drank the Kool-Aid."

"*Crap*," I say. Dani glances at me, concerned. "That's probably why Mr. Antolini is so screwed up. Devi reprogrammed his brain and sent him out to embezzle a bunch of money. His repeated exposure to whatever drug concoction she's serving must have sent him off to cuckoo-land. Where are you now?"

"I'm downtown—just leaving NWI. Where are you?"

"With Dani. We're on North Lake Shore. You're probably only five minutes away from us. Can you meet us at the Ramirezes'? I have to fill you in on the—"

I feel the impact before I cognitively understand that anything has happened. The glass shattering, the great pressure as our velocity switches trajectories from forward to sideways.

The noise is deafening. Tires screech along asphalt, then concrete, then wood. The Chevelle screams as whatever has plowed into us continues to push us toward the harbor.

I finally suck in enough breath to scream myself, grabbing the door handle and bracing my feet against the dash for a follow-up impact that doesn't come.

Dani's unconscious and limp, blood pouring from a cut along her jaw.

"Dani!" I yell, finally noticing the grille of the semitruck obscuring the entire driver's-side window. "Dani!"

"Julep!"

I hear Sam's terrified voice from the phone I'd dropped between the seat and the door. I fish for it and grab it on the first try.

"Sam! Help—"

But before I can give him any details, the Chevelle pitches onto its side. I assume that it's rolling over, that the semi has finally pushed us far enough to tumble upside down. But it's so much worse than that.

The splash as the Chevelle is pushed into the harbor looks like a tsunami from my vantage point. The displaced water rockets into the air like fireworks, and then rains down on the car with a machine-gun sound. The water is freezing as it hits my skin.

The lake is already lapping at my knees, and I have precious little time to get us out of here before we're pulled under. I drop the useless phone and yank at my seat belt, missing the release button three times in my haste. I breathe deep and finally calm my shaking hands enough to use them.

Getting Dani free is not nearly so easy.

"Dani!" I screech at her, my voice a dried husk of itself. I climb onto my seat to escape the inexorable lake. I reach for her seat belt buckle, but it's warped from the impact, and I can't unlatch the belt no matter how hard I squeeze the button.

The water is up to her hips now, which means it's up to my rib cage. If I don't get us both out of here, we're going to drown.

And as soon as I think that, a great bubble burbles up from beneath us, and the Chevelle sinks faster. The water's up to my neck before I remember Dani's gun.

I reach under her jacket and feel around for the holster I

know is there. My numb fingers finally locate it, but I have a bitch of a time unsnapping the strap that holds the gun in the holster.

I yank the gun free just as our heads sink beneath the surface. I open my eyes, ignoring the sting, and panic for a split second that I didn't take a big enough breath before being pulled under. The roof of the Chevelle is underwater with us, so there's no possibility of breathing until I get us out of this car. Us. Because I'm not leaving without her.

The thought galvanizes me, and I hold on to my renewed focus, even through the fear that the gun might not work underwater. I steel my resolve, I position Dani's gun an inch from the buckle, and I pull the trigger.

THE HOSPITAL

The gun kicks back into my hand, a bubble ballooning at the muzzle and disappearing just as quickly. The buckle shatters and the belt floats free. By now my lungs are burning and my vision is starting to go dark around the edges. I'm out of time. If I'm going to save us, it has to be now.

I circle my arms around Dani's chest, praying that none of her body parts are pinned beneath any part of the Chevelle. My heart nearly stops when her foot catches on the steering wheel while I'm trying to maneuver us through the broken driver's-side window. But her foot comes free on its own, and I get us clear enough of the car that I can risk pushing off from it toward the surface.

It feels like it takes hours to break the surface, but it's probably only a minute. I suck in a giant lungful of air, and then pull with all my strength to get Dani's head above water as well. No doubt her lungs are already full of lake, but I can't fight instinct.

"Help!" I scream. "Help me, please!"

Two splashes pelt me with more water. Hands pull Dani away from me. Other hands tug me by the armpits to the nearest floating dock. The taste of harbor water fills my mouth, and I splutter. My rescuer heaves me onto the dock. I stumble-crawl away from the edge and collapse. I cough and gasp and shiver. I can't tell if I'm crying or if it's just my water-soaked hair dripping all over my face.

As soon as I am capable of speech, I ask, "Where is she? Where is she?"

My rescuer, a bedraggled-looking woman in a waterlogged business suit, points down the dock to where an equally waterlogged Sam is performing CPR on Dani.

I drag myself to where Dani is lying like death on the cement.

"Stay back," Sam says between rescue breaths.

But I don't. I can't. I curl up next to her as Sam continues CPR. I can't remember the words she said to me. I'm sure I'll mangle them beyond recognition, because I don't know a scrap of Ukrainian. I'm going to try anyway. Anything to keep her here with me.

"*Hoўda, hoўda-hoў, nichenḱa. . . .* Don't leave me. Please, Dani. Dani, Dani, Dani. *Hoўda, hoўda-hoў, nichenḱa. . . .*"

Sam and I settle into a rhythm. Over and over. Breathe, breathe, don't leave me, compress, please, compress, Dani, Dani, compress, *Hoўda, hoўda-hoў, nichenḱa,* breathe.

The EMTs arrive in a rush of movement at odds with the slow motion inside the bubble of space around me and Dani. I lose track of Sam. There is only me and her. Even when the EMTs move her to a stretcher and into the back of the ambulance, I don't let go of her hand. No one protests as I climb in with her. Or maybe they do and I don't notice. Where she goes, I go.

The ride to the hospital exists in a temporal vacuum. The EMTs work on her, following protocols that have no meaning to me. The only thing I can do is stroke her hair and will her to wake up.

When we arrive at the hospital, I pace next to the stretcher through the aseptic halls to a pair of double doors. Then the nurses intercede. It takes three of them to break my grip on Dani and block me from mindlessly following her into the back.

One of the nurses stays with me. He's trying to talk to me, but I ignore him. There's nothing he can say that will change the fact that Dani is probably going to die. It's Tyler all over again. What have I done?

Sam bursts through the emergency-room doors a few minutes later. "What's going on?" he asks the nurse standing next to me.

I don't pay attention to the nurse's response, but I see Sam nod as he takes my hand. He leads me to a couple of chairs in the waiting area. My vision goes dark around the edges again, and I can't seem to get enough oxygen. I sink into a chair and force myself to take deeper, slower breaths. Sam squeezes my hand.

"It's not your fault," Sam says. "Don't think for a second it's your fault."

"It was a hit meant for me. How is it not my fault?"

"Whoever was behind the wheel of the semi, it's his fault. You can't make him pay if you're too busy blaming yourself."

My breath calms, comes easier. I no longer have to remind myself to exhale. As usual, Sam knows exactly what to say to make me see reason. I get up and walk to the window, then back again. Sam watches from his chair, his expression wrecked. He's still wet, but then so am I. I turn and walk back to the window. I can't hold still. I can't, or I'll crumble.

Angela comes striding through the door. She spots us and makes a beeline for me. She throws her arms around me. "Oh, thank god," she says, squeezing me tight. She pulls back and swings a tote bag from her shoulder. "I brought you dry clothes." She hands me the tote bag, and I look at it blankly.

She catches on to my disoriented state and leads me to the bathroom herself. I'm not sure how she finds it. It's down a far hall, and she works at Mercy. We're at Northwestern.

"Can you change by yourself?" she asks.

I nod and drop the bag. I make it to a toilet stall just in time to vomit. Angela grabs my tangled hair to hold it back. Her touch is soothing, and I shudder under it. She whispers to me in Spanish, and I'm profoundly grateful that I don't understand what she's saying.

Once I feel steadier, I clean myself up and change clothes. She hovers near me but doesn't interfere, doesn't demand anything. When I'm ready, she loops her arm around my shoulders and guides me back to the god-awful waiting area.

Sam leaps up when we return. He's not alone, though. Ralph is with him.

"I'm so sorry, *jang mi*. I would've prevented it if I could. I will take over as bodyguard until yours is back on her feet."

The concern on his face sends me over the edge. I collapse into the nearest chair and sob, covering my face with my hands. Sam rushes over and kneels in front of me.

"What can I do?" he says.

"Nothing."

He takes my hands so I'll look at him. "There must be something."

I shake my head, fighting to regain control. The last thing Dani needs is for me to freak out right now.

About twenty minutes later, the buzzer that the front desk gave us in exchange for our paperwork starts buzzing. With Ralph in tow, Angela and I meet the doctor in an alcove off the waiting area reserved for doctor–family member interactions. He looks capable and experienced and grave. Grave isn't good.

He starts to ask the obligatory family question, but I cut him off. "We're the only family she has," I say.

He nods and lets it go. "We managed to stabilize her. She's breathing on her own, but it took both endotracheal intubation and positive end-expiratory pressure." He goes on to talk about maintaining adequate oxygenation, shifting interstitial pulmonary fluid, and increasing lung volume. All of which sounds vaguely positive. It's when he mentions respiratory failure that I feel the freak-out starting to come back.

"So what does that mean? Is she going to . . ."

"Her chances for full recovery would be good if water aspiration were her only medical issue. But she's also experienced some amount of cranial trauma, and I'm concerned that she hasn't regained consciousness yet. Head injuries are notoriously unpredictable. She could wake up and be fine." He hesitates before continuing. "But it's also possible she may never wake up."

The bottom drops out of my stomach, and if I had anything left to throw up, I'd do it.

"What about brain damage?" Angela asks. God, I hadn't even thought of that.

"There's no way for us to know until she's conscious."

"Can I see her?" I ask, my voice like sandpaper.

"I'm afraid not. We've moved her to the ICU for now, but she won't be strong enough for visitors until the morning, if then. You can call the nurses' desk tomorrow to find out if you can visit."

I nod, my eyes burning. Angela squeezes my hand, and then peppers the doctor with additional questions. The doctor's answers are mostly vague and unsatisfactory. He doesn't know much more than we do. But he says that Dani's youth and strong constitution are compelling factors in her favor. Thanks, doc.

The doctor's phone beeps, and he checks the message. "I

have to go. But the nurses will know Ms. Ivanov's status, if you want to check in. If her condition changes, someone will call the contact number listed on her medical chart." Which happens to be Mike's, because my phone is at the bottom of Lake Michigan.

Angela thanks the doctor, but I'm too lost in a fog of anxiety and self-loathing to remember my manners. I did this. Sam's right—I have to get the assassin behind the wheel and make him pay. But Sam's also wrong. It is my fault. Because, deep down, I knew this would happen. That the bullet with my name on it would hit her instead of me. But I never wanted that. If she was going to fall protecting me, then I should have fallen, too. Why am I still here?

And then suddenly I get it. Spade is too good to have missed me by accident. He *meant* to take Dani out of the picture first. He's probably taking out my protectors one by one, in order of threat level. Which means Mike is next on his list. My guts are in knots, but I have to do something.

"Angela," I say, taking her hand. "Dani said there's a safe house. I think you should go. Make Mike go, if you can. But go now. Before—" I cut myself off, closing my eyes and lips until I regain control.

"Julep," Angela says. I open my eyes. "I'm not going anywhere. And neither is Mike." She looks like she wants to say more but is dangerously close to tears herself.

I want to insist, I want to trick her into it, but I'm not that strong a person. Instead I nod, fear of them staying washing over me even as fear of being abandoned recedes. I know that eventually I will have to face my enemies alone. It's the only way I can flush them out, and the only way I'll be able to live with myself afterward. But for now, it's enough that I can lean into Angela's soft hug and feel *home*.

• • •

Two hours later, I'm still at the hospital. Murphy and Bryn have come and gone, bringing Sam a change of clothes. Angela offered to beg off work and stay with me, but I said I'd be okay if she went. Ralph sticks around, showing no signs of leaving any time soon. Sam is still here as well, playing with his phone in a far-off section of the waiting room. One of the nurses comes over to kick me out of the alcove, but I'm leaving it anyway. I settle in the chair next to Sam's. He doesn't look up. I don't say anything. We sit like that for another fifteen minutes, each of us steeped in our own thoughts.

"I don't know what to say," I say.

"Then don't say anything. We've never needed words before."

I slide down in my seat. "You saved her life. Thank you," I say.

He smiles sardonically. "Don't thank me. It's weird."

And just that one simple thing, him reminding me of what we used to have, destroys the paper-thin protective layer I'd erected between myself and my emotional overload. I start weeping again.

Sam puts his arm around me and draws me close. "What can I do?" he asks for the second time this hospital visit.

It takes me a while to answer. "I need to see her."

Sam leaves without another word. When he returns, he waves me over to the door leading to the ICU. I follow him to the nearest supply closet, where he outfits me in scrubs, clipping a badge he'd clearly stolen from a nurse to the pocket.

"It won't fool them for long," he says. "When you get in there, remember to wash your hands. It's the ICU, not a wellness clinic."

I try to smile at him, but in my current state, it probably looks more like a grimace.

He hands me his burner phone. "Just in case," he says. He checks to make sure the hall is clear before leaving. I leave a few minutes later and walk briskly through the ICU hallway, checking the sliding glass doors for patient names. Two Smiths and a Velasquez later, I find her. Ivanov.

I walk into her room, sliding the door closed behind me. I pull the curtain to block us from view. With luck, the other nurses will think a doctor's with her, and vice versa. I use the hand-sanitizer dispenser at the head of Dani's bed, remembering Sam's warning.

The tubes crawling out of her pallid skin into machines that beep and flash make her look like an extra from one of Sam's sci-fi movies. Her tattoos stand out in stark relief, but even they seem weakened somehow, as if Dani's life force is what gave them strength. I trace the manacles on her wrist with my finger.

Tears slide down my cheeks, silent this time. *I did this.*

"I'm so sorry, Dani," I say, my voice tiny.

The cut along her jaw has been taped closed with Steri-Strips. Her left arm is red and purple from where the door of the Chevelle dented on impact, pinning it to her side. I don't see evidence of a head injury, but I'm sure it hurts like a bitch.

I crawl onto her bed, careful not to jostle her or knock any of the tubes or wires. I tuck my hair behind my ears and lay down along her right side. I stroke her cheek, her neck. I rest my hand over her heart, clinging to the ridiculous idea that my touching it will magically help her heal.

"Please, Dani. Wake up. I know there's nothing here for you really. I know Olena and the others are waiting for you, and that I'm not much compared with that. But please, please. It's not your time yet. They will wait for you. Please come back."

The only answer I get is the beeping of the machines. She doesn't move, much less wake. So I try a different tack.

"I'm still in a lot of trouble. All sorts of people are trying to kill me. You hate that."

Still nothing, but the gentle teasing makes me feel a little less like I'm bleeding internally. I snuggle in closer, inhaling the sick, aseptic smell of hospitals. She doesn't smell like Dani at all, but that doesn't stop me from kissing her ear, her temple, her nose. Then I burrow into the crook between her jaw and shoulder, finally giving in to exhaustion.

An indeterminate amount of time later, I'm jarred awake by Sam's burner phone buzzing under me. I shake off the heavy fog, trying to remember where I am. Then I remember and I'm confused, thinking a nurse or doctor has woken me and then left. The phone buzzes again, drawing my attention to my pocket. I sit up and wipe my face. I pull out the phone and press Answer.

"Hello?" I say.

"Julep, finally." It's Lily.

"Lily? What is it? I'm in the hospital."

"I know. Sam called. I'm so sorry, Julep. This is all my fault."

"All *your* fault? What do you mean?"

"It's my mom." I can hear the tears, the conflict in her voice. "She put the contract out on you."

THE DEAL WITH THE DEVIL

I wake up with a cramp in my hand and a gross taste in my mouth. I pick myself up from the nest of Dani's blankets. I didn't mean to fall asleep in her apartment, but I guess yesterday got the better of me. I snuck out of Mike's house (FBI detail didn't stand a chance) and took the "L" to Dani's, because I didn't want to have to face anyone before making my next move. I could have gone to the Ballou instead of breaking into Dani's apartment, but I wanted to be surrounded by her smell while I waited for the morning.

I managed to eke out a plan from the bare scraps of brain I have left after everything that's happened in the past twelve hours. Will the plan work? Hell if I know. But it's time to give it the old con-artist try.

I yawn the entire way to the kitchen. Dani doesn't have

a coffeepot, of course, which is a downer. I use the time to shower instead, washing all the lake grime out of my hair with her shampoo. And if the water running down my face has a higher salt content than water that comes from a faucet normally does, well, I'm not telling.

If Mike made it through the night, then he has a fifty-fifty chance of making it through the day. Especially if I don't go near him. Spade, in my grifter opinion, likes to make a point before he neutralizes his target. He took out Dani with me watching, and he didn't even break a sweat. Mike, Sam, Murphy. I'd be an idiot to think any of them are safe. But Spade won't do anything unless I'm watching. And since I won't risk my friends, I'm as good as on my own.

Lucky for me, I have plenty of enemies.

I finish my shower and get dressed for the day ahead. I brought jeans, my Converse, a T-shirt, and a hoodie with me from Mike's. I'm not a corporate intern anymore, not a Catholic schoolgirl. I'm just me. Julep. Patron saint of lost girls.

I text Mike that I'm at the hospital with Ralph and slide on a pair of sunglasses to protect my pounding head from the early-summer sun. Days like this, it's good to be a bad guy.

My first stop is the chapel. Lily asked me to meet her when we talked last night. I figured the chapel was fitting.

I pull open the heavy oak door that leads to the nave. I'm not sure what I'll find when I go in. Will she be contrite? Will she still be angry? Even more of a mystery, how will I react? When her brother betrayed me, I threw a raging hissy fit. Then he died, and I never got to take it back. What will I do when I come face to face with a girl whose silence put Dani in a coma?

I don't actually see Lily until she tackle-hugs me. She's crying like her heart is breaking. I can tell that she's not hugging me because she's sorry or because she cares for me. She's clinging to the only moss-covered rock in a storm-tossed sea. I know how that feels. I reach my arms around her and pull her close. Neither of us speaks, but we don't need to. Not about this. She used to be Tyler's sister, but she's my sister now.

After a long while, her sobs turn to little sniffles and hiccups. "She's my mother," she whispers. "I couldn't— But Tyler loved you. So I had to know. If you were worth saving."

I smile. "I guess you must have decided I am."

"Truthfully, I'm still on the fence," she says, wiping her eyes. "But no one's death is going to undo my brother's. Death just breeds more death. I couldn't be a part of that. Even for her."

"I get it," I say, bumping my chin on the top of her head.

She straightens and pulls away. "I should go home before she suspects something."

"Does she know you know?"

Lily shakes her head. "Or she might, actually. I don't think she cares if I know. She's out of her mind with grief still. She's a zombie when she's not in a rage. She spends most of her time in Tyler's room."

I shudder with guilt and sorrow before forcing my attention back to Lily. "If you're not sure, then it's not safe. Can I see your phone?"

She hands it to me, hesitant. I don't know if she'll ever trust me, but that's neither here nor there at the moment. I type Mike's office address into the nav app.

I show her the phone. "Can you get here? Buses only, cash only."

"It's not that far," she says. "Why cash only?"

"I don't want anyone tracking you."

"Okay. But aren't you coming with me?"

"I have some errands to run. When you get in the building, ask for Mike. Tell him what you told me, but don't tell him where I am. If he asks, say I'm at the hospital. Tell him I said to take care of you until I get back."

She nods. "Where are you going?"

"I'm taking my kings out of the back row," I say, nudging her arm with my elbow. Then I turn to leave.

"Wait. You still have my phone."

"I know," I say, and walk out of the church.

• • •

My next stop is the Chinese restaurant Dani and I staked out a week ago. I hate being here without her. I hate being here without the Chevelle. I hate being here at all.

The restaurant isn't even open yet, but I won't have to wait long. If Han is half as good as Dani, she'll find me.

Forty-five minutes later, Han shows up. "What the hell are you doing here? This is my territory, and I don't tolerate rats."

"We prefer the term 'criminal informants,'" I say, leaning against a fancy lamppost. "Dani's in the hospital." It's heartless to throw it at her like that, but I need to shock her into opening her mind to helping me.

She pales. "I heard about the accident. Your fault?"

I nod. "Yours, too."

"How do you figure that? I'm not the one with a contract out on me."

"Yet you knew who took the contract and you did nothing to stop it." I'm gambling that she feels some measure of guilt over this. "He was aiming for her. If he'd wanted me dead, Dani would be standing here and I'd be in the hospital. Or the morgue."

She flinches. Grifter: 1. Ex-girlfriend: 0.

"What do you want? You wouldn't be here if you didn't want something from me." Her chin inches up with each word. It's taking her considerable effort to overcome her pride.

"I need you to convince Spade to change his plans and come after me now."

"How am I supposed to do that?"

"You have the message board, your extensive underground network. Surely you can find him and convince him you have inside knowledge as to when I'll be vulnerable. Tell him I'm being sent to a safe house. That should up his timetable."

She rolls her eyes. "He's a professional. He's not just going to fall for someone willing to give him insider information. Besides, I'm not a grifter. I don't lie like it's breathing."

"Then threaten to shut him out. Start a rumor that you're

going to take me down for personal reasons before he has the chance. He'll have to follow you to make sure you don't."

"What if he tries to kill *me?*"

"Are you saying you can't evade one little hit man for the rest of the day? Didn't you say you were an enforcer or something?"

She glares white-hot daggers of rage at me. "What's to stop me from actually killing you? For 'personal reasons.'"

"I'll take my chances," I say. "Be at Bar63 on North Broadway by nine tonight." Then I end with, "For Dani." Because I can't not.

• • •

My last errand is the one I've been dreading, and that's saying something since I just came from a tête-à-tête with Genghis Han.

The president's house is a beautifully renovated turn-of-the-century Tudor about a mile from campus. I've never been inside. Had I a choice, I wouldn't be trying to get in now. But if enemies are the only allies available to me, then I'll take them.

I ring the bell. It's actually kind of normal-sounding. Not the overly dramatic cathedral bells I'd anticipated.

A young aide opens the door. "Sister Rasmussen has been expecting you," she says.

"I'll bet she has," I say.

"Please, follow me."

The aide takes me to the kitchen in the back of the house. This is hardly comforting. There are lots of knives in the kitchen. And any screaming is not likely to be heard from the street. Not that I think she'll try to kill me. Probably. She's my grandmother, after all.

"Can I get you a drink?" the aide asks.

"No, thank you," I say, thinking about Persephone and pomegranate seeds.

The president keeps me stewing for almost fifteen minutes. I suppose it's a demanding profession, running the largest Catholic high school in Chicago. Or dominating the international criminal underworld. Or both.

When she does finally deign to grace me with her presence, she is still wrapped head to foot in the nun getup. "Ms. Dupree," she says with her usual aplomb.

"Sister Rasmussen," I say, just as calmly.

"Come to ask for another favor?" she says, arching an eyebrow.

"I've come to ask for help in protecting your investment."

"What investment is that?"

"Me."

"I see." She skirts the opposite side of the kitchen island, keeping the polished countertop between us. "Difficulties with your summer internship, I presume?"

That's right. Rub it in, why don't you?

"A few. And I was hoping you could help me resolve one or two of them."

"Exactly how would the president of a preparatory school do that?"

"I'm sure you have all sorts of resources at your disposal."

"Suppose I could offer you the resources you need. What would you give me in return? Or are you going to throw the school into jeopardy again so you can rescue it?"

"Harsh but fair. No, I don't have a badger game prepped this time. I'm hoping family ties still mean something in the twenty-first century."

She gives me a warning look, but I haven't pushed her so far as to make her brush me off. I have to tread carefully. She still hasn't admitted anything I can use against her if this all goes south.

"If you do not have collateral to bargain with, then I have a suggestion."

"I'm listening," I say, suddenly even more leery of wolves in nuns' clothing.

"The Brillion internship is still open." She smirks at me. It's a small smirk, but it's definitely there. "I'll give you what you need if you agree to take the internship for the rest of the summer."

I pretend to consider her offer. In truth, a summer internship is nothing for what I'm asking. But my daddy didn't raise an idiot. My sentence would be to the Moretti family business, or my name isn't Julep Dupree. . . . Okay, well, you know what I mean.

"Fine, I'll do the internship, if you help me today *and* if you make the New York investigation against Sam for that safe-deposit-box theft go away."

She pretends to consider my counteroffer. I'm sure she doesn't give a crap one way or the other about whether Sam goes down for the safe-deposit box, and I highly doubt sabotaging an investigation would take more than a drop of her considerable power. It's more a show of good faith on her part than something that would take any real effort. It's a good deal for her, and it's not a terrible deal for me.

"Done. You start on Monday. Brillion office, eight a.m. sharp." She clasps the delicate gold crucifix hanging around her neck. "I think I have just the resource you need."

Did she just call someone simply by touching her necklace? I am seriously impressed. I want one of those.

I hear the door to the back hallway open and close, followed by footsteps on the marble tile floor. I'm surprised to not hear heels, though. I guess I assumed Fake Mrs. Antolini would still be in the same outfit she'd come to my office in.

But it's not Fake Mrs. A who rounds the corner.

"Ralph?" I say, shocked.

"Thank you for joining us, Mr. Chen. Ms. Dupree has a problem for which she needs to make use of your considerable talents."

Ralph bows to me, silent, expression completely neutral. No guilt, no surprise, no affection, nothing. He's not playing it like he doesn't recognize me, either, which no doubt means that my grandmother knows our whole history. She was probably the one who sent him to watch me from the beginning of his friendship with my dad. She probably knows things about me that I don't even know. The thought makes me shudder.

Get it together, grifter.

"Well, this is unexpected," I say, ignoring the million questions crowding my brain. Right now, only one thing matters. "Shall we get started?"

THE BAR

Most people think that the trick to the three-card monte is the sleight of hand, the dealer's ability to switch the lady out for a worthless card without the mark noticing. But prestidigitation is just a tool. It's a necessary part of the game, but it's not *the trick*. The trick is getting the mark to believe he can win.

In my case, Spade already thinks he can win. He's had the upper hand since he took the contract. But I'm not his usual kind of target. I don't run to my friends or the police or even strike out on my own. I'm craftier than that, and he'll likely underestimate me. Ackley will be harder to lure. He's easily as crafty as I am and will be tougher to tempt out of his lair. But it certainly helps that I know what he wants. I can pretend I have it and he'll have to face me to find out if I do.

I unlock and open the door to Bar63. The bar is uncharacteristically empty for a Saturday evening. The Closed sign on the door probably has something to do with it. I had Sister Rasmussen close it for the occasion. It's amazing the places you can get into when you have the key.

I check Lily's phone for the time: 8:19 p.m. I open the text app. I tap Ackley's *Phony* number into the *To* box, and then type the following message:

I have the encryption key. If you want it, meet me at Bar63 at 9:00 tonight. Come alone.

I tap Send and take a seat on a barstool at the empty bar. Now for the waiting.

I could call the hospital, find out how Dani is. But I think it's better if I don't know. If she's awake, I won't be able to concentrate. If she's not, the same. But if I don't know, I can hold off thinking about it. I remember the Chevelle, and my heart thumps painfully. There'll be no saving it from the impound lot this time. *Good car,* I think, stroking its hood in my mind.

Time passes as I swipe through memory after memory of friends and jobs and St. Agatha's and Mike and Angela. Tyler, too. I linger on him now, remembering the boy and not the pain. But it's like looking at someone else's life. A different Julep from a parallel dimension.

I stop myself before my sappiness gets to the puddle stage. I pick up Lily's phone again and type in Dani's phone number. I hold the phone to my ear and wait. Her phone is either at the bottom of the lake with the Chevelle or waterlogged past repair, but I'm not really trying to call her.

This is Dani Ivanov. Leave a message.

I take a deep breath, the bands around my chest loosening for a half second before ratcheting down even tighter. I end the call and redial the number, listening as it rings before the voice mail picks up. I repeat the cycle several times, a junkie on a binge, before deciding I should leave an actual message. Who knows what will happen tonight? And if she does wake up, I want her to know—I don't know. Something.

This is Dani Ivanov. Leave a message.

"It's me. I—" I close my eyes, listening to a second tick by. Two. I don't actually know what to say. She wouldn't want to hear me say I'm sorry. "I'm going to fix it, Dani. When you get this, if I—" My voice cracks, damn it. "If I'm not around, I just want you to know that I'm thinking about you." Man, as last messages go, this one really sucks. "Tell the others I'm thinking about them, too." I pause and then laugh at myself sardonically. "I'm a grifter, I should know how to do this better. I never was any good at being real. Except with you." I pause again, wanting to say more but not knowing what. I end the call.

Han takes the barstool next to me with lethal grace. It must be later than I thought.

"Nice message," she says, unwrapping a stick of gum and folding it in her mouth.

She heard. Fabulous. That's just . . . perfect.

"You're the reason we broke up, you know," she says, alternately wadding up the wrapper and smoothing it out.

"Dani said it was because you asked her if she loved you and she said no."

Han clenches her jaw, then keeps chewing. "Yeah. Why do you think she said no?"

I dig my nails into the polished wood of the barstool. "Are you trying to make me feel worse?"

"Maybe," she says.

Well, I did ask.

"What time is it?" I say.

"Showtime." She nods at the door, which is nudging open as we speak. "Break a leg, grifter. Or both legs." Then she's gone.

I slide off the stool to face the fate I made. *Keep your eye on the lady.*

My mark walks into the bar.

"Aadila," I say.

"Julep," she says, much less surprised than I am. She's wearing black. Black cargo pants, black crew-neck sweater, even a black skullcap. No hijab, I notice. And she's clearly not here for the chicken wings. "Expecting someone else?" she taunts.

"How did you—? But the footage. The fairy." I'm stumbling over my words like a moron.

"Ackley was a stooge. Easily manipulated to do things I wanted him to—like go to Duke's office at a certain time for no good reason. I told him to ask about the blue pixie to hook you. Almost as easy to manipulate as you with your weakness for the young and marginalized. Throw a scarf over my head, whip out a pithy sentence or two, and you were eating out of my hand."

I scowl at her. "So I'm guessing Aadila isn't your real name."

"Nope," she says, smiling. "But I picked it because it means 'just,' 'honest,' 'upright.' Isn't that kind of poetic?"

"What do I call you?"

"Aadila works," she says. "Or Your Highness. Whichever."

I need to get this conversation back on track. Spade could show up any second.

"If you're here, where's Ackley?" I ask.

"The canal, probably. I killed him and his mother so no one could sound the alarm for a few days. I changed his address on the employee directory to send you to a house that looked like a front. And I planted that phone number for you to find. *Phony*. Get it?" She chuckles. "I kill myself."

"Why go to all that trouble? Why not just kill me, too?"

"Come on, Julep. We're the same, you and I. Except I'm slightly better than you. But in any case, I figured if anyone could find the encryption key it would be you.

"How'd you get it out of him, anyway? I interrogated the sneaky bastard for two days and got nothing. The poison I used on him should have rendered his brain completely useless, but I guess he clung to that one thing until he could tell someone he trusted. Intriguing. I may have to do a study on it. You know, when I get into med school."

Is she talking about Duke? But he was shot, not poisoned. And he certainly didn't have a chance to tell me anything. She just admitted to killing Ackley. So who the hell is she talking about?

"Where's the flash drive?" I ask. "I'm not giving you the encryption key until I see it."

"That's not true. You'll give me the encryption key as soon as I ask. But I'll humor you." She lifts the chain she's wearing around her neck. The blue-fairy flash drive is attached to it like a pendant. I feel a slight measure of vindication in predicting that a person who'd leave me a taunting note with their contact info wouldn't be able to resist taunting me with the drive itself.

"I know you're not working alone."

"Well spotted. Maybe there's hope for you yet."

"It's Devi Raktabija, isn't it? She was Duke's right hand and got too greedy, watching all those people with access to millions waltzing in and out of NWI. She couldn't resist."

Aadila laughs. It sounds a lot like a cartoon-villain laugh.

"Just a note: criminals don't really laugh like that anymore."

Her smile broadens. "I like you. Too bad he wants me to kill you."

"He?" I ask.

"He," says a new voice behind me. Joseph enters the room.

I nearly fall off my stool in surprise this time. I really need to turn in my detective-in-training badge. I *suck* at this. I manage to keep it together but only just. Any time now, Spade. Really.

"So Devi's a patsy, too?" I ask, stalling.

"Devi's an idealistic fool. She actually believed in that garbage Duke was selling about self-actuation and manifesting your fullest potential." Joseph snorts. "Sanctimonious bullshit.

No one *gives* you a leg up in this world. The only advantage is the one you take when no one else is looking."

"That whole sob story about being out on the streets? That was all a lie?"

"Yes and no. I did come to them as a street punk, but it was a cover."

"What's the blue fairy to *you*?"

"A paycheck. I'm a contractor. Sort of like you." He smiles at me, his eyes crinkling at the corners. I can't believe I never noticed how crazy it makes him look. "Unfortunately, you showing up kick-started Duke's flabby grifter instincts. He knew things were heading south the second you set foot in the building. He began suspecting me after I instituted the relaxation exercises. I tried to rope Devi into planning them to throw off Duke's suspicions, but he saw through that eventually. Which is why I had to kill him before I could get the blue fairy. But I'm a grifter of many gifts, so I figured it was only a matter of time before I found it."

"Devi had no idea what you were doing?"

"You had no idea what I was doing," he points out. "I'm just that good."

"But why even bother going to so much trouble manipulating the NWI initiates? Wasn't the blue fairy your objective?"

"It wasn't my only objective," Joseph says, flashing the charismatic grin. "And I really *can't* tell you any more." He nods to Aadila. She smirks and pulls out a black velvet bag. "I think it's time that we get down to business. You have the encryption key. I want the encryption key. Hand it over."

"Where's your gun?"

"I don't need a gun. You're going to hand it over to me of your own free will." He lifts his hand and points at me. I focus on his finger and watch as he moves his hand to the side.

"Sleep," he says softly. And I do.

• • •

"Wake."

I come to cross-tied between a table leg and a ceiling support, my arms wide and unmovable. I blink rapidly, trying to remember what just happened. Oh, right. Joseph.

He smiles at me. "Your more authentic self told me that you don't actually have the encryption key. That rather upsets me. So here's what's going to happen: I'm going to leave Aadila to play with you while I go make a phone call." He pats my head and turns to Aadila. "No need to leave her mind intact. I'm sure they'll bargain for her with or without her sanity."

Joseph strolls off humming to himself like a crazy person, which he clearly is. Crazy and really, really good.

"I am very much looking forward to trying out my special compound again," Aadila says, squatting next to me. "It's taken me years to perfect. I started working on it when I was twelve."

"How does a kid become a poisoner?"

"Oh, same old story," she says. "I answered an ad on Craigslist."

"You're sick."

"Am I? Or is sympathy the sickness? You can't honestly say

that you don't see your gaping chasm of compassion as a weakness."

I can't honestly say that, no. I've always considered my feelings to be my grifter's Achilles' heel. But faced with Aadila, with the atrocities she's committed, I can't help but recognize myself in her.

Is this who I'd become if I could stop myself from caring? If I could block out my guilt over what happened to Tyler, eradicate my feelings for Dani, use up and throw away Murphy, Bryn, and Sam? Is that what I want, really?

"Well, Julep? Are you a grifter or a phony?"

I am the patron saint of lost girls.

"They may be sheep, but they're *my* sheep," I snarl. "Just do whatever it is you're going to do already. I'm losing brain cells just listening to you talk."

She chuckles and pulls out a wicked-looking bowie knife. Running the flat edge along my cheek, she says, "This is going to be fun."

I close my eyes, prepping myself for pain, when the door creaks open. I can't see who has come in since I'm facing away, but I can see Aadila's reaction. Her eyes widen and she grips the knife tighter as she stands up. I'm desperately hoping it's my second guest and *not* the cavalry. Though, if it were the cavalry, they'd probably have announced their presence loudly and a lot.

"What do you want?" Aadila asks.

"Your prisoner," says a cool, dispassionate, and undeniably feminine voice.

"I hate to disappoint you, but I had her first, and I have obligations to my employer."

"As I have to mine."

Click. Same sound, different gun. A round slides into the chamber.

THE THREE-CARD MONTE

"**W**ait," Aadila says, raising her empty hand. "Maybe we can come to some sort of compromise."

"I'm not interested in compromise," the woman says. "Give me my target and walk. Otherwise, I'll take her and you'll be carried out in a bag. Your choice."

All doubt of the woman's identity evaporates with her use of the word *target*. *Spade*. A *woman*. The rumors must be part of her cover. I hope she's as good as they say. Well, almost.

"Who's the girl?" Aadila asks, clearly stalling. Wait. Girl? What girl?

Faint whimpering sounds behind me. "She's none of your con—"

Sounds of a scuffle erupt. I crane my head to see, but the booth blocks my view. Joseph must have gotten the drop on Spade, damn it.

"Julep!" cries a terrified Lily.

Oh, *crap.*

"Lily!" I shout back. "Get out of here!"

"I can't!"

Aadila leaps into the fray with Spade and, I presume, Joseph. The tussle turns into a battle with objects breaking and shrapnel flying through the air.

I fight to get out of the zip ties. Unfortunately, being tied spread eagle makes breaking out a challenge, but I might still be able to do it. I manage the wriggling necessary to line up the locks, and with a couple of sharp yanks, the ratchet on the table-leg tie breaks, freeing my hand. Without hesitation, I grab the ruined zip tie to shim the tie holding my other hand to the pole. But it slips in my fingers and lands on the floor, skittering just out of reach.

The fight tumbles onto the floor in front of me. I yank back my legs just in time to keep them from getting squashed under Joseph, who springs to his feet at once, although he's holding his ribs and there's a bleeding cut on his forehead. Aadila isn't faring much better. She's lost her knife in the fight, but the blue fairy is still dangling around her neck.

Spade is a relentless blur of black Lycra, the bottom half of her head shaved close, the other half sporting a braided knot at the apex of her skull.

If I could just get free of this last zip tie, I could snag the blue fairy and take off while they're distracting each other. That was the original plan, anyway. The plan that is now blown to smithereens because I hadn't counted on Lily.

"Lily!"

"I'm here!" she calls from behind my booth.

"Get over here, now!" I say.

The bench moves, opening a small gap wide enough for Lily to squeeze through and under the table.

"What are you doing here? How did she get you?"

"She caught me on the way to the bus stop. Julep, I didn't get a chance to tell Mike."

"Never mind that," I say. "I need the zip tie on the floor over there. Can you reach it?"

Just then, Spade whirls a back kick into Aadila's stomach, sending her flying through the air and crashing into the bar. The shelves along the wall behind the bar shiver for a split second and then break apart, sending a hundred or more bottles of booze crashing to the floor. The noise is deafening.

Joseph launches himself at Spade, but she's ready for him. They grapple, both crashing to the ground again, though Spade is a hair quicker. Joseph is covered in cuts and is limping. Spade doesn't have a mark on her.

"Now, Lily! Get me the tie, then get out," I hiss.

She scrambles for the tie, fumbling it in her haste. I want to shriek at her to slow down, be careful, but I know if I do I'll draw unwanted attention. So I swallow my backseat rescuing and wait for Lily to come through.

After what feels like an age, she hands me the broken zip tie. I shove it into the locking mechanism and pull. It won't budge. I reposition the broken end and try again.

"Go!" I push her with my shoulder.

"Not without you," she says.

"I don't have time to argue with you. Go! Now!"

"No!"

I break the last zip tie just in time to see Spade scoop up her gun and point it at me. Aadila is unconscious on the floor in a pool of blood, and Joseph is lying facedown on a table, his neck bent at an unnatural angle.

I have time for only one move. I wrap my arms around Lily and roll to the right. Spade fires, the shot's crack, earsplitting even with the silencer on.

Unfortunately, I don't roll fast enough.

A white-hot bolt of pain rips through the muscle of my left shoulder. I scream but force myself to keep rolling. I haven't got a prayer of disarming her. I'm not trained for hard-core combat the way Aadila and Joseph clearly were. Our only way out now is to run.

I push Lily to her feet and stumble to mine, bending to wrench the blue fairy necklace off Aadila with my good hand and scoop up her dropped knife with my bad hand as we pass. I pull Lily to the right once we round the booths. The front door is out, since that's Spade's territory. But there's a back door, and I'm going for that. Spade doesn't make a sound, and she doesn't waste a shot. When she kills us, we won't hear her coming.

I shove Lily through the back door, into the alley. One shot clips the doorframe next to me. But once I register the layout of the alley, I realize why Spade let us run. She was herding us here. It's a blind alley—no outlet at the other end. If we keep running, she'll pick us off for sure.

I slam the door behind me, wedging it closed along the hinge side with Aadila's knife. It won't hold Spade for long. Two, maybe three solid kicks to the door at most. We need to get up one of the walls and out of the alley. I'd kill for a Dumpster right now, but none presents itself.

"What are we going to do?" Lily says, crying.

"We've got to get on top of the building," I say.

"Are you *crazy?*" she asks, looking up.

The shortest wall looks to be about twelve feet high. Been there, done that, but not without help. Which means only one of us is leaving this alley alive.

"Lily, I need you to listen to me," I say as I drag her to the wall. I blink my eyes to clear my vision, which has started speckling. Numbness spreads through my left arm as I hand her the blue-fairy flash drive. "I've done this before. It is possible. Just do everything I say and you'll make it. Do you understand?"

"You mean, *we'll* make it," she says fiercely.

"Of course," I say. "Step into my hands." I cup my hands at knee level, and she dutifully steps into them.

"Your shoulder," she says.

The bar's back door shudders in its hinges as Spade kicks it.

"I'm going to count to three, and you put your weight on me. Reach up as high as you can and *pull.* Got it?"

Lily nods. Tears are flowing down both our faces at this point. I wouldn't mind a little cavalry right now.

"One, two, three."

Lily leans her full weight into my hands and reaches up the wall as ordered. My shoulder is both excruciatingly painful and somehow covered with a strange, cold emptiness. I dig deep, and with all the adrenaline and drive and need coursing through my body, I muster the strength to lift my hands up to chest height. I shuffle-pivot and grab Lily's other foot, then cheerleader-press her up over my head. My arms are unsteady at best, and I can't straighten the left one. My knees wobble, and I fight desperately against the urge to sink to the ground.

"I can't reach it!" Lily shouts, her voice despairing.

I'm about to give up when suddenly the weight is gone. Lifted off my shoulders as if it never was. I collapse to the ground, shaking.

I hear another kick, and the door breaks open. Spade is coming for me, and I hurt so much that I don't care. I shiver and bleed and wrap thoughts of Dani around me like a blanket.

"Get up, *jang mi*! Get up and jump! I will catch you!"

Ralph. Ralph's here. *Finally*. With superhuman effort, I push myself up to all fours. Shots ring out, and for a second, I think they're aimed at me. But the sound is wrong. Ralph must be shooting at Spade, forcing her to take cover and buying me time.

I use the hope that I might actually make it to fuel what's left of my ability to move. I back up to the opposite wall, gauging the distance through long, slow blinks. It's laughable to think I'm ever in a million years going to make it over that wall. But I see shadows moving at the top. I have to trust my team. They'll get me out.

I shut my eyes and take a deep breath—in through my nose, out through my mouth. And when I open my eyes again, I can see more clearly. I can feel desperation tensing my muscles. I will do this or I will die trying.

I run as fast as I can on trembling legs, pumping my arms and focusing on the task ahead. About two feet from the wall, I launch myself into the air with the last of my remaining strength, reaching up as far as I can with my right hand. I smack painfully into the bricks and scrabble desperately for a fingerhold. But just as I start to slide down the wall, a strong hand grips my wrist and pulls. My face scrapes against the bricks, but it's the best thing I've ever felt.

"Give me your other hand!"

Sam's voice. I swing my left hand as high as I can. It isn't very high, though. I try again, but my arm feels even more noodly than my legs do. I bite my lip, fighting giggles. I inch my hand up instead of throwing it and finally, finally Sam manages to grab it. He pulls, and it feels like someone is forcing sticks of dynamite into my shoulder. I scream.

An eternity of seconds later, I collapse onto the roof with Lily, Sam, and Ralph. Ralph crouches next to me, examining my shoulder.

"You're late," I say, slurring.

"You're shot," he says back.

And then I black out.

THE TAKE

The next time I wake up, I feel like I've been run over by a freight train hauling a herd of elephants. My eyes are gummed shut, and I can't move either of my hands. Something about zip ties filters through my fuzzy brain. Something about . . .

"Dani," I say, forcing my eyes open and trying to sit up.

"Don't move, *milaya*. I'm here."

The fluorescent lights are blinding. Medical equipment crowds my bed, looming over me like aliens. I recognize some of it from when I visited Dani, but that's hardly comforting.

Dani's holding my right hand, which is why I wasn't able to move it. She's sitting in a plastic chair next to my bed, dark circles under her eyes and a barely healing red gash across her jaw.

"You're awake," I say, relaxing into the concrete mattress. I smile, though even smiling hurts. "How long was I out?"

"Two days," she says, a worried frown tightening her face.

"How long have you been awake?"

"Long enough to nearly have a heart attack when Sam told me you had been shot." With a pained look, she drops her gaze to the scratchy white sheets. "I am sorry I was not there to keep you safe."

I inch my butt back so I can sit up taller. There are lots of things I could say that would all be true, but only one thing that will irritate her out of her guilt. "I wouldn't have let you come anyway."

She scowls at me. I take the opportunity to pull her hand to my cheek. She doesn't resist, but the pained look is back. I let our hands fall to the sheets, though I keep our fingers firmly entwined. We have all the time in the world for fixing us. I'll chase every particle of her pain away if it takes every grift in the book, and she'll keep me safe while I do it. But that's a battle for another day. I can feel my energy ebbing, and there are things I need to know.

"Did we get them?" I ask.

"You almost got killed. You are lucky Spade is still on the run, or Ramirez would be here, grounding you to kingdom come."

"I'm okay with being grounded. I can't imagine wanting to leave the house anyway. I may develop a healthy case of agoraphobia."

She smiles, but it's guarded. There's something she's not telling me. Like a coward, I let it lie. For now, it's enough that she's awake. We all made it out alive this time. I just want to coast on that for a little while.

"How's Lily? She didn't go home, did she?"

"She is fine. Mrs. Ramirez is with her. You should stop worrying about everyone else and start worrying about yourself. You almost died." Her expression twists when she says it. I try to squeeze her hand, but it's a pathetic attempt. I'm still more noodle than bone.

"I had everything under control at first," I say. "My plan just sort of . . . fizzled."

"Fizzled?" Dani says, her eyebrows shooting up. "You had to be airlifted to the hospital. *Airlifted*." She grips my hand with both of hers now. "I need you to stop putting yourself in these situations. Please."

I want to promise her whatever she wants. I almost do, that's how hopped up on narcotics I am. But I know that I can't keep that promise. Certainly not with the deal I made with Sister Rasmussen, my grandmother, whatever. So I continue my questions as if she hadn't spoken.

"What about Joseph and Aadila?"

"Both dead."

I should probably feel bad about that, but I can't say I really do. They were truly evil. More so than Spade, even. I won't be crying at their funerals.

"I got out of zip ties," I say, trying to lighten the mood. "Aren't you proud of me?"

"I am always proud of you." She strokes my hair. "Whether you are a grifter or a gardener. But I prefer gardener."

"I'll consider it," I say, rolling my left shoulder experimentally. A sharp pressure stabs the muscle but no pain. I eye the

IV bag with more respect this time. "What did the doctor say about my shoulder?"

"Three hours of surgery to get the bullet out and repair the damage. You owe Ramirez about a million dollars."

Ugh. Fantastic. "And you? What did the doctor say about you?"

"Full recovery, for now. There's a risk of infection, but if I stay on antibiotics and away from large bodies of water, I should be fine. Moderate concussion. Nothing serious enough to keep me here."

I study Dani's face, drinking in her features. She's haggard and worn, but seems okay. I pull my hand free of hers to trace the cut along her jaw. She doesn't pull away this time, which kind of surprises me, actually. She closes her eyes and shivers, tension sloughing off her to reveal the tired, relieved, damaged girl underneath.

"I love you." It just sort of pops out of my mouth. I didn't mean to say it. But now that I have, I feel so free. It almost doesn't matter what she says back. Almost.

She leans forward, resting her forehead against mine. "*Ya tebe kohayu.*" Then she kisses me. *Finally* kisses me. And it's different from any other kiss I've ever experienced. It's softer and sweeter and at the same time there's something aching in it.

I reach up to touch her face, to pull her closer, but she breaks the kiss. I start to protest, but the look in her eyes when she opens them instantly silences me. It's unguarded, unwavering, overwhelming. I shiver with exhilaration under just her gaze. But I want more.

I kiss her again, cradling her face, taking care not to brush her cut. I don't want anything disrupting this. I want the world to fall away. I've saved it twice now. It owes me this.

Dani deepens the kiss. Not too much, but my body starts to protest anyway. I ignore it. I slide my good hand around her neck to draw her closer. She wraps her arms around my waist and pulls me up, supporting me like she always has since before we even met.

The kiss lasts forever and is over in a flash. Time moves funny when we're this focused on each other. "Say it in English this time," I whisper, closing my eyes, ignoring my pain.

"I love you, *milaya*," she says. "I have loved you my whole life. I just didn't know it."

I sigh happily, a drop sliding down my cheek as I beam up at her. "Then none of it matters. We made it. We're here."

Her smile fades as cares pile back on her shoulders. I could kick myself for reminding her, but it had to happen sometime. At least we can face the fallout together. I'm probably still trouble, but she will always be Dani. She will always have my back. And I can do anything as long as she's with me.

I let go of her neck to take her hand. "I'm sorry about the Chevelle," I say.

She lifts my hand up to her lips and kisses it softly before pulling it to her chest. "You should have left me," she says quietly. "You could have died trying to save me."

"Don't be dumb. I would have died anyway without you. Just slower."

"Don't say that," she says, her voice rough. "You have the Ramirezes, your friends. You would be fine without me."

She's rubbing my hand, working up to something. The drugs can't mask the alarm climbing my spine. I almost ask her not to tell me. I don't know if I'm strong enough to handle whatever's causing that look on her face. But bad things only get worse when you hide from them.

"Why does it sound like you're trying to say good-bye?" I say, panic edging my voice.

She opens her mouth, but it's not her who answers.

"Because she is," Petrov says as he saunters into the doorway of my room and leans casually against the frame.

A machine next to me starts beeping faster.

"Petrov." My fingers fumble for the nurse's call button.

"By all means, send for help. Unfortunately for you, I haven't broken any laws since I was released from prison three days ago."

"You were *released*?" I gape at him. How is this possible? He was supposed to be incarcerated for the rest of his natural life.

He straightens, adjusting his jacket lapels and fiddling with his left shirt cuff. "I found the long hours of idleness in prison didn't agree with me. And I still have a friend or two in high places."

"It would have taken a presidential pardon . . ." But even as I say it, I know it's not true. I grifted my way into an off-limits area of a high-security facility with almost no effort. Getting out would be tougher, but not impossible for someone with Petrov's connections.

"You'd be surprised who owes whom favors," he says.

I scramble for an angle, my normal grifter instincts dulled and slow from the drugs. "We're in a public place. You can't just—"

"Calm your pretty head, Ms. Dupree. I'm not here to kill you. Dani and I have come to an arrangement."

Oh, god. The deal.

"Whatever she promised you, I will double it if you leave us alone."

He laughs. "You forget. I'm familiar with your negotiation strategy—you overpromise and underdeliver. Besides, Dani's giving me exactly what I want. You can't double that."

"What are you giving him?" I ask her.

She looks miserable but resolute. I remember what Han said about her mulishness. I'm not going to be able to talk Dani out of this. But that doesn't mean I won't try.

"I promised to go with him. To work for him again," she says.

"What?" I turn back to Petrov. "But why would you want that? She betrayed you. She shot you. She hates you."

"Exactly," he says, his triumphant smirk making me sick. "What I want is revenge. I can be persuaded not to kill you, as long as the price is right. And today, my price is your suffering. I thought, what better way to make you suffer than to take someone you care about away from you? And forcing Dani to work for me, the person she loathes most in the world, well . . . that's two for one."

"You can't do this, Dani," I say, pleading with my entire being. "We can beat him like we did before. You don't need to protect me from him."

"Yes, I do. This was the bargain I struck for the name of the first contractor, and for Petrov's assurance that he would not come after you when he was released."

"Why didn't you tell me?" I accuse, though I don't have the right to be angry. I guessed at the time that she wasn't giving me the whole truth. I should have forced it out of her then. "I can't let you do this. I need you too much, Dani." It kills me that we're having this conversation in front of Petrov, but at this point, I'd do anything to keep her from leaving.

"My duty has always been to protect you." The *even from me* hangs between us, and I want to tear the words to shreds.

"*Please*, don't do this," I whisper, hopeless tears staining my face. "Please stay."

She rests her forehead against mine, then kisses me lightly, lingeringly. "Do not look for me," she says. "Just live your life. Be happy."

I swallow hard. "It's like you don't even know me."

"At least try," she says, smiling weakly.

"You're really doing this?"

She squeezes my hand. "Good-bye, *milaya*."

Then she follows Petrov through the door and out of my life.

THE NEW WORLD

"Keep your eye on the lady."

I show the Queen of Hearts to Lily, and then start juggling the cards on the rolling bedside table between us. The concrete bed is starting to feel more like a pile of boulders the longer I stay here. I get to check out tomorrow, a week after checking in. And I'll never again be so happy to see Mike's guest room.

Though *happy* is not really a word I'd use to describe my general state of being. It had taken Angela one look at my wrecked face after Dani's departure to realize something was desperately wrong. She'd called in reinforcements, but there was nothing we could do. Petrov had told me the truth: he'd been legally released and was free to come and go as he pleased.

"I don't get how this works," Lily says, drawing my attention back to the game. "It seems like the player should win every time."

It does seem like that, doesn't it? It seems like I should win every time. I am the best grifter in Chicago, after all. I should have seen through Joseph's ruse. I should have seen Petrov coming.

"Where's the lady?" I say, pushing back my hurt. She points to a card and I flip it over. Jack of Spades.

"What?" she says, incredulous. "I was watching really closely that time. I swear you put the queen there."

"It's a trick," I explain. "When I'm juggling the cards, I pick up two cards in one hand. Like this." I show her the correct hand position with one card directly on top of the other. "When I'm moving fast, I can drop either the bottom card or the top card in that hand, and it's impossible for you to tell which one I dropped. Like this." I slow down the move for her. "And even if you happened to pick the right card by accident, I can switch it without you realizing it and show you the wrong card."

"It's like magic," Lily says, impressed.

I shake my head. "The magic part is hooking the mark. If you're good, you can get a mark to believe he can win even when he knows it's a scam."

I shuffle the cards into the deck and ache for Dani. I remember how it felt when she kissed me. Pain steals my breath, and not for the first time I regret a whole host of choices. I don't know what I was thinking. I stupidly believed I could love, even when I know love's not in my cards.

I deal out a hand of Go Fish for something to do. If I don't keep busy, I'll go crazy.

"Got any sevens?" I ask, arranging my cards into chaos.

"Go fish," Lily says.

Lily seems to have made it through okay. She's staying with a nearby aunt temporarily. She has to testify against her own mother, which makes me want to throw up every time I think about it. Girl must have nerves of steel, though I've seen her pale out of nowhere sometimes, and I imagine it's a stray thought about what's ahead for her.

Another day, another orphan. Both parents in prison. Brother dead. I wish I could tell her it'll be all right, that I'll make sure she gets to choose her living situation. But I don't have that kind of power. I can rescue a hundred Ukrainian immigrants, but I can't save this one friend. Of course, what fun's a cause if it's not hopeless?

"Got any threes?" Lily says.

I pass her two threes.

"Can I ask you something?" I say.

"Go fish," she says, smirking.

"Cute. Look, I haven't really talked about this with the Ramirezes yet, but if staying with relatives doesn't work out long term, would you want to maybe—"

"Yes! I mean, yes," Lily says, smiling. "I'd love to." She looks down at her cards. She might still hate me for Tyler's death. She might even also hate me for taking her mother away. But it doesn't feel like it. At least, not all the time.

"What are you going to do now?" she asks.

"I don't know. Try to find Dani. Try to find my mom. Do that silly Brillion internship. It's already set up, and I'm still in the hospital, for Pete's sake."

Lily lays down three aces. "I meant about where you're going to live."

"It's up to the Ramirezes, I guess," I say, shrugging. "I cost them a crapload of money. I put them in danger. I'm a liar and thief and I never hang up my towel." I scrape at a pen mark on the rolling table with my thumbnail. "They don't have to keep me if they don't want to."

"Keep you from what?" Mike says as he maneuvers through the door, arms laden with packages of varied size, shape, and type—balloons, flowers, baskets, chocolate, bags of gourmet coffee.

"What the hell is that?" I ask. "I'm leaving in a couple of hours, not a couple of years."

"It's all the stuff my interns had to comb through to make sure there were no explosives, poisons, wiretaps, booby traps, and nasty notes."

"This is all for me?" I look at the stuff Mike has strewn on the bed, picking up a book called *How to Survive Just About Anything* and putting it down again. "Where did it come from?"

"Your fans," he says as if it's obvious.

"What fans?" I say in horror. Oh, god. I may never be able to work in this town again.

"She's decent," Mike calls out into the hallway. Three respectable-looking young men plus Sam, Murphy, and Bryn walk in bearing, impossibly, even more stuff. Well, except for Bryn. She's carrying her purse.

"That's debatable," Sam says as he unloads on the upholstered chair Lily vacated for a spot on the bed.

"Can I keep the Best Buy gift card?" Murphy says. "Bessie needs an infrared upgrade."

Bryn crosses her arms. "My glasses-cam upgrade is a much higher priority than your dumb van's night goggles. It way stretches the bounds of credibility that I would ever wear something so 2013."

"This is insane," I say, staring woefully at a balloon that says GET BETTER SOON, TIGER with the word *Tiger* crossed out and *Grifter* written in Sharpie next to it. "Send it back."

"Oh, no. I'm getting something out of all of this," Mike says, snagging a candy bar from a gift basket. "I chased that contract killer all the way to Texas."

And he did. Personally. But Spade managed to escape the trap they'd laid for her. Mike finally returned at Angela's request to help with all the hospital stuff. I assume the FBI is still hunting her, but there are only so many resources they can put on a lowly contract killer. Besides, now that Mrs. Richland has been arrested and all her funds seized, there's no possibility of Spade getting paid. The contract is officially off.

"What the hell is going on in here?" Angela says as she walks in, looking as horrified as I did.

"I know, right?" I say, gesturing at all the stuff. "Tell them we're not keeping it."

She ignores me and turns her disgruntled look on Mike.

"She's supposed to be resting. Not entertaining hordes of people. Out. Everybody. Out. That includes you, Lily."

Lily sighs and follows Sam out into the hallway.

"And don't come back until it's time to check out," Angela says sternly as she shuts the door. Then she turns back to me, a completely serene version of herself, and leans a hip against my bed. "How are you feeling?" she asks.

I take a deep breath, assessing. "Tired," I say. "Sad."

"You miss her," she says.

"Part of me is just gone," I say, gripping the covers. I don't want to cry anymore.

Angela places her hand on mine. I turn my hand over to let her hold it. She's more my mom than my mom is. I wonder if she knows that.

As if reading my mind, she says, "We need to talk about what's next for you."

I nod, dreading the topic. "Do you want me to move out?"

"We don't want you to move out," she says, squeezing my hand. "We want you to be happy."

I close my eyes. "Even after everything that's happened? Putting you guys in danger all the time and staying out too late and the medical bills and holding your plumber at gunpoint?"

She laughs. "Yes. Even after holding my plumber at gunpoint. There is one condition, though," she says, sobering. "It can't be 'Mike and Angela's house' anymore. You can't call it the guest room. It's your room. It's your house."

"That's it?" I say.

"That's it."

I pretend to mull it over. "I can live with that."

• • •

It's weird sitting in the New World Initiative waiting room. Any second now, I expect Joseph to saunter around the corner, giving me busywork, or a pearl of wisdom, or a hug. I can't help but layer con man Joseph over my memory of NWI Joseph, and the juxtaposition is jarring, to say the least. For the first time, I wonder if that's how other people see me. But it's a heavy thought, so I set it aside. I'm not here about grifters. I'm here to see a guru.

I thumb through an issue of *Car and Driver*, because obviously. *"I read it for the articles,"* I hear Dani say, and then ignore the sharp tug in my chest. I focus on being annoyed that the damn thing keeps sliding off my lap. Every time it does, I jerk my arm instinctively to catch it, and a jolt of pain shoots from my left shoulder into my arm and chest. But I suppose I'll take pain over the alternative. The doctor said I almost lost use of the arm entirely. Mike loved hearing that one, let me tell you. He brings it up every chance he gets.

"Ms. Dupree?" Brigitte says, as if she doesn't know me. Though, to be fair, I think she looked at me twice and never once spoke to me the whole time I was at NWI.

"Dr. Raktabija will see you now."

I follow Brigitte's rigid back to Duke's—I mean, Devi's office. Brigitte shuts the door behind me, and I have to take several breaths before I can force myself to step more than a foot into the room. My gut is churning, and I'm not sure I won't hurl all over the gorgeous new Berber.

"You remodeled," I say, trying to distract my nightmares.

"It's okay, Julep," Devi says as she comes out from behind the desk. "It took me a while to get over it, too. Let's go somewhere else."

I follow her back the way I came, but instead of going down to the lobby, we go through a side door I hadn't paid much attention to before. We emerge on a balcony overlooking the city. The cool evening wind brushes my shoulder with a consoling caress.

"So what did you want to see me about?" Devi asks. "The report you gave the police was pretty detailed. Was there more?"

"Yes," I answer truthfully. "But that's not why I'm here."

She waits patiently for me to continue. I clear my throat, gathering my thoughts.

"First, I wanted to apologize," I say. That's not quite what I mean, though, so I tackle it from a different direction. "I wanted you to know—though it's too late now, really—that I get it, what Duke was all about. I respect his aspiration."

Devi reaches for my hand and squeezes it. "You carry so much sorrow, Julep. The world is not a weight one person must bear alone." "*Let someone else watch the world while you sleep. . . .*" Tyler's voice this time. So many ghosts, so little left of me to carry them. "Besides, it is never too late to come home."

I give her a pale shadow of my usual smile.

She gestures to an upholstered armchair next to a small bistro table. She folds gracefully into the chair on the other side of the table. I follow her example, clasping my hands in my lap.

"I also wanted to thank you for getting Mr. Antolini out of holding and into a good care facility." I still feel awful for him. His brain damage is permanent. Therapists are working with him, but there's no guarantee he'll regain even a tenth of his abilities.

"The paperwork still isn't finalized, but we'll take care of him," Devi says. "He is one of us. Like you."

My heart thumps painfully at that. Devi might consider me family, but it doesn't mean I belong here. Maybe I don't belong anywhere. Any time I get close to belonging to someone, I lose them.

Devi leans back in her chair, reading on my face what I haven't yet said. "You didn't come here for just a heart-to-heart, did you?"

"No," I say, laying my metaphorical cards on the table. "I came to ask a favor."

• • •

The "L" rattles me from the Loop through Near West Side and North Lawndale. I stare out the window without seeing the buildings blurring by. I'm empty. Numb. There's nothing internal left to witness the external. There's barely enough to notice the lack of noticing. I think I should be sad about that. But I've been sad for weeks now, and it doesn't seem to change anything.

My conversation with Devi went well enough. She said she'd consider my request, which is better than the gentle rejection I thought I'd get. She's a tough lady with a tender heart. Unless she's evil, of course. Though aren't we all a little of both when it comes down to it?

The "L" shudders to a stop. My stop. The doors open and close again, and the "L" moves on with me still inside. I could tell myself I just missed it, but I'm not that good a grifter. The truth is that I can't move. I'm stuck. I'll be sitting on this hard plastic seat until the train stops running and the tracks rot beneath me.

You'd think it couldn't get worse than being responsible for the death of someone you love. Turns out, it can. There are worse things than death, after all. And with Tyler, at least I have a grave to grieve beside. Dani's just gone. The wind took her, and I don't have any idea where to start looking. She could be in another country by now, or right next door. And it might as well be the moon, because even if I do manage to find her, I won't be able to convince her that she's worth fighting for.

The doors open and close. Open and close. People get on and off. Or maybe I'm the only one on the train and I just never noticed. I close my eyes.

Two or three or ten stops later, someone sits down next to me and takes my hand. I lean my head on his shoulder and breathe in his coffee-and-cedar scent, as familiar to me as my own. At least military school didn't take that away. He pockets his phone, which he no doubt used to find me, and rests his head on mine without a word.

• • •

"I'm in," Sam says from Murphy's desk an hour or so after he finally peels me out of the train.

"Already?" I'm cradling a Ballou latte, sipping it slowly, because my stomach is grouchy with me.

"Wow, you really must have been hacker-slumming it while I was gone. It's just the no-fly list."

I give him a sour look and then open my mouth to say it's his fault I'm not used to competence, when I'm interrupted by the bell above the door.

My heart leaps and dives in less time than it takes me to turn toward the sound. I know it's not her, but that doesn't stop my subconscious from hoping it's her for the millisecond it takes my conscious mind to catch up and crush it. Stupid subconscious. There's a reason *hope* is a four-letter word.

But even as the adrenaline fades, it kicks right in again when my brain finally registers who our visitor is. . . .

Fake Mrs. Antolini.

Only this is not the woman I remember. This version is dressed in a starched and pressed steel-gray suit with blood-colored heels. Her posture is poised, confident. Her expression is cool and collected.

"Ms. Dupree," she says, acknowledging me with a nod. "We meet again."

"Who are you?" I say.

Sam must hear the fear in my voice, because he jumps out of his chair. He stops there, looking to me for direction. But I can't tear my eyes off the woman who set me up.

"I am Helen Dare."

"You work for my grandmother, don't you?"

"No, I do not," she says. "Do you truly think your grandmother is the only one with plans for you?" Then she turns to Sam. "Mr. Seward."

She hands me an envelope, then nods again and leaves. I remember that night, about how she wept and cajoled me into taking the case. Who does she work for, and why is the blue fairy so important if no one knows what's on it?

Sam looks confused. "Who was that?"

"That's the woman who sent me after the blue fairy," I say. Then a thought occurs to me. "Are you sure she didn't send you after it first?"

He thinks for a moment, but then shakes his head. "Sorry, Julep. I wish it were that easy, but hers definitely wasn't the same voice. The woman who called me, her voice had a slight rasp to it. Like yours."

I sigh. We still have such a long way to go, and I feel so lost.

Sam reads my mood and nudges my arm. "Come on, partner. We got this."

I smile gratefully at him, ignoring the sting in my eyes.

He gestures at the envelope in my hand. "You going to open that?"

The envelope she gave me is plain, but clearly from an expensive stationery set—ivory, side-seamed, heavyweight. Executive grade.

I lay it on my desk and push the flap open.

"Wait," Sam says, taking a step closer but pulling himself up short, as if he spoke involuntarily. I raise an eyebrow. "Are you sure you want to know what that says? It could be anything. It could be bad."

I trace the edge of the envelope with a finger. "What choice do I have?"

He takes a breath and holds it, as if preparing for a grenade to go off. He's probably right. It probably is a grenade. But I'm right, too. I don't have a choice.

I pull the single slip of paper from the envelope with unsteady hands. But it's not a threat, or even a demand. It's a check for a hundred thousand dollars. Enough to repay Mike and Angela for my hospital bills with a little left over. And I'd bet Bessie's state-of-the-art surveillance system that the handwriting on this check matches the writing on the check I got last year to cover my St. Agatha's tuition.

And just like that tuition check, this one has a note in the memo line. Only this note's not in Italian.

Lodestar.

"What is it?" Sam asks, touching my arm.

"Another message," I say. "Does 'Lodestar' mean anything to you?"

He thinks for a moment. "It's a company. I think it provides IT services for the government."

"Wait a sec," I say, cogs clicking into place in my head. "Mr. Antolini worked at Lodestar. Fake Mrs. A mentioned it in our first meeting. But why put it on the check?"

"Holy shit!" Sam says, grabbing his phone from the desk and swiping its screen furiously. "Lodestar is special because it runs one of the country's fastest supercomputers. *It's the numbers*."

"The numbers . . . ?" And then I catch up. "The numbers! Sam, you're brilliant," I say as he pulls up the text I sent him after visiting Mr. Antolini in his prison cell.

That's who Aadila poisoned. Not Duke, not Ackley. Mr. Antolini. He wasn't embezzling money for Joseph. He was decrypting the blue-fairy flash drive for Duke. The embezzlement was a frame job to cover up the truth.

"I've got it!" Sam says, setting his phone down and pulling the blue fairy out of the safe I'd had installed just to house it.

"When you're ready."

"I'm ready," I say, though maybe I'm not. Duke died for whatever it is we're about to open. It could just be a personal letter. Or it could be a threat to national security. The only way to find out is to use the encryption key Mr. Antolini paid for with his sanity to open the file for which Sam risked going to prison.

We each take a seat in front of the monitor, side by side as if it were any old job from the days before my life went completely off the rails. Sam types the encryption key in the password field and is about to hit Enter when I grab his hand. He looks questioningly at me, and I give him a half smile in return.

I'm still holding his hand when I press Enter.

ACKNOWLEDGMENTS

If I thought creating a first book from scratch was difficult, repeating the miracle was an even greater challenge. I would not have been able to do it without the encouragement, enthusiasm, late-night Google chats, brainstorming sessions, coffee-club rescue missions, character vivisections, and ad nauseam reassurance from all my amazing and talented friends, family, and fellow writers.

First, I have to thank my tireless critique partners, who, on a moment's notice, would read the entire manuscript and give me the precise feedback I needed within—not kidding—forty-eight hours. Marie Langager of the coffee-club rescue mission mentioned above—I owe you big-time. Thanks also to Alexa Donne, my late-night word-sprint buddy, who got me through my second draft; Rachel Potts, for a line-edit talent that is seriously uncanny; Laura Ferrel, my longtime BFF and the voice I always hear in my head, telling me the right way to grammar (my drive to do my characters justice, no matter how much time it takes, comes from her); Emily Lloyd-Jones, my soul sister of nefarious protagonists, who saved my plot-hole-riddled bacon with her devious brilliance; and Terry Bell, who I'm pretty sure shares my brain. To all of you: I hope that when the time comes, I can return the favor with comments as targeted and on-point as yours.

Next, I must express my undying love and gratitude to my

publishing and agenting teams. I worship you all. Wendy Loggia is a joy of an editor. With this book, I took the envelope I was trying to push and set it on fire. Wendy gave me the time and space I needed to let my imagination run wild and naked over the moors, and then patiently helped me shape the story into what I truly wanted it to be. Laura Bradford, my amazeballs agent, continues to be beyond awesome and always in my corner. She's just as crazy as I am but with a megadose of cunning that makes her invaluable to all her authors (but me especially).

I also want to thank (from the Delacorte Press team) Beverly, Colleen, Tamar, Stephanie and Ashley, Trish, Krista (!), Alison, and Ray (of the brilliant cover design)—y'all are all right in my book. And to the agenting team—Brandy Rivers, Taryn Fagerness, Natalie Lakosil, and Sarah LaPolla—I cannot thank you enough for your tireless efforts on my behalf.

I also owe a debt of gratitude to the larger community on several fronts, without which I'd be up the drafting creek without a paddle. April Henry, bestselling author and jewel of a person—half my local connections come from her (you rule, April!). The One-Four KidLit debut group has kept me sane this past year. Second Book Syndrome became Second Book Shazaam! thanks to these fine folks who shared their experience, their support, and their gorgeous books with me. Special shout-out to Michelle Krys, my editor sister, who dropped everything to answer my questions about the publicity end of the authorial life.

The YA blogosphere at large is the most amazing, supportive place I have ever encountered. I am where I am today because of the collective, collaborative genius that only a bunch of fannish book nerds would have the ability and the generosity of spirit to share. In specific, I want to thank Nikki Wang, Crystal, Amy Trueblood,

Celeste P., and Sabrina Kooy. I <3 you guys. I also want to thank my Facebook crew for their constant support and cheerleading—Kim Beach Kenney, Rachael Byington Nuzzaco, Nick Heap, KT! Eaton, Meg Stocker, Kristen Ketchel-Bain, Rebecca Moses, Jacque Justice, and everyone else who has shared my posts and encouraged me over the years.

Thanks, too, to my home away from home, Ava Roasteria Café, for supporting a schedule-challenged author by being open 24/7 and serving me delicious coffee whenever I need it. Progress Ridge, represent!

Last but not nearly least, my family. I can never repay them for allowing me the time to write this book on top of doing my day job, at the expense of being there for them when they otherwise needed me, and for indulging me every time I needed reassurance or an ear to help hash out a plot point or to revel in some new success. Thanks go specifically to my mother for early-morning international-phone-call brainstorming sessions while I commuted to work; to my siblings, Christopher, Elizabeth, James, and Will, for psyching me up; to my wonderful in-laws, Lisa and Cal, for their unfailing support and excitement; to my father, my stepmother Daryl, and my other stepmother Milla, for inspiring me to shine; and to my daughter, Caelan, for her patient understanding whenever I'm not there to kiss her goodnight.

And of course, most especially, I owe my heartfelt thanks to my beloved wife, Miranda, for all the late-night "You can do it!" texts and surprise chocolate-chip cookies and many loads of dishes quietly done in my absence—not to mention her timely, sharp, and insightful critique. This book, quite simply, could never have been written without her.

ABOUT THE AUTHOR

MARY ELIZABETH SUMMER is the author of *Trust Me, I'm Lying* and its sequel, *Trust Me, I'm Trouble*. She contributes to the delinquency of minors by writing books about unruly teenagers with criminal leanings, and has a BA in creative writing from Wells College. Her philosophy on life is "You can never go wrong with sriracha sauce." She lives in Portland, Oregon, with her wife, their daughter, and their evil overlor—er, cat.

WANT MORE JULEP DUPREE?

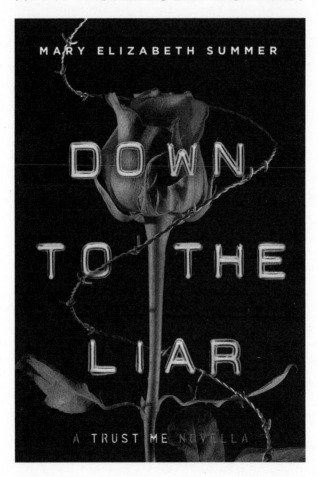

Read this all-new digital novella told from Julep's point of view—nothing she has been through could possibly have prepared her for the truth behind her next con.